About the Author

Adam Gillespie had a fascination with motor vehicles from early childhood and this led him to follow a career in engineering. While vehicles and their design characteristics were the focus of his attention, he soon realised that interaction with his colleagues was vital in carrying out his work activities. Understanding people was also vital if the goals of the job were to be achieved.

The Human Machine at Work

Adam Gillespie

———————————————

The Human Machine at Work

Vanguard Press

VANGUARD PAPERBACK

© Copyright 2024
Adam Gillespie

The right of Adam Gillespie to be identified as author of
this work has been asserted by him in accordance with the
Copyright, Designs and Patents Act 1988.

All Rights Reserved

No reproduction, copy or transmission of this publication
may be made without written permission.
No paragraph of this publication may be reproduced,
copied or transmitted save with the written permission of the
publisher, or in accordance with the provisions
of the Copyright Act 1956 (as amended).

Any person who commits any unauthorised act in relation to
this publication may be liable to criminal
prosecution and civil claims for damages.

A CIP catalogue record for this title is
available from the British Library.

ISBN 978 1 80016 898 5

This is a work of fiction. Names, characters, businesses, places, events and
incidents are either the product of the author's imagination or used in a
fictitious manner. Any resemblance to actual persons, living or dead, or
actual events is purely coincidental.

Vanguard Press is an imprint of
Pegasus Elliot Mackenzie Publishers Ltd.
www.pegasuspublishers.com

First Published in 2024

Vanguard Press
Sheraton House Castle Park
Cambridge England

Printed & Bound in Great Britain

Dedication

To Alan McMunnigall, editor of Glasgow-based publisher thi wurd, and my tutor in creative writing at the University of Glasgow.

Acknowledgements

I should like to acknowledge the support of my editor in helping me choose wording that would assist the reader in looking further into the minds of the characters.

Part One
Adulthood

Chapter 1
After the day's work

Jason, the depot engineer, said, "Things are getting really unpleasant now." Stephen knew that they were, but he was surprised to hear Jason admit it. It was only Monday morning, so not the best start to the week. Some people reckoned that Jason was difficult, but when you took the trouble to watch him at work – the way he spoke to his staff – you quickly realised why his depot, the largest, the most demanding one, always performed better than any of the others. It sounded like bullying but the interaction between him and his team confirmed that they didn't see it that way.

They knew that maintaining two hundred vehicles and keeping them available for earning money was a difficult, relentless job for all of them, but they found it satisfying when they got through each day without too many problems: it made each day worthwhile. They also knew that he took the flak from management – these new people with new ideas. Sadly, these ideas weren't new to the people who had been in the job for a while, sometimes their entire career. Long ago, they had been tried and found wanting, and worse still, most of them were now totally irrelevant to the business. The blind leading the sighted.

It just confirmed what everybody believed. The folk at the top thought about themselves but it was the folk at the coal face who thought about the business; they delivered the profits that the accountants added up and boasted about, except they weren't boasting at present.

"I've seen them come and I've seen them go," said Jason. "You used to be left to get on with your job, but now all you get is 'Why are you over budget'?"

Stephen knew exactly what Jason meant. The group was now much larger than before and while that might explain why people wanted to join the organisation, it didn't explain why they had been selected. The main board now had more outsiders than directors with experience in the industry but at least one of them, Harold, the divisional engineering director, had finally been found out and dismissed. Even then, the main board refused to admit to his shortcomings. Doing so when they did finally get rid of him would only have confirmed their own shortcomings by having appointed him in the first place.

Happily, Jason's boss, Sandy, was ultimately responsible for all depots in this operating company and he, like Jason and Stephen, knew the business inside out. And, like Jason and Stephen, he had always enjoyed the job. Not anymore..

*

"Is it true?" asked Stephen.

"Is what true?" said Sandy.

"That you're leaving."

"Who told you that? It's meant to be confidential. I've told our board, but it wasn't meant to be announced until they'd found a replacement. Anyway, I can't wait to get out of here. It's a truly horrible place now. Poorly specified vehicles, non-genuine replacement parts, too few spare vehicles, and when the people who caused all of that finally realise that there's a problem, they'll point the finger at me."

"But you've seen things fixed before," said Stephen, "and it can happen again."

"When you were involved," said Sandy. "But now that you've been sidelined, there's no chance. I'll send you a postcard."

On his way back to his desk, Stephen tapped on the purchasing manager's door. Felix was reading through a report with one of his staff, so he simply looked up and pointed in the direction of the coffee machine.

By the time that Felix was free, Stephen was back at his desk and so Felix joined him there.

"You've heard about Sandy?" asked Stephen.

Felix laughed. "I heard last week."

"Have they found a replacement for him?"

"We'll see. They've got their eye on someone from another of our operating companies. You should lift your head more often."

Stephen did, so how had he missed that? "Who tells you what's about to happen next?" he asked.

"My boss," said Felix, "Derek."

"And what about our MD? Is he thinking about moving on? Everyone else seems to be leaving at present."

"Clerk?" asked Felix. "No, he thinks he was the chief executive's chosen one."

"I'm sure he is. I think Eadie did choose him," said Stephen. "Somebody I knew at head office said that Eadie had liked the way Clerk stood up for himself at the first meeting they had."

"Someone as difficult as Eadie is?" said Felix. "A man after his own heart?"

"Nobody could be as difficult as Eadie. But, yes, he probably interpreted Clerk's confidence as ability."

"You can't say that Eadie had any ability," said Felix. "He's just a big bully who switches people off."

"Well, that's an ability. The ability to switch people off."

"Your coffee's getting cold. I'll catch up with you later."

Stephen's phone rang. It was Jason. "Have you seen that e-mail about the new group engineering director leaving?"

"Harold? I'm aware that he's leaving but I haven't seen an e-mail. While you're on the line, I've just finished a report for Sandy about your mid-life vehicles with the overheating problem. I'm just about to develop a solution for you."

"Never mind that. Open the e-mail. You won't believe the rubbish the main board has written. We all knew that he'd be hopeless but the board obviously didn't. Remember, last year, when they told the press that we were lucky to have attracted him to head up engineering in this division? He had been responsible for maintaining vehicles, but not like ours. The board obviously didn't understand the difference, and I don't think that he did either. But it wasn't just that, they allowed him to specify depots that our business can barely operate from. And it's only just dawned on them. Do you think they'll admit it? It took them a whole year to realise that he was hopeless and for the next few years we'll have to live with the problems he created. Any problems at the coal face, and there will be, and we'll be shown the door."

"Right, I've found it."

"Read that paragraph, 'The post of divisional engineering director will now be based at head office, and unfortunately, Harold will be unable to relocate'. Is anyone really expected to believe that? Why don't they admit they should have known better than to appoint him?"

"People seldom admit to their mistakes, and in some ways, I would agree with them. But that's the way things are. I just hope his replacement is better. And it's certainly true that his legacy will linger on. A big step backwards. Anyway, I've got to get my report on your vehicle overheating problem to Sandy. Are you sure you don't want me to tell you what I've recommended?"

"No thanks. Just show me when you've done something."

*

"I've just read your report," said Sandy. "Jason was on about it again last week. Is there a practical solution?"

"You'll have seen the extent of the problem," said Stephen, "so we certainly can't ignore it. As soon as I'd handed the report to you, I went down to the central workshop to discuss it with Joe. I believe that all it needs is a fairly simple modification, and he agrees with me."

"Good timing," said Sandy. "Our MD's been on to me again about vehicle availability. What do you propose we do?"

"The radiator on this vehicle type blocks up with road dirt every two years or so. Being mounted where it is, it's vulnerable to that. It can't be cleaned in situ, and removing it, cleaning it and refitting it is a two-man-day job. But, if we rotate the radiator through forty-five degrees by modifying the support brackets, we could reduce the remove-and-replace time from two days to two hours. And you'll get longer transmission life. If the gearbox casing runs too hot, it expands and internal oil leakage increases, making gearshifts more sluggish."

"What are you waiting for? One of Jason's vehicles has to go into Joe's section for accident damage repair. I thought we could kill two birds with one stone. Would you tie up with him and have your modification carried out at the same time as the repair?"

"Will do."

*

"What are you up to?" asked Stephen.

Felix looked up. "Have you given Sandy your report yet?"

"I've just left his office."

"And was he happy with it?"

"Yes. He says that I've to go ahead right away. What I wanted to ask was if Jason had called you about Harold."

"Harold?" Felix almost choked on his coffee. "What an episode that was. Yes, Jason did call me. But listen, there's more. I've found out who Sandy's replacement's going to be. It's from a reliable source, but I've been sworn to secrecy."

"Then I'd better buy you a pint tomorrow. Derek told you, didn't he? We can't have secrets between friends. Anyway, until then, what do we know?"

"I'd forgotten I'd told you who my source is. Yes, we do know who he is, and his present fleet's similar to ours, so he should settle in without any problems."

"It's bad enough when they change managing directors." Stephen sighed. "Do you know, we've had three since I started back here nine years ago?"

Felix thought for a moment. "For the whole eleven years that you were away, we only had one. He knew the business, knew the competitors, and most important of all, he knew us. And he was as sharp as a razor."

"It's worst of all when you get people from outside this business. They feel that they need to stamp their authority on the place, make their presence felt. But since they don't know what they're doing, they introduce ideas that seem to be taken from management-for-beginners books. And as well as getting in the way, they switch people off."

"I agree," said Felix. "It's difficult remaining committed to the place when you see so many wrong decisions being made."

Stephen went back to his desk to collect his camera and a measuring tape.

*

"Where's Joe?" Stephen asked.

"He's not here at the moment but the vehicle's over there," the foreman replied.

Stephen was familiar with this vehicle type. What he now focussed on was how the radiator could be relocated on the chassis to allow it to be removed and replaced quickly, even if there were a vehicle on an adjacent pit.

Same old story, he mused. A vehicle is only built once, but it's maintained every day for the rest of its life, and next to no thought is given for the people who'll be asked to do that.

"What are you up to?" Joe had arrived.

"Sandy's project. How do we remount this radiator in order to reduce its replacement time?"

"Sounds ambitious."

"Not really. If you can get somebody to remove the whole thing, we can design new brackets that allow it or the intercooler to be slid out independently. Designing the brackets won't take long. Just let me know when it's been removed."

Joe said that he would.

*

The following morning, Stephen's phone rang.

"It's Joe."

"Is the radiator out?

"It was, and it's going back in."

"What?"

"Apparently someone from head office was going through the stats on vehicle availability and Jason's depot stood out. Sandy got a phone call and he phoned me. It's to be back in service as soon as possible."

"Looks like we'll never save all these two-day labour bills, or the costs of all the failures that resulted from the preventative maintenance that wasn't carried out as a result of them."

"But just imagine the satisfaction that somebody got from making that call."

"And I take it that nobody was willing to tell him where to go?"

"People would sooner hang onto their jobs than try to fix the company. That's what it's come to," was Joe's response.

"Sandy should have explained why we needed to make the modification. It's not as if he had anything to lose. I'll tell him that the next time I see him." Stephen put down the phone.

"Come and have a coffee. You look as if you need one." Stephen looked up and it was Felix.

"Joe phoned me first," Felix said. "He was wondering how best to give you the bad news. I said I'd give you some counselling, the high caffeine kind."

"It's more than counselling I need. Every decision they make these days sets the business back years. And then we have to work out how to get back to where we started."

"One sugar or two?"

"None. Comfort eating's bad for you."

*

That afternoon, Felix appeared again. "Open your e-mails and tell me what you think."

A new divisional engineering director had been appointed and the news had taken everybody's attention.

"Who is he?" asked Stephen. "He's got to be better than Harold."

"I don't know him," said Felix. "His name's Millar. Probably just a lackey to the big chief."

"To whom?" asked Stephen.

"Eadie."

"Then heaven help us."

After so much excitement, everybody just wanted things to get back to normal. One of the recent incidents had been a fire on a vehicle and Sandy had asked Stephen to find out how it had occurred. While there was a great deal of damage, the area where the fire had started was quite evident. An exhaust leak had ignited some engine oil.

"What caused it?" Sandy asked, when Stephen got back to the office.

"The immediate cause was exhaust gas blowing from a failed pipe. The pipe had failed because a support bracket had received one shock too many from the exhaust constantly hitting the kerb. It's very difficult to see this bracket during routine inspections and the lesson for us is that we'll have to give our vehicle examiners time to remove seats in order to obtain a full view of the engine compartment. I'll draft a set of revised inspection procedures."

"Is there any good news?"

"Well," Stephen replied, "the problem could have been avoided if the vehicle had been specified differently."

"Then draft a letter to the manufacturer. I'll forward it to the central engineering manager and ask for his permission to send it.

"I'll do that just now."

*

The following Monday, Stephen had barely installed himself in front of his computer when Sandy appeared at his side and said, "About that vehicle fire – I'm getting no support from the central engineering manager."

"From Jack?" Stephen asked. "He's moving on; he's maybe moved on already. Did you really expect a response?"

"Yes. I did. He did this job before me and he knew exactly what I'm up against, what we're all up against."

"He's now probably too near the top. He'll have to watch what he does, what he says. And I don't suppose he'll want to be viewed by suppliers as difficult. That might get fed back up the tree."

"So how do we deal with things like this?" asked Sandy.

"You could leave a note for your successor telling him where we've got to with the problem and let him know that I've drafted a letter and I can make any changes that he might want."

"Thanks," said Sandy. "I've to attend a meeting just now, but I'll catch up with you when I've finished."

*

"Come in." Sandy said, looking up from a desk that was tidier than usual. "Are these the draft inspection procedures? Just put them down over there. I'll come back to you when I've had time to read them."

Back at his desk, Stephen got a phone call.

"Hi. It's Felix. Sandy's planned a farewell night out the week after next. Once the drinks have loosened tongues, we'll maybe hear the truth about why he decided to leave. And he's invited some friends who work for competitors of ours, so we'll maybe also learn how they see us. And we might even learn if any of them wrote those remarks about us in the trade press. They can't all be better than we are."

"It depends on what you mean by 'we'. You, me, Jason, Joe?"

"You know what I mean," said Felix. "The main board."

"When exactly is the night out? I'll put it in my diary."

*

"The procedure's fine," said Sandy. "So, here's hoping. You could also put the incident on the agenda for the next quarterly meeting with the manufacturer."

"I've already done that. But, while I'm here, who exactly is Harold's replacement?"

"Millar? I'm sorry. I can't tell you. But he is somebody who's grown up in our organisation, so he should be a great improvement."

"Are you sure you can't tell me more than that?"

"Eadie's decided and that's that. And if you find out more, Eadie will assume that I told you."

"In that case, I'll try to be patient."

*

After the day's work that Friday, Stephen crossed the road and met Felix in the bar.

"Where's Joe?" asked Felix.

"He's just locking up," said Stephen. "He'll be here in a minute."

"What are you drinking? The usual?"

"Yes please. Are you off between Christmas and New Year?

"I am. Are you?"

"Too much to do, I'm afraid. Sandy got me involved in these two last projects and I've fallen behind on all my routine stuff. At least the office should be a bit quieter now and I'll have no interruptions."

"Interruptions from what?" Joe had arrived.

"From Sandy, mainly, but to be honest, he was just passing on messages from above," replied Stephen.

"Our MD, or the main board?" Felix asked, before signalling the barman for a pint for Joe.

"Both. The board contacted Sandy through Clerk about some issues and directly about others."

"So, Clerk might have been thinking that Sandy didn't have too much on his plate when the reality was quite the opposite?"

"Exactly. That's good management for you, isn't it?"

"Thanks Felix," said Joe, picking up his pint. "So, what do you think about Stephen's radiator project?"

"I wasn't directly involved, but after it was called off, Jason phoned me. He was raging. He's got thirty of these vehicles in his fleet, so losing a significant number of man-days through that problem makes life more difficult for him. And he reminded me that he's got other avoidable problems to deal with beyond normal repair and maintenance. What do you think, Stephen?"

"Obviously, I don't get stressed in quite the same way as Jason since, unlike him, I'm not on the front line, but I do find it very frustrating that we don't sit down with the manufacturers and agree a detailed specification before we place orders for new vehicles."

Joe butted in. "That reminds me of when we first met. When was that? Nearly twenty years ago?"

"About specifying the bodywork?" said Stephen. "Yes, it must be about that. Eadie was our chief engineer then and I had persuaded him to go beyond simply specifying colour and layout for our next intake of new vehicles and deal with a structural problem that we all knew about. It was time-consuming to live with but easily resolved with a simple design change. The manufacturer was understandably a bit defensive at first but soon agreed to introduce them when they saw that we weren't going to make an issue of it."

"It was a big problem for us," Joe said, agreeing, "but after these changes it just slowly went away. That's obviously how to do things."

Felix had been listening attentively. "It was and it still is how to do things. So why don't the folk at the top do that today?"

"I think the answer to that is quite simple," said Stephen. "They don't know enough about this business to understand how it operates. They want results. When I studied business, I was taught that a business is that which exists to make money. And while that may be true, you still have to decide what you want to achieve in business, and obviously, how to go about it. Everything that needs to be done in the organisation needs to be understood by someone. No one individual is likely to be sufficiently well informed so the head of the organisation needs to surround himself with the appropriate people. Easy if the organisation needs a particular tradesman to produce a specific product or supply a specific service, for example, but less easy to ensure that all other necessary aspects of the business are fully understood."

Felix interrupted. "We're all aware that, collectively, the new folk in the main board don't know everything about the business, but Eadie should have ensured that we didn't lose that ability. He should have selected people with more care."

"But that's exactly the problem," Stephen went on. "Eadie began his career in the business but he wasn't trained to do anything. He simply made his way up the ladder by being pushy. If he'd been brighter, he'd have been aware of all the skills that were necessary for the business to succeed. And, even if he didn't have these skills, he should have ensured that they were all contained in his team. But, as we're all very well aware, he couldn't, and he didn't. But I've got a question for you."

"Before you ask, I'm not naming Sandy's replacement."

"In that case, you can get the next round as well."

Chapter 2
Curiosity

"Happy New Year."

"Same to you." The greetings were repeated across the office.

The team was back for another year. New, or more of the same? It was dark outside when people came to work and again when they went home, but the psychological effect of the new year seemed to have lifted everyone's spirits. For one thing, starting back on a Wednesday meant that Felix, Joe and Stephen would be going for their traditional after-work drink in only two days' time.

"Have you looked into that gearbox problem, the one that everyone seems to be talking about?" asked Felix.

"Yes, and I was just about to go over to see Jason and tell him what I saw," Stephen replied.

"Where?"

"I visited the manufacturer's agent to see one being overhauled. Nothing to it, really, but they did recommend we ensure that one or two things get checked from time to time."

"No need to change supplier, then?" said Felix. "One or two people have been suggesting that we should."

"Definitely not," said Stephen. "That would be catastrophic."

Before he could reach Jason's office, Stephen was called over to look at a vehicle being repaired under warranty by the manufacturer's agent.

"Broken bolts," said the foreman, "just like the previous model."

"I'll bring that to Jack's attention," said Stephen. "By the way, who's that?" He pointed over to someone being shown round the workshop.

"Don't know. He's been here for about half an hour."

Later, when Stephen bumped into Jason, he asked him the same question.

"That's our new engineering director. Mike. He's good," said Jason.

"How do you know?" asked Stephen.

"I've known him for years. He worked here while you were away. Then his career took off. He's been everywhere."

"Why would he want to come back?"

"He was engineering director with one of our other operating companies. Millar asked him."

"Has he accepted the job?"

"Not formally, but yes, he told me he'll take it."

Jason's word was good enough for Stephen. He went back to the main office and added the bolt problem to his list of actions.

The phone rang.

"Could you come along to my office?" asked Felix. "Sandy's with me."

When Stephen got there, Sandy looked up. "I've just given Felix formal confirmation that I'm leaving."

"Tell us some news. Is there anybody who didn't know that? By the way, I've just seen your replacement," Stephen replied.

"Mike?" said Sandy, rather bemused. "How did you know? Nothing's been announced."

"The informal organisation," was all that Stephen said.

"Good luck in the future," said Felix. "The last few years have been fun but things are certainly changing for the worse."

"The blame culture certainly is," said Sandy, "and the new people are nearly as good at it as Eadie."

"Very true," was the consensus.

*

There were even more people present at Sandy's leaving night than Stephen had expected. They were gathered in small groups of friends who had not seen each other for a while – years in some cases. Some had left to work for a competitor, but now they just seemed to be continuing the conversations they were having when they last saw each other.

A familiar face caught Stephen's attention: Joe, who, on seeing Stephen, raised a glass from the other side of the room. And the fellow Joe was talking to looked over and did the same – another former colleague, now with a competitor, a very good competitor.

What a small world.

His attention was then caught by Sandy waving across to him. A gesture said that he was being offered a drink. Stephen signalled that he would be happy to accept.

He made his way through the crowd, and when he reached the bar, a glass was put into his hand. "Thanks, Sandy," he said.

"Thank you," said Sandy, "for all the help you've given me – us – over the years. I can't believe that Eadie's treated you the way he has."

"That's life," said Stephen. "But more importantly, good luck in your new career."

"Yes, I'm looking forward to it. On the whole, I really enjoyed working in this industry, but I've found a position somewhere else. It's not the same grade as I have here, but to be honest, I could do without the hassle. I'll still be managing a team of people, but the focus here will just be on maintaining vehicles. No politics getting in the way."

"How can you be sure of that?"

"Well, I probably can't be sure, but all the vibes I got during the interview were very positive. Everybody was polite to me and they all seemed to get on with each other. As you always advised, I tried to read between the lines of what everybody was saying and there were no signs of anything other than a group of people who enjoyed their jobs and took satisfaction from carrying them out."

"In that case, all the best. Cheers."

"Cheers."

Stephen was about to continue when someone he didn't recognise came over to talk to Sandy. Probably time for him to go home.

*

The next morning, Mike was brought round the office and introduced to everyone. He seemed slightly remote, as if already thinking of the changes he intended to make.

When lunch time, or, effectively, the second coffee break, arrived, Stephen went along to Felix's office where the two of them could shut the door and catch up on what was happening.

"It's sad that Sandy felt he had to go," said Stephen. "I'll miss him in some ways; he was a genuine guy, but to be honest, it's as if he was never here. Mike's settled straight into the role. No one's questioned it. Where is he just now?"

"I saw him just before you came along," said Felix. "He was leaving to go around the depots to see his engineers face to face and find out exactly how they're managing on a day-to-day basis. Obviously, he was going to see Jason first. But listen to this: there's a divisional board meeting here tomorrow."

"How do you know?"

"Derek told me."

"You're unbearable. Anyway, I've to prepare the minutes for a supplier meeting next week so I'll catch you later. But thanks for the biscuit."

*

The following morning seemed no different to any other, but everyone knew that the boardroom would be full. Not that the visitors themselves would be of any interest, but the team knew that there would be trays of sandwiches available after they had gone. Before they left, however, a few familiar faces appeared on a walkabout, stopping here and there to ask questions: not particularly meaningful ones. Probably people just wanting to appear polite rather than find out anything about the business.

When the party had moved on, Stephen's IT colleague Henry appeared at his desk. "Are you leaving, too?" Stephen asked.

"I am, actually. Too much interference from the centre. But the reason I'm here is to ask you if you would write a note to Eadie on the problems we're all experiencing?"

"Why should I? I still haven't been paid for the last time."

"Because that's your job, because you care," said Henry. "Eadie's down for a conference next week and I've made an appointment to meet him, to say goodbye, but also to tell him why I'm going. When I hand the note over to him, I'll just say that people knew I was seeing him and I found it lying on my desk."

Stephen went back to his list of tasks.

At midday, he got a call from Felix. "Do you want to go for a walk to the sandwich shop and get some fresh air?" Felix asked.

"Thanks," he replied, "but not today."

When he saw Felix leave the office, he went over to the machine and got a coffee. Back at his desk, he began typing out a list of current issues, and the costs associated with them, before describing how each in turn could be addressed and resolved.

He had been through board papers with Sandy often enough to know what the current issues were. Get your costs down. How? Reduce your workload. How? Make everything last longer. Fifty minutes later he laid three and a quarter pages of bullet points on Henry's desk.

"I knew you would," said Henry.

More changes at the top. An e-mail was circulated from head office announcing the appointment of a new group purchasing director and it wasn't long before it became the subject of office chatter.

"I hope he's better than the last one," said Stephen. "He simply removed some suppliers from the approved list. And not a word to the folk who were counting on the stuff to get vehicles back on the road – to earn money."

"But he wasn't there to earn money," said Felix, "he was there to save it. And he did, didn't he?"

"He reduced spend in some areas, but he caused more increases in other areas. He was a net disaster. He shouldn't have done anything if he didn't know the effect it would have on the business."

"Calm down," said Felix. "I was just joking. Yes, if you don't know the effect your actions will have, you shouldn't do anything. Not until you understand what the result will be. And he didn't. End of story."

Two weeks later, Stephen was surprised to see a number of strange faces in the office. They must be here for another divisional meeting, he thought, but it can't be another board meeting. What was going on?

"That's Millar," whispered Felix, who was observing the visitors from behind Stephen.

A number of e-mails later, it was almost lunch time. Stephen had noticed the sandwich trolley being pushed towards the boardroom. They'll soon all be out for a comfort break, he thought. Engrossed in an e-mail from a colleague in another operating company, Stephen was suddenly aware of a figure beside him. It was Millar. "How are you getting on with Mike?" he asked.

"Very well," Stephen replied, but it had seemed a very odd question. He didn't know Millar and he wondered if it was simply that Eadie had asked him to find out, or that Eadie had suggested to Millar that Stephen was somebody dangerous, somebody to be handled with care, not to be trusted.

A new e-mail. This time from Felix. It read 'Jack's just undone the last group contract that we set up.'

'So, I see,' Stephen typed in response.

Another e-mail from Felix: 'Open the new one from Millar. He's supported Jack and he's reduced Mike's budget; everyone's budget, in proportion to the average parts price reduction.'

'Does Mike know?' Stephen wrote back.

'Yesterday's meeting must just have been Millar working his way round all the opcos. in this division and telling folk how he wants to proceed. Mike was there so he must know. He'll be furious.' Felix wrote.

The phone rang. It was Felix. "Because it will be the same old scenario. The new purchasing people count the savings on last year's usage multiplied by the price reduction. But, in nine cases out of ten, the service life is shorter, usage goes up, labour is soaked up removing and replacing more of them, and as a consequence, routine maintenance suffers. And those at the coal face get the blame," said Felix. "There, that saved you saying it."

"What I was going to say," said Stephen, "is that the law of gravity acts downwards, not upwards and it's a never-ending task fighting it off. Ask an aeroplane about the realities of flight."

Mike came through to Felix's office and asked him to invite Stephen to join them.

"They're insane," said Mike. Do they really not understand what they've done? Anyway, I want you two to make up a list of all the diagnostic tools that we have and those that the current fleet needs. Tell me how long it will take you to get them and how much it will cost. Three diagnostic technicians will soon be joining us."

When Mike left, Stephen and Felix looked at each other before Felix said, "We seem to be going forwards again, or is that upwards?"

The following morning, Stephen was called to Mike's office. "I want you to do something for me," Mike said.

"Sure," said Stephen.

"Remind me where we are with that vehicle that suffered fire damage just before I came here. I'm under pressure to remain within budget and the estimate for the repair is quite high."

"This was an issue that had been discussed before, but Jack didn't pursue it," said Stephen. "The vehicle could have been better designed, and equally it could have been better specified. And maintenance staff could have been better familiarised with it. However, the facts of the incident were not in dispute. I'll forward to you the letter I drafted for Sandy in case he didn't leave it for you, and you can see how far we got."

"Thanks. I'll follow it up."

Stephen had always found that confrontation was not as successful as looking for a win-win situation. Both companies, they and their supplier, depended upon each other in the commercial world, and although they were totally independent, their relationship was almost akin to vertical integration. Discussing the detail design of the vehicle would give some credence to the request for assistance.

Both companies would hopefully learn from the incident and a goodwill contribution by way of parts supplied by the manufacturer was worth more to the operator than it cost the manufacturer. Surely it wouldn't be too difficult to find a solution here.

"A result," was all Mike said as he walked through the main office one afternoon not long afterwards. Mike was results driven and people respected him for that. And he stood out from many of his fellow directors by knowing his job inside out.

*

When Friday came, there was now even more for Felix, Joe and Stephen to discuss. They said nothing to each other during the day; all three simply kept their heads down to ensure that they had dealt with all their outstanding tasks before the day ended.

Stephen's first reminder that the weekly pint was now imminent was the sound of Felix locking his office door. Time to log off. "I take it that Joe will make his own way over the road?" he asked.

"He's just locking up as we talk," Felix replied.

Stephen's mind was still racing, and he looked around to see if there was anything that he should be taking with him. No, there wasn't.

The air was fresh outside, but it wasn't raining. The two of them just walked briskly across the road and into the bar. Home from home.

Felix pointed to one of the taps and said, "Three of them, please."

The barman hadn't really needed the request, but it had come out automatically.

"What were you doing today?" asked Felix.

Stephen's mind seemed to be elsewhere, and it took him a few seconds to reply. "Mike sent me an e-mail asking me to list all the problems we have that arise directly from all the poor-quality spare parts that the last divisional purchasing manager had thrust onto us. He also wanted me to give him an estimate of the time that we would lose through replacing these parts more frequently than the original equipment parts used by the vehicle manufacturer. I assume Jason told him that I had a background in work study in my early years with the organisation."

"And did you manage to tell him?"

"Yes. It was a bit tiring, but I managed."

Felix was about to ask another question when Joe turned up. "All he wants is good news," said Joe.

"You're talking about Mike," said Felix, handing Joe his pint.

"Who else? Cheers, by the way. But that's a good thing. He never complains, in fact he doesn't react at all if you give him bad news, but he always smiles and says, 'Well done', or something like that if you give him good news. I think that's how he gets the best out of us."

This time Stephen interrupted. "That reminds me of something a psychology student once told me. A lecturer had been telling them about the different effects that people smiling and people frowning can have on other people's reactions. Apparently, the lecturer used to pace backwards and forwards across the platform in the lecture theatre while talking and some of the students conspired to play a trick on him.

"During the next lecture, they all smiled as he walked to the right and frowned as he walked to the left and progressively, the distance he walked to the left reduced. He was finally pinned in a corner."

"And did you believe that?" Felix asked.

"There was no doubt some exaggeration but yes, I did believe it. And it's exactly what Joe has described."

Felix nodded, before asking a question. "I'm just curious why we haven't discussed this before. Joe, do you think Mike is the first person we've met who behaves like that?"

"I'm not sure," said Joe. "I've never been aware of anyone behaving like that, but maybe I simply hadn't noticed. Perhaps no one's ever had to behave like Mike because, until relatively recently, there haven't been the problems that there are now. The blame culture really only started when we became part of the group.

"But it doesn't surprise me that Mike doesn't blame people," said Stephen. "He knows the reasons for these problems and he simply wants to encourage people to get back to carrying on as they did before. And he'll be looking to any additional resources he needs from outside. Jason told me that Mike began his career here. I didn't know him then; I had probably left to do my business course. But he seems to have got to understand the job, and of course the industry, while he was working his way up the ladder with other companies."

"That'll be why he's settled in here so quickly," Joe replied. "He knows what our problems are and he'll be looking around for the means of resolving them." He then went up for another round.

"That's your beer, Felix," Joe said when he returned. "Drink it before it heats up. Anyway, Stephen, I was about to ask what you've been getting involved in this week."

"Funny you should ask. I got a call from one of our property people. Harold's new depot is due to open on Monday—"

"You mean the one with no inspection pits," Felix interrupted.

"Quite so," said Stephen, continuing. "They tried to drive a vehicle into it yesterday and it ended up like a beached whale. The ramp in from the street was too steep. One rear wheel was off the ground and the thing ground to a halt."

"So, what did the guy want? The loan of a jack?" Felix asked.

"No, I sent him the dimensions of the vehicle wheelbase, front and rear overhang, approach and departure angles, et cetera. He's probably out with a bag of cement as we speak."

Joe put down his glass and said, "What did you get up to, Felix?"

"Stephen was right. Mike gave me back the list of diagnostic tools for the new vehicles. He said, 'Go ahead'. Apparently, he's got his technicians starting on Monday, so he wants the stuff pdq.

"How was Mike able to find these technicians so quickly?" Stephen asked.

"What did you say to Sandy?" said Felix. "The informal organisation? Anyway, most of the tools are available off-the-shelf. Only three of them are on back-order. That means most of the stuff will be here by the time that the new people start. Not bad."

"Oh, I forgot to say," said Stephen. "Joe and I bumped into Clerk in the canteen at lunchtime today. He'd never spoken to me before, but he said that he was leaving. He seemed concerned that we might think he was running away. Apparently, he had asked his boss, Taylor, for a salary increase and been turned down. He's going back where he came from."

"It seems a bit drastic just to get a salary increase. I mean, he's well paid already, isn't he?" said Joe.

"He's probably just making a point. But I'd already heard he was leaving," said Felix. "Although I was told to keep it under wraps. Derek is going to be our new MD."

"That's a piece of good news," said Joe.

Chapter 3
Life at the mill

"Checked your e-mails?" asked Felix. "We've got another divisional MD, but again, it's someone from outside our business."

Stephen looked up. Felix and Joe were both at his desk. "They've obviously learned nothing from the Taylor episode," Stephen noted.

"I'd almost forgotten about him. Did he jump or was he pushed?" asked Joe.

"Neither," said Stephen. "After the Harold fiasco, the board obviously didn't think they'd get away with another high-profile departure. Taylor's probably been moved gently sideways and given some meaningless project to keep him busy."

"Busy at what? Counting his six-figure salary? I wish I knew as little about this business as he does. I could have asked for the same punishment," Felix mused. "And have you seen this one from Jack? He's trying to wriggle out of the problem with unsupported laminates."

"Not surprising," Joe answered. "It's nearly a day's work to replace one. Do you think he'll want to be associated with that?"

"That should have been dealt with in the new vehicle specification," said Stephen.

"I know," said Felix. "In fact, I think that one of your old specifications is still downstairs in the archive."

"Brilliant," said Joe. "It's there in black and white, but who's going to tell him?"

"You are," said all three at once.

"I'll send Jack an e-mail," said Stephen. "He won't like it, but he could still try to have the original specification re-introduced on future vehicles."

"He'll probably throw one of his tantrums," said Felix. "Keep your door locked."

"I don't have a door," said Stephen. "But remember, the laminate's the least of our problems on new vehicles at the moment," he continued.

"I'm aware of that," said Felix. "Colin phoned in this morning about that new batch of vehicles that he's got: wiring, air systems and radiators."

"I'll go down and see him this afternoon," said Stephen.

*

Amazingly, Colin was on good form when Stephen arrived at his depot. "What's the saying?" Colin said, smiling. *"Noli illigitimi carborundum?"*

"That's it."

The manufacturer's field service engineer was already there, and they both knew him well. He had already explained the electrical problem and arranged to have all the vehicles in the batch checked to avoid future problems. "I'll work my way through the list of vehicles as fast as I can, but you'll have three vehicles off the road tomorrow."

"I'll go and tell the operations team," said Colin.

"While you're here," said Stephen to the service engineer, "it's worth mentioning that the air filter shouldn't be installed like this. It pulls engine oil in here because of the pressure reduction that's caused by the turbocharger. I've got a depression gauge and I can show you on a road test."

The manufacturer's engineer replied that he was too busy at present; he could perhaps follow that up some other time, but Stephen knew that he understood exactly what the problem was.

Colin was having a coffee when Stephen went back to bring him up to date. Colin pointed to the machine. "Grab a cup and I'll show you the radiator I was telling Felix about. This vehicle had a bump yesterday, so we took off the body panels. Look at the radiator. Three months from new and it's badly blocked with road dirt."

"I see what you mean," said Stephen. "I'll get a photograph and note the mileage. A fast-fit radiator would have been ideal on this vehicle type."

"And on a few other new vehicle types," said Colin.

*

Back at the office for a meeting with the MD on vehicle breakdowns, Stephen put his head round Felix's door and asked, "Who's all going?"

"Just Derek, you and me."

All three arrived at the boardroom at the same time.

"You've read my e-mail," said Derek. "Who's going to start?"

"It's the new batteries that the group contact has brought in. They're not a heavy-duty specification," said Stephen. "They've probably been bought on price. In fact, they are not really heavy at all," he continued, smiling.

"What does that mean?" asked Derek, sensing that he was missing something.

"The savings have been obtained by using less lead. And it's the lead that holds the electrical charge."

"At least they'll be easy for the storemen to carry," quipped Felix, "and Health and Safety will be happy."

Felix often made light of things, but everyone probably accepted that laughing was better than crying.

Derek looked at him briefly before turning back to Stephen. "How does that affect vehicle reliability?"

"Normal lead acid batteries don't like deep cycling; that is, they don't like being discharged too deeply, but this is inevitable in our stop/start operations. Modern vehicles are also clever enough to avoid allowing a driver to try and start the engine when the battery charge is low enough to risk damaging the starter motor, hence the large number of vehicles failing to start. And, as these batteries don't like deep cycling, they last less than half the time of those provided by the vehicle manufacturer."

"And the solution?" asked Derek.

"Easy," said Stephen. "Just go back to original equipment specification and the problem will stop. Your spend on batteries will reduce, so you'll save money. The vehicles will be more reliable, so you'll earn more money. You'll need less overtime for the road recovery team, so you'll save even more money. The main board will stop moaning at you for excessive overtime spend. And all you need to do is ignore the group battery contract."

"Fat chance," said Derek.

*

"We don't often see you," said Joe when one of the new technicians appeared. "I'm just in to see Mike and give him a report on what I'm up to," he replied.

"So, what's the latest?" Joe asked.

"I've found something really interesting. There's a batch of vehicles where the transmission warranty is just about up and I've been asked to give them a health check. Some of them had low oil pressure and I phoned around to see if anyone I know had seen this before.

Apparently, it's an internal oil leak. And, if you don't get it corrected, you lose the transmission, so I'd better get on and give Mike the good news. But, while I'm here, what are you up to?"

"More of the usual. It's bad paint at the moment. Takes ages to dry and it fades in no time. Another problem inflicted on us by the new group purchasing director."

"At least I won't get dazzled if I see one in the street," was the response. "See you. Keep smiling."

Among Stephen's new e-mails was one from Jack asking for agenda items for the next meeting with one of the vehicle manufacturers. He gave a quick reply confirming that he was producing a report on three new items, and then amended his things-to-do-today list accordingly. That would keep him occupied for the next few hours.

He had barely started when Felix appeared at this desk. "Want to hear the latest? They're moving the glass contract, after all the effort we put into the current one."

"I was told earlier," said Stephen, "but I didn't want to depress you. Apparently, it's strategic."

"What kind of strategy reduces your access to a distress product? Wait 'til Joe hears about this. He's directly responsible for getting vehicles back on the road."

"It's certainly interesting to watch the changes made by the new head of purchasing. You've met his new deputy?"

"Yes," said Felix. "Derek introduced us to Alistair the day he started. I see that he sits next to you."

"How else do you think I keep up to date with all the changes they're making? Alistair carries out his business in a very professional manner and it's interesting to see how he goes out of his way to keep his boss in the picture. More than I would have expected. I assume that the boss is a control freak."

"Maybe," said Felix. "He certainly appears to be trying to run the whole show. Apparently, he was a bit pushy at the last divisional board meeting. Trying to muscle in on every other director's patch."

"Either he feels he's being protected by someone higher up, or he won't last long. Watch this space. But more interesting than that is listening in on Alistair's telephone conferences with his own team. I don't sense any nastiness; it seems to be quite a happy group of people. Their main project at present is reducing the number of suppliers."

"Yes, that's at Alistair's level," Felix said, "but the really big project is at main board level: the introduction of a central store."

"That's unlikely to work. And, even if they did manage to make it work, it's not necessary."

"But listen to this: they intend to abandon most of our current suppliers and look for cheaper alternatives."

"Say that again. Abandon our current suppliers? Stop buying sophisticated components that have been designed by specialists and have evolved over the years to give us the reliable vehicles we have today? Vehicles that we operate for our customers, vehicles that we depend on for our living. Do you not remember the phrase from the olden days in motoring, 'Get out and get under'? We can't go back in time, can we?"

"Don't worry, Stephen, you're not alone. Mike went crazy when he first heard them raise the idea."

"Did he tell them?"

"Even at his level, you have to watch what you say. But I'm sure he'll be lobbying whenever it's safe to do so."

"I think I'd better listen in on more of these telephone conferences. Come on, we'll grab a coffee on the way back to your office. This can't be ignored."

*

"Shut the door and sit down. I'll check my e-mails while you rabbit on," said Felix from behind his computer. And Stephen took up Felix's offer.

"This is unbelievable. When we first met, my role was to investigate problems with our vehicles and develop solutions in order to keep them running reliably and affordably. We needed that, and still do, for our business. Vehicle components have an expected life, and if that isn't met, an investigation takes place. It could be that our operating environment is unnecessarily harsh, possibly our preventative maintenance could be improved, or it could be that there is a design weakness with a vehicle type or a component. We had to determine which one it was.

"We used to hold meetings with vehicle manufacturers, and I would take along the reports that I had produced, setting out the problem, the weaknesses identified and my proposed solutions. We weren't the only organisation doing that. Other major competitors did so, and one outcome of that was the manufacturers often developed solutions in response to feedback.

"It was evolution, and things worked very well that way. But what's being proposed now? That we go back a hundred years? The purchasing guy's insane."

Felix's head reappeared. "What was it you used to say? All problems are solved backwards?"

"Those weren't simply vehicle problems I was talking about. Any problem, but especially larger ones. It was while I was doing word puzzles in newspapers that the analogy came to me. Do you know these puzzles where you're asked to change one word into another in five or six moves? You change one letter at a time, and each change should result in the creation of a real word.

"That really is like a major project. Ideally, just like the word puzzle, you should know exactly where you are at present, and you should be sure where you're going before you start making changes. And your business has to remain fully operational at all stages of the project.

"That's a useful discipline, because I've seen many projects in which it was recognised that there was a problem, but no consideration was given to the desired outcome before changes were devised and implemented. The focus was simply on improving the problem. People often ended up in a position that was worse than before."

"Yes, I remember now." Felix had abandoned his e-mails. "It was more for major projects. And this central store idea is such a project, isn't it? Why have they started it? Where are they going? To save money, I suspect. But, as you've always said, it's not the cost of a component, it's the life cost, including the cost of removing and replacing it. I can't wait to tell Derek."

Derek's leadership was tested a few weeks later. An incident during the night put the main office block out of action. When people turned up in the morning, they found that they were locked out and Derek was there, taking charge of proceedings. "We've got the IT people setting up computers in the conference suite," he said, "but anyone not involved may as well go home."

Nobody moved. How can we help, was the question.

While the computers in the open plan office were down, people drifted off to catch up with colleagues they had not seen for days, if not weeks. Stephen and Felix went over to see Jason and hear first-hand how his depot was operating.

"Not too badly, but have you heard they're sending in consultants?" said Jason. "I think they want to see how hard we're working."

"Oh dear," said Stephen. "I hadn't heard, but that might be my fault. A few weeks ago, I passed on a note about what the problems are and how they can all be addressed. They probably didn't understand the point about you having a shortage of labour. Here's what they'll be looking for."

Stephen sketched out the work study-based approach that he assumed the consultants would be taking and he indicated how the depot should operate while they were there.

"Got you," said Jason.

"It was lucky that we went over there," said Felix on the way back over to see if the conference room had been set up for everyone.

"Too true. All the board would need was some disinformation from an external source and they'd feel free to carry on as before."

When they got back to the conference room, it was like being back in secondary school. The room was full, with people seated at tables set out in rows. Everyone had a computer, and most were already busy reading e-mails or typing replies.

Stephen and Felix sat together, and some colleagues they seldom saw were seated not far away. "Let's see what they do for a living," whispered Felix.

The first item Stephen and he had to deal with was another group contract. Purchasing had again promised savings, so now Stephen called up a template of the previous year's contract. He keyed in the new allocation of vehicle types while Felix contacted Charles, the supplier, in order to give him the bad news.

"I'm way ahead of you," he replied. "I've been abroad sourcing cheaper products after receiving a call from group a few weeks ago. I should be able to send you a list of the new part numbers and prices by mid-afternoon."

"In that case," said Stephen when he heard, "we'll have our report ready by the end of the day."

Both he and Felix had sighed internally when they first heard of the latest call for price cuts. The industry was well known for having negotiated tight prices over the years, but the new people didn't seem to be aware of that. They would simply be setting out to stamp their authority. Quality would be down, and usage would go up, but at least in this case they were retaining a valued supplier whose technical support was invaluable.

Another e-mail. Another main board initiative.

"Look," said Felix. "Just what I told you. I bet they don't ask for input from the coal face; ask why these suppliers were appointed, and the pros and cons of each."

"They probably think that would slow down the process," said Stephen.

"I'm sure it would speed it up," Felix responded. "There are only five of us across the division and we've worked closely together for years, optimising specification, price, availability and after-market support. The only complaints that we get relate to things imposed on us by these supposedly cost-saving schemes."

One week later, they were back in their own offices. In some ways, it had been inconvenient working elbow to elbow with colleagues from a number of different departments, but it had also been fun. And it had been very informative seeing them go about their business, playing their part in keeping the operation going. And after work on Friday, Felix, Stephen and Joe were grateful to relax over a pint.

*

"This week was much less exciting that the one before. All back our own desks, just doing our bit to keep the place going," Joe said.

"I think we'll be having to try a lot harder from now on with all these changes in our purchasing procedures," Felix replied. "Do you agree?"

"I've never been involved in purchasing procedures. I've only ever been interested in their outcomes. Is the stuff I get fit for purpose and does it arrive on time? But I'm having problems with both of these requirements at present. What do you think, Stephen?"

"I agree that, if you're not directly involved in purchasing, there's no need to know how it works. In my role, problem solving, there shouldn't be any need either, but unfortunately purchasing's been the cause of a number of problems, so I agree with you. And I agree with Felix that things are going to get worse from now on, a lot worse. When I first started here, the purchasing manager worked closely with engineering to ensure that everything we bought was fit for purpose while he negotiated to drive down the price of the approved items, so I assumed that was how purchasing worked. I thought no more about it. But, Felix, do you remember that I had to attend a group purchasing meeting on your behalf last year while you were on holiday? The last manager was just nasty. And he didn't do the group's reputation much good either."

"I remember you telling me what you thought of him," said Felix. "I never told you, but I think everybody had the same opinion of him. I was glad that he left, or was forced to, and now I'm hoping that the current guy has the same fate."

"I'll drink to that," said Joe. "I just want to be left in peace to deal with the challenges that my job brings without having another department cause even more problems. So, tell me, what new difficulties are we about to experience? Felix, you go first."

"It's just what Stephen said. The company used to describe to the purchasing team exactly what it needed, and then purchasing went out to the marketplace to get the best deal for exactly that requirement. Now, they only seem to be focussing on purchasing procedures, how to go about things, all packaging and no content, with the single aim of showing that they've succeeded in getting a price reduction. But the one thing that's so very obviously missing is the detailed description of what's to be bought. I knew the purchasing manager Stephen's talking about so I'm totally aware that we needn't be in the mess we're in. And, I said, this is only the start."

"Would somebody buy me another pint?" said Joe. "I feel a sudden need."

"I think we all do," said Stephen. "I'll get this round."

While Stephen was at the bar, Joe asked Felix if he thought that there was anything that could be done.

"To be honest, I don't. The best option would be to get Stephen to sit down with Eadie and take him through exactly what's happening."

"Have you asked him to do that?"

"I did, in a sort of playful way, just to see what his reaction would be."

"And?"

"He just said that was no longer his role."

"Pity."

"One pint," said Stephen. "I'll just fetch the other two."

As soon as he went back to the bar, Joe asked Felix if they should raise the question again. Felix just shook his head.

"Here's yours, Felix," said Stephen. "Now, what have I missed?"

Felix replied, choosing his words with care. "We were just talking about the way our team rallied together last week. There's nothing wrong in principle with being part of a group, but last week proved that we as an operating company should simply be given a broad remit and then be allowed to do it our way."

"A good answer," said Stephen, "You've dealt with two important issues arising from being part of a group. Economies of scale and diseconomies of scale."

"If you say so."

"I do. The possibility of having more resources on board, a benefit, but the chances of the message being lost in transmission, a disbenefit."

"'Send reinforcements, we're going to advance' becoming 'send three and fourpence, we're going to a dance'?"

"You've got it in one."

Chapter 4
Impatience

On Monday morning, Stephen's computer was only just booting up when Joe arrived at his side. "Have you heard about this new guy, Lockhart?"

"Don't think so," said Stephen.

Joe took control of the mouse. "Come on, come on."

He passed it back to Stephen. "Log into your e-mails." They seemed to take forever to come up. "That one there."

Stephen read through it carefully. "That's incredible, I can see his job title, but I don't know him. He's trying to make a name for himself, that's obvious."

"And look at all the letters after his name."

"Eadie won't like that," noted Stephen. "I think we're looking at naked ambition. Not much useful content, but he's certainly trying to catch someone's attention."

"Well, as long as it's somebody sensible enough to see through him."

"Time will tell. Anyway, I've got my 'things-to-do-today' sheet to get through. I'll catch you later."

Before dealing with the next item on the list, Stephen looked round the office in case he was missing anything. People were settling in at their desks, starting to type on their keyboards or checking their computer screens. Alistair was just beginning one of his telephone conferences.

Should he listen in? Perhaps not: some of the discussions he had heard in recent weeks had annoyed him so much that he'd been tempted to interrupt. He'd rather not hear anything stupid that he couldn't readily influence.

There were actually two sheets of tasks for him to deal with. He made a start.

Item one. Millar was sending one of his team to visit all operating companies and lecture the engineering teams on how to do their jobs and Stephen had to be there. That would be the following Wednesday: he put that in his diary. Half past ten at Colin's depot. What would everyone make of that?

Item two. Jason had reported recurring problems with one type of vehicle. It had been reported for running out of fuel although investigation of the breakdowns had found no reason for the problem. It had reached Derek's level, and no doubt someone at the centre had latched onto it. He'd better deal with that today.

Item three. Speak to Mike. He'd do that just now.

The walk through to the directors' suite took him past Felix's office. What was he up to? Stephen looked in but there was someone with him. He'd catch up with him later.

Stephen knocked on the door and Mike looked up. "Come in," he said. "Take a seat. I want you to do something for me."

"Of course."

"A member of the main board says that he's invested in one of our minor suppliers and I've been asked to ensure that we don't forget to put some business his way. Do you know this firm?"

Stephen's first reaction was one of disbelief. It must also have been Mike's. "I do," he said. "How do you want me to deal with this?"

"Just make an appointment to visit them and ask them to give you a list of all the services they offer and then type up a brief note for me. That's all."

Stephen nodded and left the room. Felix was still busy on the way back and so he headed back to his desk and that inevitably led past Alistair, earphones on, and in one of his many telephone conferences. Stephen had too much to do to be distracted today.

Item four. But before he could read the full note, Felix appeared at his desk. "I saw you looking into my office. Anything interesting to report?"

"I was just along to see Mike, but if you'd been free, I'd have asked you if you'd seen this."

"What?"

Stephen pulled up the e-mail that Joe had brought to his attention. "Read that and tell me what you think."

Felix began reading and quite quickly started to smile. "What an idiot. Who is that guy?"

"He's a new manager in one of our other opcos. Apparently he's been the talk of the town this morning. Colin wrote to us as soon as he saw it and Joe brought it to my attention first thing this morning."

"What's his background? One of us, or another outsider? I certainly don't recognise the name. He could be from a competitor, but I doubt that any of them would be interested, considering the state we're in."

"No doubt we'll have more comment tomorrow. I'll let you know if I hear anything interesting."

*

As with most days, the morning had continued from the previous afternoon. The same people at the same desks doing the same things. A treadmill. Stephen went back to item four. A response to the agenda points for the supplier meeting that was scheduled to take place the following week. A batch of vehicles in operation across the division was about to come out of warranty cover and depots had been reporting problems with them. It was Stephen's responsibility to collate this information and present it to the supplier in such a manner that each issue could be explained clearly and a response obtained from them. He found it satisfying work, problem solving. Like a crossword puzzle or a Sudoku.

He would pass this work on to Jack, who would then forward it to the supplier in anticipation of a meaningful response at the meeting. Mike would be copied in.

*

After he'd forwarded his report, Stephen looked back at the list and item one caught his attention again. Why hadn't he paid more attention to it the first time round? He couldn't believe what he was reading.

Millar had formed a team of people that was to visit all operating companies in the division and advise them how they should be carrying out their day-to-day tasks. A range of standard operating procedures was also being introduced.

Who were these people? Retired and respected former colleagues? No, they had all been taken from the young team that had built up around Millar in his former role, and he himself wasn't particularly experienced. Eadie had probably appointed him to ensure that someone quiet and malleable would take over the role of the disgraced Harold. The team was scheduled to visit them next week.

*

Joe knocked on Felix's door. He said, "I'm up here because I got a call that my main supplier's been changed. Your team are just checking who the new people are."

Felix called Stephen. "Have you got a minute? We've potentially got another quality problem."

"It's not the first time that this has happened recently," Joe went on once Stephen had arrived, "but it's the first, no, second, time that it's caused serious problems for me. Parts don't fit. I can't get vehicles back into service. From what I can gather, it's strategic."

"That word again," said Stephen. "Pass me the dictionary. These new strategies must have been well thought out because they've been very successful in making things worse. Ignoring batteries, I think that electrical equipment is the only area that hasn't suffered. In fact, the new supplier is really very helpful."

"Couldn't disagree," said Felix. "But most other suppliers are completely fed up. No one goes out of their way to help now when we report a problem."

"Good will is becoming a thing of the past," said Stephen.

"But what about my problem?" Joe interrupted.

Felix walked over and had a word with one of his administrators. "Someone's on the case. I'll let you know when we get a response."

"Thanks."

When Joe had gone, Felix explained to Stephen that Joe wasn't the only manager having to deal with delivery or quality problems. "In order to rationalise the list of suppliers, the central team has given a vastly increased range of products to a company we've dealt with for years. We know their sales representative quite well and so we can ask him to follow up specific concerns, but I sense that he's been overwhelmed by the sheer volume of complaints. I've spoken to colleagues in some of our other opcos and they confirm that we're not alone.

"Another problem is that paperwork isn't as well managed as it used to be. Their sales people are probably also under pressure to cope with the step-change in volume. If they can't invoice us as quickly as before, we can't pay them as quickly as before. And then they put us on stop for non-payment and our depot staff then struggle to get vehicles back on the road to earn the money in the first place."

"A bit of exaggeration there, but I know what you mean," said Stephen. "And do their finance people not realise the importance of solving the problem? It's in their interest as well as ours. I went through a similar problem some seventeen years ago and it's not too difficult to resolve. All it takes is some good will on both sides."

"I thought accountants were meant to understand good will."

"Pass me the dictionary again," said Stephen.

"It's the new head purchasing guy. He's moving too quickly for the business and he'll probably move on before the shit hits the fan. Then everyone will be left to clean up the mess. We've had to do that quite often."

"At least we've become quite good at it," said Stephen.

"And meanwhile," Felix went on, "the folk who know what they're doing get the blame and then they're sacked. And you'll never be able to replace them."

"That's Eadie's philosophy: 'If you can't do it, I'll get somebody who can'. But, unfortunately, what that really means is that, if an experienced job holder stumbles, doing his best to meet the impossible demands of his boss, he'll be shown the door."

"You're meant to be able to attract and retain the right people."

"That's what the literature suggests. And develop these people. Some managers go as far as forgiving, if not encouraging, mistakes."

"As long as you learn from the mistake and make sure it isn't repeated."

"But that's one of Eadie's big failings. He's so insecure that he won't allow anyone close to him if they know more about the business than he does. And he's not good at accepting advice," said Stephen. "I've learned that to my cost."

"So, what do we do?"

"There is an answer. It's not ideal, but it works. Never criticize anyone; that will really put their back up. But if you have a solution to a problem, just plant the thought. When they finally understand what you've said, they'll adopt it as their idea and see it all the way through. It's painful, but it does solve the problem."

Felix thought for a moment. "It's effectively looking for a win-win situation, isn't it?"

"You've hit the nail on the head," said Stephen, "That's exactly how I try to deal with issues. It was when I was first involved in meetings with vehicle manufacturers, and that would be around the time that I first met you."

"Twenty-five years ago – twenty-six to be exact," Felix said.

"It must be," Stephen agreed. "Life's short, isn't it? Yet another reason to try to do your best every day. Achieve something. Anyway, when I identified a problem area with a vehicle, I was aware that the manufacturer's representatives were very non-committal. But when I thought about it, they were only defending their organisation in the same way I was defending mine. We wanted a vehicle component to be free of a particular weakness, and no doubt they wanted the same thing. So, when I showed them my analysis of the problem, I focussed more on the possible solution.

"We had a vehicle type with a certain weakness, but as a result of this investigation, we now had an answer. If we asked for all similar vehicle types to be upgraded free of charge, they would refuse. But, if we asked for the modification to be built into future vehicle purchases, they would agree, and similarly, with the specification of the relevant replacement components purchased from then on.

"I took that as a win-win situation. And, having made that discovery all those years ago, I find that it's still a very effective approach today."

When the agenda for the next meeting had been dealt with, Stephen turned his attention to his e-mail inbox. What to deal with next?

There, at the top, was another epistle from Lockhart. It must have taken him a full day to write it; had he no work to do? Or was it simply that he didn't know enough about his new job to be of any use to anyone?

It went on about the need for change – a good opening gambit for someone as impatient as he seemed to be, and someone who could offer no sound advice on improvements possible in the present situation.

Felix had to see this. Mike was already copied in and no doubt he had already forwarded it to Jason, Joe, Colin and the team. Stephen pressed the send button then sat back and read it again.

Not unexpectedly, the phone rang. A quick response from Felix. "He's unbelievable, isn't he? Is he implying that everything that has evolved over the years in this industry should be abandoned so that he can now tell us all what to do? It reminds me of playing snakes and ladders when I was a kid.

"While I'm on, there's some big cheese coming down from head office tomorrow to discuss vehicle availability with us, particularly repeating defects. Derek's just called me. Mike'll be there, of course, and

I gather he's already got Jason producing the information for the last financial period. Failing to prepare…"

"Got the message," said Stephen. "I haven't been asked to get involved, but I'll go over and see how Jason's getting on. It's amazing the number of problems that could have been avoided if we'd been involved in specifying our vehicles before they were ordered."

"No, wait. We've both to be present," said Felix.

"Yes, I've just seen that," Stephen replied.

The agenda for the meeting was vehicle reliability and availability.

"We're to stop doing what we can to fix things, and instead tell him what the problem is. He should know what the problem is," said Jason when Stephen went over to his depot to find out what the latest position was. "He's part of it."

"What are you complaining about? You're not even invited," said Stephen.

"But when the minutes come out," Jason countered, "I'll have to go through my maintenance records and write a report on where we are. That reminds me, while you're here, we had another of these vehicles run out of fuel last night. When it was towed in, I drained the tank myself and there was plenty of fuel left. It always happens when they're going uphill."

"What was the vehicle registration number, and where did it break down?"

*

The meeting was as bad as Jason had predicted: 'What have you done about this? What have you done about that? It had better be fixed before I come back.'

The next day, Stephen phoned Felix. "Do you want to go out for a sandwich at midday? You'll need your car."

"Sounds exciting," said Felix. "Come along to my office when you're ready."

Stephen went downstairs to see Joe. "Can I borrow a small sheet of aluminium, a spirit level and a scribe?"

"Sure, but what for?" said Joe.

"I'll show you when I get back."

*

Felix parked the car where Stephen suggested. He stood at the roadside and watched as Stephen dashed out and back again between the vehicles that were driving past and scratched the gradient and the road camber on the aluminium sheet.

"All done," Stephen said. "Let's go and buy the sandwiches."

*

"You're back," said Joe, as he appeared at Stephen's side. "What are you up to now?"

"I'm making a scale drawing of the vehicle's fuel tanks and then I'm going to rotate it through the angles of the road camber and the gradient. Jason's removing the fuel standpipe as we speak, and I'll then add it to the drawing."

"To achieve what?"

"It'll tell you how much fuel was left in the tank when it dropped to the level of the standpipe. Remember, the pipe is at the front of the offside tank and there could be quite a lot of fuel left when the tank was supposedly empty."

With the position of the pipe added to the drawing, the quantity of fuel still on board was calculated.

Stephen took the drawing over to Jason. "How much fuel did you drain from the tank?" he asked.

"About five gallons," Jason replied.

Stephen showed him the drawing. "How about twenty-six point six litres or five point eight five gallons?"

"That's it," said Jason.

"So, for the moment," said Stephen, "you just have to assume that the vehicle's tank capacity is six gallons less than claimed by the manufacturer. The permanent solution is to move the standpipe."

"Brilliant," said Jason. "When are you doing something about these radiators?"

"I'm glad you're pleased."

At the next meeting, nothing was said about this issue no longer being one of the reasons for breakdowns. There was no interest in the fact that this problem could have been avoided if someone had sat down with the manufacturer before the order had been placed. Someone who knew what they were doing, of course.

*

Again, Stephen had no idea of the time passing until he became aware of someone standing beside him. It was Felix. "Lunchtime. Time for some fresh air. A walk to the sandwich shop?"

"Again?" Stephen sounded quite impatient.

"That was yesterday," said Felix. "This is today. Put your jacket on and forget your computer for a while."

Stephen followed him out of the office, saying, "How can I forget it and all the rubbish that keeps flooding in? I can't even forget it when I'm at home."

"That's yet another reason to clear your head. And Derek asked me to update him ahead of the next board meeting. Spend is increasing, so he asked me to get the team to avoid any major spend until the next financial year."

"That's imminent, isn't it?"

As they left through the main entrance, Felix nodded before looking round to make sure it was safe to cross the road.

"Hello, Felix."

It took a moment or two before Felix could identify the person who had spoken. Somehow, recognising Felix hadn't been a problem for him. It was the new group purchasing director standing outside on the pavement and smoking a cigarette. Why was he there? Neither Felix nor Stephen was aware of any group meetings that day.

"I was wondering if you would be interested in monitoring a prototype vehicle in service," he continued.

Stephen was about to say that it would be more useful to agree the specification with the manufacturer before committing to anything. Felix must have been reading his thoughts. He'd seen prototypes come and go in the past, but they had simply been some kind of publicity stunt. No one had ever asked for meaningful feedback.

"It might be better to ask Mike," said Felix.

*

Yet another meeting on vehicle downtime was arranged, but the visit by Millar's team to educate them all had been postponed. There wasn't a round of applause, just a shaking of heads. And the guy from the centre wasn't present for the meeting on downtime. Derek chaired it, and the conversation was more open this time. "By the way," he said to Felix and Stephen when the meeting was over, "there's some money to be spent before the end of the financial year."

Both of them knew exactly what to do with it, and an order was placed.

Jason was first on the phone. "I hear that we've got some real batteries in stock. How many can I have?"

Felix was logging off when there was a light tap at the door. It was Joe. "Come in," said Felix. "We were just talking about you. We assumed you'd be late for your pint. Just as you usually are."

"We had to shut up shop on time today," said Joe. "That new supplier's still giving us problems."

"Just look on the bright side," said Felix. "You'll have a pint in your hand in exactly four minutes. Let's go."

*

With drinks in their hands, they made their way over to their seats, Felix in the lead. He seemed his usual mischievous self. "Cheers, Joe. Cheer up, Stephen. Hello, are you still with us?"

Stephen was deep in thought, but Felix had managed to catch his attention. "Sorry, I was just wondering if we should be dealing with things in a different way."

"Like what?" Felix asked.

"By reporting every problem that has resulted from non-genuine spare parts that have come in via the changes that group purchasing have made." Felix put down his pint. "Like bad batteries, for example. Jason's reaction summed up the mess we're all in at present. Everybody in this company and no doubt all the others in this division. That's easy. Just bypass the group purchasing director. Go directly to Eadie."

"On you go, then," said Joe.

"Well, Stephen, you've heard what Joe said. Get on with it." Felix laughed.

"After the mess that advising him got me into. No chance."

"So, he'll just be left in the dark," said Felix. "No, one'll tell him what effect these problems are having on the business right across the division and how easily they could be fixed. If he's just looking at the bottom line, he'll know there are problems but his first reaction will simply be to get his team to go around and threaten everybody, and then we'll have two problems. Bad parts and low morale. Great. But one thing I forgot to ask. How did the visit go of Millar's high-flying consultants to Colin's depot?"

"It was postponed," was all that Stephen said.

Luckily, the conversation turned to how the current problems should be addressed. The university of life had taught them and their colleagues the answer to most of the issues that might be encountered in this fast-moving environment.

So, from now on, whenever one did crop up, especially if it had been created by these new directors, the team would advise Derek. The information would then no doubt end up in a board paper and make its way up the chain.

"What do they say?" said Felix. "By your pupils you'll be taught?"

"Maybe not in this case, if you're thinking of Millar's team," Stephen replied.

"Not funny," replied Felix.

Chapter 5
Mine!

It had been a full year since Derek had been promoted, and life in the operating company had become less stressful. People in all departments were fully occupied – it was that kind of business – but they were also comfortable in their roles. It was a happy place again.

There were still occasional visits by members of the main board asking for progress reports regarding vehicle reliability and engineering spend, but there were never any issues that demanded immediate action.

Mike had also played a role in reducing stress. His focus was on managing the engineering workload by ensuring that the needs of the vehicles were met by appropriately training and equipping his staff. In the past, changes in the vehicle fleet had not always resulted in such action being taken. This was not because the engineering director at the time had been unaware of its importance, but rather that his request to make the necessary investment had been turned down.

Derek was not an engineer, but he trusted Mike's judgement and left him to manage as he saw fit. To be more specific, he had kept an open mind when Mike was appointed, but informal chats with Felix, Jason, Joe and the others had completed the picture for him. They all knew that Mike was a good manager who understood the operation along with its strengths and weaknesses. And if he thought that something was not quite right, he would say so immediately and set out the action he required.

As well as being in Derek's team, Mike reported to Jack who was known to blame people when problems arose. However, this might have counted against him.

When Jack was moved to another division not long afterwards, there was initially some rejoicing amongst those who had worked with him most closely. However, this stopped immediately when it was announced that Lockhart would replace him.

What about his e-mails? Surely these should have been a warning to the board, but no, he now had a central role and he wanted to appoint a team around himself. Some people would be made redundant while others would report directly to him. It was truly difficult to say which was the worse fate. Certainly, had Stephen been able to afford to leave, he would have done so.

The new team was created, and Stephen was part of it. All members were called to a brief meeting in Lockhart's office, along with representatives of major suppliers. Out of earshot, both groups expressed amazement that they had all been asked to travel, in some cases long distances, simply to hear Lockhart describe the changes to the structure. It was not lost on anyone that, of those present, he knew least about the business. Even much later, this remained a topic of conversation.

There now began a number of military-style projects. None was necessary and none, as it would turn out, was destined to be completed. They were all named after seabirds and the first one was to set up a meeting with an engine re-manufacturer Lockhart knew from his previous job. The majority of the team was obliged to attend, but at least the host company was very welcoming, and before lunch, they provided a tour of their workshops. Knowledgeable staff were happy to explain what they were doing as the party moved from one workstation to the next. A genuine rapport built up between the team and the supplier's representatives.

The next stage was to agree what type of engine would be re-manufactured or, rather, to endorse the type of engine that Lockhart had already selected. Of all the engine types in the fleet, this one was the cheapest to own in pence per mile operated. It was more or less trouble free, but of more concern to Stephen, the vehicle type that used it had been in the fleet for over twelve years. It was now due to be phased out. Therefore, by the time the trial was completed, the majority of them would have been scrapped.

Stephen looked around the room. Surely everyone was well aware of the other engine type in the fleet that had the potential to benefit from this exercise. But better still, a win-win situation could have been sought with its manufacturer. Stephen had already done the work necessary to allow that project to proceed.

But deep in his heart, he knew that this was the beginning of the end of everything that he and his colleagues had achieved in the industry. Should he say anything? He could certainly say nothing now: it was not the done thing to contradict a colleague in public. But would advice from anyone ever be accepted? No. Lockhart had told the world that this was what was happening and to change now would be loss of face.

"I've got a spare unit," said one of the team. "I won't need it back, but I'm certain one of my colleagues would put it into service for evaluation."

"I'll do it," said another.

The unit was duly provided, re-manufactured and put into service. That was the last that anyone heard of it.

Time-wasting charts and techniques were now being implemented by Lockhart. The temporary office accommodation used after the incident last year had reminded Stephen of secondary school. These new charts now reminded him of primary school.

The impression they gave was that Lockhart was trying to teach himself the business while trying to give the impression that he was teaching his new team. Stephen was sure that no one in the team, or elsewhere in the organisation, had been fooled – except the main board, of course.

*

"What are you doing?" asked Felix.

"Look at that," said Stephen. "Absolute rubbish. Engineering made simple. We're all to follow these time-wasting techniques and charts."

"You're joking. This is a real step back and here was I thinking the place was getting better."

"We all were."

"Have you told Mike?"

"I'm not allowed to. I've been reminded, threatened, that I don't work for him anymore."

Felix just shook his head and walked back to his office.

The new team had now to set out and submit problem-solving diagrams for each of the enumerated issues. The tricky part was manipulating the logic, if that was the word, within these diagrams to ensure that it arrived at the known solution.

Stephen was asked to deal with one issue as a matter of priority. He read the report submitted by the operating company and it was exactly the same problem that Stephen had earlier identified and drawn to the attention of the manufacturer's technician in Colin's depot, the design of the engine's air filter. This problem wasn't yet top of the list, but it was good that it had now been raised formally.

With Jason's help, he carried out an experiment on a vehicle similar to the one in the report. And for his part, Jason was grateful that a potentially time-consuming problem was now being addressed.

Stephen was therefore able to reply that it was an issue that was no fault of the operating company that had reported it but was certainly one that required raising formally with the manufacturer. Would now be the time for him to reveal his suggested solution?

The response from Lockhart? None.

"First, he confronts the supplier and makes them defensive, and then he backs off and lets them walk all over us," Stephen complained to Felix when they met at the machine for their afternoon coffee. "We've moved back about fifty years."

"I'll take your word for that," murmured Felix between sips.

"When Jack was moved on, there was almost nobody left at the centre capable of understanding the business, far less contributing to it. But it's fascinating watching them wriggle and posture. They want to exercise their authority, but they've got nothing to contribute."

Felix looked up again. "That seems to be true of all the new senior people these days. No matter where you look, there's somebody asking irrelevant questions. For example, that new finance guy who was down last week. He talked nonsense while he was here, and then he phoned as he was driving home and said that he'd seen that one of our vehicles needed re-painting. 'Just trying to help', he said. What were we meant to do? Re-write the paint programme?"

"Ignore him," said Stephen, "if we acted on all the rubbish that gets hurled at us, we'd be out of business. It must just be ego that drives them. 'I'm a director. I'm magnificent. I'll make them show me some respect'."

"That's so true that it's not funny."

Despite the constant background noise in the open-plan office, Stephen was keeping up with the endless list of e-mails that he found on his computer screen. He was engrossed in one of them when Alistair asked if he would have time for a drink after work some time.

"When?" asked Stephen.

"This evening?"

"Of course."

That was a surprise, but it would be a good opportunity to find out what Alistair thought of the organisation

At the end of the afternoon, they went to a hotel in the middle of town. It was a relaxing, but interesting evening and Alistair did most of the talking. Purchasing was his discipline, and he was passionate about it. And from what he was saying, and from what Stephen had already overheard, he was a good manager. His team were expected to behave professionally, and he seemed to be a supportive manager.

Where he felt it was appropriate, Stephen expanded on some of Alistair's points, but in the context of this industry. And context was the key issue. Would all of

Alistair's actions be correct in this environment? Stephen reminded himself of one of his sillier thoughts. Is three a good number? Good if it's the points on your lottery ticket, but bad if it's the number of points on your driving licence. He didn't say that.

The following morning, while his computer was booting up, Stephen went through to see Felix and report on the previous evening. However, the moment he walked into to his office, he could see that there was bad news. Very bad. Derek had been sacked by the new divisional MD. What had he done to her? Did she think she was helping the organisation, or was she just trying to show the board how nasty she could be? Felix said nothing more and Stephen simply went back to his desk.

Later that day, the news was official. Derek had left the organisation and one of his team would be taking over while a replacement was found. Although wounded, the company would be able to keep hobbling along, but the next change would be critical.

Stephen's e-mails were almost all now from Lockhart, or one of the new central team. At least they knew what they were talking about.

An e-mail appeared, from Lockhart. There would be another meeting that the new team had to attend, and this time it was with the company's major supplier. The team members were given instructions to analyse the performance of the latest vehicle type provided by this supplier and compare it with that of one from a competitor. A few phone calls between the team members and the summaries were typed up and forwarded to Lockhart. The date of the meeting was confirmed, and Stephen made his travel arrangements.

*

The meeting was held on the premises of one of the group's operating depots, and arrangements had been made for one example of each vehicle type to be made available for inspection at some point during the day. Some of the supplier's representatives were well known to the team but there were now also some people from their head office. They were taking it seriously.

The day began with coffee and biscuits, and people took the opportunity to talk to each other and explain what their roles were. The agenda had been set out with care and it was followed to the letter. The team assumed that embarrassment wouldn't be far away, and soon enough, it came. Lockhart announced that the reliability of 'his' vehicles, 'my vehicles', was at the core of the business. What planet was he on? He'd only just been appointed to his position and people still couldn't work out why. Now he seemed to believe he owned the place. There had to be a medical term for that.

How had the others reacted, the other members of the team and the manufacturer's representatives? It was impossible to tell, but it seemed even more difficult to take Lockhart seriously after that. And by coincidence, at another meeting shortly afterwards, Stephen met someone who had worked with Lockhart in his previous organisation; he was apparently notorious for stealing other people's ideas and presenting them as his own. That was useful to know.

*

Felix was at the coffee machine when Stephen arrived at his desk the following morning. "How did it go?" Felix asked.

"Difficult to say. At least the manufacturer got a guided tour of their vehicle and one from a competitor and got our opinions of each of them."

"That sounds like a successful day?"

"Part of it was. But what's been happening while I was away?"

"Clerk's back as our MD."

"Interesting."

Felix put down his cup and pointed to Stephen's screen. "Open that one," he said.

Stephen did as he was told, and there it was in black and white. "He wasn't away very long. Did he ask to come back, or was he invited?" he asked.

"Invited by whom? Eadie? Maybe. But it could be that he'd enjoyed his time here and maybe assumed that he could eventually replace Taylor."

"The fellow who wouldn't give him a pay rise?"

"The fellow we thought wouldn't give him a pay rise," Felix corrected him. "Anyway, the deed is done.

It's a pity about Derek; having him in charge was one of the best moments recently. He had come from the team; he knew everybody and therefore whom to approach in any situation. At least he's got a new job; that was one bit of good news. He was snapped up by someone as soon as the news broke. And we've worked with Clerk before so we know how he operates. Here's hoping."

"Yes, Clerk just concentrates on the business side of things, and in the past, if he had any questions for us, he'd just ask the engineering director: Alan, Jack, Sandy and now Mike. So, I assume that will continue and we can just get on with our own work."

"Let's hope so. Derek and I were always close so I was able to understand where we were at any point in time. That helped me plan ahead for my own team and so his departure was quite a shock for me in a number of ways. For one thing, future changes will be more of a surprise to me than they were in the past. Anyway, changing the subject, tell me more about the meeting Lockhart summoned you all to attend."

"In its own way, it was nearly as shocking as Derek going. We were all embarrassed that we should be associated with such an idiot. Maybe humiliated is too strong a word, but certainly embarrassed. And it made our organisation look ridiculous. What must have been going through the minds of the supplier's team, some of whom occupied very senior positions? An organisation that had appointed someone like him and failed to monitor his behaviour. It doesn't bear thinking about. Will they be able to take us seriously from now on?"

Felix nodded in sympathy. "A new low," was all he said.

Lockhart had obviously enjoyed meeting the manufacturer. Everyone in his team was told what an important step had been taken and they should now take advantage of the manufacturer's renewed involvement in the day-to-day operation of their vehicles.

However, chatting to some of the manufacturer's representatives, their team had received different feedback. They would now have to be more cautious when discussing issues at a local level. They would still keep in touch, but now only to receive information and not to offer verbal advice. That was a pity.

The coming weeks now took on quiet but steady sending and receiving of e-mails. Clerk's aim, as usual, was to grow the business, and he was good at networking locally.

One day, quite unexpectedly, Stephen was asked to go through to see him. "I've been given a project by the chief executive and I want you to get involved," said Clerk.

Stephen sat down while Clerk took him through the plan. It was a local project in relation to environmental improvement, so not necessarily something that would also involve Lockhart or Mike. Stephen did of course ask if the project had their approval. Apparently it did.

The project was interesting in concept, although only at an early stage, but it reminded Stephen of a similar situation some twenty-five years earlier and he was keen to learn more. He would have to wait until the originator arranged to visit him in the office.

When he was back at his desk, the phone rang. It was Colin, and Stephen tried not to sound too disappointed. "I'm having some problems with some of these vehicles that have just been transferred into my depot," Colin said.

"What kind of problems?"

"Occasionally, the brakes come on when we're reversing."

"When the steering's on full lock?"

"That's right. How did you know?"

"It's not a problem, I'm afraid. It's how they're programmed. You'll just have to get used to it. All you needed was some training from the manufacturer's local team. I can't arrange that for you, but if you mention it to Mike, I'm sure he'll set up something for you. Meanwhile, if I see him first, I'll mention it to him. It should really have been carried out when Clerk called for them to be transferred to you in the first place. Hope that helps."

"Thanks, Stephen. I'll give Mike a call just now."

*

The phone rang. It was Clerk's secretary. Would Stephen be free to join him for a drink one evening? That was as unexpected as Millar turning up out of nowhere to ask him if he was getting on well with Mike. The first time Clerk had been with the company he had no contact with Stephen until the chance encounter in the canteen the week before he left. But now this? Why?

Stephen had no idea what Clerk had planned to discuss with him, but he prepared a list of current issues that might, from Clerk's perspective, be relevant to the current operation of the business. He wouldn't want a microscopic view of what was going on but the details on which Stephen focussed did have outcomes at the macroscopic level.

Stephen now began to wonder if Eadie had asked Clerk to tell him if he believed that Stephen was a danger to the business. However, later that week, they met in a club of which Clerk was a member. After clinking glasses, the first topic of their conversation, somewhat unexpectedly, was the problem with the vehicle type that was prone to running out of fuel. It was an engineering issue of course but also one that would be apparent to anyone monitoring the reliability of vehicles in service and any problems that would immediately affect customers.

The evening moved on comfortably and ended up with a meal in a local restaurant. Conversation now was more general. It could have been that Clerk knew of Stephen's passion for cars, one make in particular, but when he mentioned that many years earlier, he had shared a flat with one of the industry's great influencers, he really struck a chord.

Yes, Stephen did know of that family and the beneficial influence that they had had on that make of car. Small world. Very small.

A few weeks later, Stephen met the project manager and learned what the trial would involve. It wouldn't be too difficult to have a few vehicles modified and put into service to be monitored. That was added to his things-to-do-today list.

The next e-mail was a shock. Clerk had sacked George; someone Stephen had known since he first joined the organisation thirty-four years earlier. What on earth for?

The e-mail hadn't come from Clerk but from Felix. Why hadn't it been announced officially?

Stephen picked up his phone. "What's all that about?" he asked.

"Apparently he saw George as 'difficult'," replied Felix.

"Difficult? Never. He was pedantic, that's for sure, but he filled his role perfectly. I didn't envy him in that role, but somebody had to do it. That's frightening. Do you think I had a lucky escape when Clerk invited me out for a drink? Who knows?"

"It certainly won't do morale any good anywhere in the company. Everyone else will now be looking around all the time to see if they're going to be next. I'll try to find out more, and if I do, I'll let you and Joe know when we go for our pint tomorrow."

*

The shadow made Stephen look up. Felix pointed to his watch. "Just let me finish this and I'll be with you," said Stephen.

Felix simply said that he'd see Stephen over the road.

*

"That's yours," said Joe. "Good health."

Stephen and Felix toasted him in return.

"So, who's going to take over from George?" Joe asked.

"No idea. Who'd want a new legally required bureaucratic role like that?" Stephen replied.

"Not me. But he was good at it."

Felix put down his pint and spoke. "I phoned George when he got home. He was devastated. He honestly couldn't think that anything he did was wrong. He'd been with this company all his career, earning money to look after himself and his family, paying into his pension to make sure he'd be secure in retirement and then somebody does that to him for no reason that he could think of."

"I can't think of any reason either," said Joe. "He was always available to look at any issue that my team had. He'll be missed."

"I told him that when we spoke," said Felix. "That might have helped a bit but if it did, I picked up no signals. Poor boy. But it makes you wonder how people can be so thoughtless in their treatment of others. What do you think, Stephen?"

"It's a big question. An organisation needs a leader. People are programmed to follow a leader who, in turn, requires attributes that are appropriate to the situation. Our business is relatively simple, but as with any other business, it needs to understand what product or service it has decided to provide.

"The leader needs first of all to retain the confidence of the employees, but he also needs to understand the market and how to meet the market's expectations. Not many individuals are able to fulfil all of these requirements so, for the second two, if he does not have the necessary training or experience, he needs to design a team around him that is capable of fulfilling them. And that's where the problems can begin. It can be a long and hard journey to the top, so they have to be determined to make it. That can mean thinking of themselves before others."

"Do you mean a psychopath?" Felix asked.

"No, I wasn't meaning that. But some of the literature does use the term psychotic. A managing director is dealing with a bigger picture than other members of the organisation. Decisions are made at a high level, but I believe that, in a civilised world, there should be some function in every organisation to look after employees as best it can. An individual may be part of an organisation, but the organisation is part of the community, civilisation.

"I don't believe that he should have got rid of George, but do you remember the university experiment with students playing the roles of prisoners and jailers?"

"I've heard of it. People behaving badly." Felix said.

"Such behaviour is innate in people," Stephen continued. "Think of road rage. I used to call that bad behaviour, now I call it natural behaviour. A squirt of adrenalin; that's natural, but in our global community it's no longer acceptable. I would say that civilisation is the thin veneer over innate behaviour, but if people can't be taught to compromise their innate responses, then mankind won't be able to reap the benefits that civilisation can bring: food, shelter, healthcare, education."

There was a silence for a few minutes, until Felix broke it. "On a more humorous note, our divisional MD's kept her head down until now, but according to a reliable source, she made complete fools of us all at a top-level meeting with our major supplier. Whatever she studied at school, it didn't seem to include the laws of motion. She seems to want our new vehicles to be able to ignore them. And, to make the point, she apparently stormed out of the room. Do you remember Princess Tantrum on children's television? It seemed to be a bit like that."

"Well, if you didn't understand Newton, how would you make your point?" asked Stephen.

"Never mind that," said Joe. "How did all this begin?"

Felix put his pint down. "You're too young to remember. But Stephen and I met at what was then the head office exactly thirty-three years ago. I was a management trainee just out of school and Stephen moved up from the central workshop in a technical role. He'd just started the year before in the work study department. That's right, isn't it?"

"Yes," said Stephen. "I remember it as if it were yesterday. I was fascinated by the idea of job design and the ability to make things more efficient. But I wanted to work with vehicles in a more direct way, so when the technical job was advertised, I applied and got it. And the rest, as they say, is history. But maybe we should be more concerned about what next week will bring. What the latest news is."

Felix put down his pint and smiled . "It's my birthday next Friday. You and Joe come up to my office at coffee break and bring a cake with you. And then you can buy me a pint after work."

Part Two
Reflections upon childhood

Chapter 6
Pause

After completing his engineering degree, the young Stephen wondered what direction his career should take. His dream had always been to design motor cars, and perhaps that should have led him to apply to a manufacturer, but for whatever reason, it didn't. One of his fourth-year subjects had been work study, a discipline including work measurement and method study. And it was when trawling job advertisements in newspapers that he found a vacancy for a work study practitioner in healthcare. He applied and was accepted.

The organisation had taken him on as a trainee, and he and another new staff member were quickly placed on a formal course. His interest in the subject grew as the weeks passed and it was as fascinating as he had hoped, particularly method study. He couldn't wait to get back to the office and start his first assignment.

The following eighteen months were enjoyable and offered him the opportunity to put into practice the theory he had been taught. The only thing missing was an engineering environment, and one day, another advertisement caught his attention. A work study practitioner was required by a vehicle operator. Were people meant to move on so quickly? Perhaps not, but he couldn't turn down the opportunity to put his training into practice in an engineering environment.

The interviewers representing human resources, the work study function and engineering were all very polite and their questions seemed very straightforward. He was asked if he understood the design and operation of vehicles and if he was familiar with the two main disciplines of work study. No question took him out of his comfort zone. Two weeks later, he received a written offer.

The head of the department introduced him to his new colleagues, and all of them appeared genuinely welcoming. He would be based here in the office but would be required to visit the operating depots from time to time in order to follow up specific projects. Another of the requirements was that he should attend evening classes in the discipline. That would be no problem and he would not be alone; two of his colleagues would be doing the same thing.

He was now a team leader reporting to the deputy head of department, and the job involved creating job times in a vehicle maintenance environment in order to allow an incentive bonus scheme to be rolled out through the company. He quickly sensed that the organisation's work measurement programme was unlikely to be completed and his interest in method study continued to grow. He likened it to a learning curve. The potential for improvement was almost limitless.

One thing he had not anticipated was the close working relationship that the department had with the trade unions. He was introduced to one of the shop stewards who would be involved in agreeing the job times that the department produced; he seemed quite straightforward.

The first few weeks passed quite quickly. New things to learn, new people to meet. The department closest to the office was the one in which vehicle components were re-manufactured and this is where Stephen initially became involved.

One morning, the foreman appeared at Stephen's desk. "We've got another job that we'd like your team to measure," he said.

"Of course," said Stephen. "When would you like us to do it?"

"Whenever your boys are free, but maybe you could look at it first. It's an axle type we get to re-work, but there are problems with it. Major cracks form, and then all we can do is scrap it."

They went down to the workshop.

"Look, there's an example," said the foreman.

"Fatigue cracks," said Stephen. "That radius is too small. You could increase it to fifteen millimetres since the component that is pressed onto it is formed to allow that. Any questions, just let me know."

"Will do. But, while you're here, we've got another problem for you. These brake drums are queuing to have all the wear marks machined out of them and have their internal diameter taken out to the dimensions supplied by the vehicle manufacturer. The vehicle then goes back into service using increased-thickness brake linings. I can't see what we're doing wrong, but drivers complain about vibrations during braking. They call it brake knock, and the depots are blaming our drums."

"Can I see one that you've finished? But, before we do that, what machine do you use to carry out the work?"

The foreman pointed to a vertical boring machine at the other side of the workshop.

"And how do you machine the drums?" asked Stephen.

"Just one pass, from top to bottom."

Stephen looked at the reworked drum before feeling the surface with his fingers. "There's your answer," he said. "The machined surface on the drum is acting like a screw thread and the brake shoe will be pulled off centre before jumping back to its normal position. That will keep repeating while the vehicle is moving and the brakes are applied. The drivers will experience a bump, bump, bump sensation."

"Is there any answer to that?"

"Yes, you could simply tell the depots to be patient, since the surface of the drum will eventually become smooth, but the ideal answer is for you to carry out two passes on the borer, one down and one up. You'll be left with a diamond pattern on the surface. The shoes won't be pulled off centre. I'll get someone to time the revised job, so you'll still get your bonus, but no complaints from the drivers."

"That's more like it. Thanks."

*

Weeks turned to months but the job remained as enjoyable as ever. The evening classes were also enjoyable and very relevant to the work of the department. Stephen was now quite comfortable in the daily routine. He attended meetings, made decisions, and produced weekly reports for his line manager. And he felt that he was pulling his weight; he could contribute to discussions and offer advice where his training and experience were relevant. But, for much of the time, he was still learning, either through reading between the lines of what was being said, or by being mentored by a colleague when appropriate.

Experience is important, he thought, very important. Training too, education. But probably experience is the more important of the two.

Another aspect of activity in the workplace was that everyone seemed quite happy. There were no confrontations, no strained expressions to be seen. Ever. This seemed too good to be true. And to some extent it was. The shop stewards he spoke to, whether socially or during formal meetings, were usually very pleasant. There was one exception, however.

Stephen had been curious to see if there were any brake drums that had been machined as he had suggested. It hadn't been a formal change, but he wondered if it had been carried out, even just to see how the resulting finish looked. As he looked around, one of the machinists came over to ask if he could help. Before Stephen could reply, another figure appeared.

"If you want to talk to any of my men, ask me first. Understood?" The character in question was someone Stephen hadn't met before. "Just remember that," he snapped, before turning and walking away.

"Ignore him," said the machinist. "He's one of the shop stewards – just likes to keep management in their place."

That was the only time that Stephen had met anyone in any way confrontational in the workshop. When he thought about it later, he was actually surprised that he hadn't encountered hostility more often. Back in the office, he mentioned the encounter to one of his team.

"They run the place," was the reply. "They've got no reason to be difficult. Mind you, if they didn't like something, they'd soon let everybody know. The guy you met is just grumpy by nature. Nobody bothers about him. They probably think it's good that somebody goes out of his way to keep management on their toes."

Not long afterwards, he was invited to his boss's office to attend a meeting with the principal engineer. As he made his way past the desk of Matt, one of the older members of the team, the two of them made eye contact. Matt leant forward in a conspiratorial manner and Stephen stopped to hear what he was about to say. "Work study does not ask what is done; work study asks what is achieved."

He then sat back in his chair, implying that Stephen was free to carry on. But what was the message? He paused to think about it. It was the first of his many epiphany moments. It expressed exactly what he felt he wanted to achieve in his career. Why couldn't he have thought of that himself?

He had almost forgotten that he was now in the meeting.

"I hear that you've cured our axle problem." the head of department said.

"It wasn't difficult," said Stephen. "Just a small change to the machining process."

"There's a vacancy for a technical engineer. You should apply."

Meeting over.

Another interview. Four faces to address. Two of them were familiar: they had been present at his previous interview, and if he were successful, one of them would be his line manager.

The questions were searching, some outside his comfort zone, but he was able to deal with them more calmly than he had feared. Was it experience or adrenalin talking?

The interview went well and Stephen was appointed.

On day one, he was taken around by his new manager and introduced to the team. Fifteen faces and fifteen names. How long would it be before he could remember which ones went together? The engineering teams offered electrical, mechanical and civil engineering support to the organisation and they, in turn, were supported by the office administrators.

The rest of that first morning was spent with Jim, his line manager who described the current workload, and most specifically, the projects in which Stephen would initially be involved. Back in the main office after lunch, the senior administrator took him round the support team, this time more slowly. They introduced themselves again and described in detail their typical day. The last to be introduced was the new management trainee. "Hello, I'm Felix," he said.

*

The job seemed potentially more satisfying than the advertisement had implied. He would be involved in the operation of vehicles, their specification, purchase, repair and maintenance. He had always been fascinated by machines, how they operated and how they were designed and he hoped that his engineering training would allow him to contribute to the business. However, he was also looking forward to seeing what he could learn. That's what life was all about.

On his second day in the job, he wrote some names and phone numbers in his diary. While he got 'up to speed', probably a polite way of telling him that he wouldn't immediately be of much use, Jim had suggested that he visit all the operating depots and introduce himself. He had already gone to some of them in his previous role, but it would certainly be useful to visit them again and learn what issues were of concern to them. He thought that he'd start with the smallest one – fewer people to interrogate him.

Since he hadn't previously met that depot engineer, he chose a time of day that should avoid any peak activity and allow him to learn how the day-to-day operation functioned. The white coat identified his host, and Stephen walked over and introduced himself. Perhaps not surprisingly, the engineer wanted to learn as much about Stephen as Stephen had hoped to learn about the depot. What exactly was his background; what experience, if any, did he have with this type of business; how did he think he'd be able to help?

In his work study role, he had been involved in the daily repair and maintenance activity, if only from the point of view of classifying job types rather than reviewing their content from a vehicle design perspective. That seemed enough for him to keep some credibility during their chat.

Someone waved from the other side of the depot and made his way towards them. "That's Ian, my foreman," said the engineer.

Stephen was introduced and the two shook hands, but he was very, very aware of Ian looking him up and down as if to say, 'Who on earth is this? An asset or a liability?'

"I'll leave you two to get on with things," were Stephen's words on his sharp exit.

The following week, he got a phone call. It was Ian. That afternoon Stephen went over to the depot. "We've noticed that the front brake linings on this vehicle type wear out much faster than the rear. We'd hoped that they would last just as long. The depot engineer was wondering if you could advise us if there's anything we could do about it," said Ian.

No idea, thought Stephen, but this feels more like a test than a request. "Leave it with me," was all he could say.

Back in his office, Stephen reached for the workshop manual for this type of vehicle. He was very familiar with hydraulic brakes in cars, but he'd never familiarised himself with air-operated brakes. Fascinating. Moving from page to page, he sketched out the layout of the braking system before reading up on the characteristics of all the component parts.

Lights going out in the main office made him look at his watch. Time to go home. He still didn't fully understand what would have caused the problem he'd been shown. That would be his homework.

The next morning, he arranged to visit the depot again. "I noticed from your fleet list that you've got two versions of this vehicle type," he said.

"That's right," said Ian.

"The older ones, the type you were complaining about, wouldn't have the problem if they were used more on the open road. Around town, the driver will be doing a lot of check braking rather than bringing the vehicle to a complete halt. The air flowing from the brake pedal will apply the front brakes a second or two before it reaches the rear brakes, so, if the driver is just touching the pedal briefly, the front brakes will often work without the rear ones assisting. The more recent versions of this vehicle are fitted with a relay valve to make sure the rear brakes respond as quickly as the front, so no problem with them."

"So that's what's happening," said Ian.

Stephen went back to the office.

The admin team looked up and smiled when he arrived and so he simply smiled in return and sat down at his desk. Yes, he seemed to belong here.

There were some new memoranda in his in-tray and he looked through them. The first one was a request from the purchasing manager. Would the technical team review the quotations that he had received for the annual brake lining contract?

What would that involve?

He was fascinated to see the formality of the supporting documentation. He had entered an adult world. Having read all the documentation, he went downstairs to see the purchasing manager and confirm exactly what would be expected of him. Luckily, very little.

Quotations had been sought from the all the main manufacturers in that industry after they had been provided with the predicted usage in the next financial year. Stephen's colleagues in vehicle operations had already confirmed their predicted vehicle mileage for that year and so he simply re-read the documentation that he had received.

As it happened, the lowest quotation was for the make of brake lining that the vehicle manufacturer had specified for the main vehicle type in the fleet following their evaluation at the vehicle design stage. No complaints had been received from the operating depots and it seemed a straightforward task for Stephen to inform his line manager of his endorsement of the purchasing manager's recommendation.

However, the task was not totally straightforward. There were three other vehicle types in the fleet and the manufacturers of two of them had recommended a different lining material from the one proposed by the purchasing manager. How should Stephen address that?

Stephen had no information on the brake performance of these vehicles with the material that purchasing was recommending. He read through all the documents again, and after a few quick calculations, he found that leaving these two vehicle types with the materials specified by their manufacturer was more expensive for them, but the overall result was still a saving in comparison to the current year.

Had there not been an overall saving from the quotations that the purchasing manager had obtained, Stephen might have been under pressure to approve some changes. But he was lucky. He'd got away with it, but it did teach him that he would have to be better informed when future contracts were submitted for his approval. What next?

A letter in his in-tray, this time one from another vehicle manufacturer suggesting that their local service engineer visit. Stephen called him on the number provided and they agreed a date the following week. The voice on the other end of the line had sounded very friendly. Was that a characteristic of all service engineers? Probably.

But having arranged the meeting, Stephen knew that he'd better get up to speed with the vehicle make that he'd be discussing next week. He had heard people say that it wasn't particularly reliable but there were forty examples of it in the fleet so more homework would be necessary, as would arranging to visit the depots in question and getting the experiences of the staff who maintained them. A workshop manual went home with him that night.

Most of the vehicles in the fleet had metal leaf springs but this one was different. How did that work? The manual, in fact, set out quite clearly how the vehicle was designed, and in particular how the air suspension worked. Yes, the vehicle had an air system for its brakes, he knew about them now, and the same system provided air for the suspension. The tricky thing was that air was compressible, and if the load in the vehicle was increased, the suspension sagged and if the load decreased, the vehicle increased in height. How did the vehicle remain its correct height all the time? It had levelling valves which were there to keep the vehicle at its correct height all the time. They simply admitted the air and exhausted it as required. This was going to be a long read.

*

The following morning, Jim called Stephen to a meeting with the chief engineer. "We're discussing the short life of gearboxes on the vehicle type that now makes up the majority of the fleet," he said.

The chief engineer started by describing the 'very difficult shift from first gear to second'. I'll never keep up with this, Stephen thought, panicking. Again, he was very familiar with car gearboxes, but this thing was huge and again, operated by air. He paid attention and took notes, and at the end of the meeting he was told, "The project's all yours now."

That evening, he took a workshop manual home again. A glass of red wine reduced his stress levels. An epicyclic gearbox with air-operated band brakes. Yes, he had heard of this.

Luckily, the failed gearboxes were overhauled in the central workshop, and over the next few weeks, he made a number of visits to examine the individual component parts. It was becoming less complicated by the minute. Even better, the head of quality control let him read a summary of all the failures that had taken place over the last twelve months. The pattern of these failures was very simple.

He presented the initial findings to his manager, Jim. "Twenty-five percent of failures are broken brake bands, and that should never happen. Thirty-five per cent are worn band linings, fair wear and tear if it occurs at a high mileage. Of more interest, another thirty percent of failures are reported as 'stuck in top gear' and that requires further investigation. Seven percent are broken pull-rods and the last three percent are miscellaneous. So, for the time being, there are only two main failure modes to follow up. When I examined the gearboxes reported as 'stuck in top gear', I found out that the cause was planet gears fracturing, and this results in the transmission locking up. From the failure date I was given, this is a relatively new problem, so I'll see if I can work out what changes there have been to the gearbox itself or the way we're treating it."

"Good work," said Jim. "Give me a progress report next week and we'll see if we can give the chief engineer an estimate of the time required to complete the project."

Back in the workshop, Stephen asked if he could examine some of the gearboxes that had been stripped down and set aside for overhaul. Again, the majority of the units had no problem with the planet gears, but he soon found one that had. He looked carefully at the broken gear and then at the bearing that supported it. The parallel rollers supporting the planet gears had apparently worn through the aluminium cage that was there to keep them in place. Examination of another gearbox awaiting overhaul showed that there was no problem with the planet gears, but of more interest, the bearing was of a different design and displayed no signs of distress.

Stephen then checked the information on the labels attached to these and the other gearboxes in the queue. Yes, the aluminium cages were introduced on new vehicles approximately three years ago and were now, for the first time, accounting for the percentage of failures shown in the vehicle examiner's records. The new method of mounting the gears seemed to have been introduced purely to save time, and hence cost, during manufacture.

The evolution of this type of gearbox now became the focus of the project. It had first been used on lighter, less powerful vehicles, and apparently it had been regarded as trouble free. As vehicle weights had increased over time, and engine power was raised in response, the air pressure used to apply the band brakes had been increased. That seemed logical. But the failed brakes showed all the classic signs of fatigue failure and that suggested to him that the air pressure was now too high. The band brakes were now stressed beyond their fatigue threshold.

Stephen went back to Jim and told him, "I've done some calculations to estimate the stress on the bands and I'd like to involve the local university to get the exact figures under normal operating conditions."

"Well, you've got a supplies and services budget," said Jim. "Off you go."

While waiting for the university to respond, he looked again at the transmissions with planet gear fractures. Examination of more data on gearbox failures confirmed that the collapse of these gears was a relatively recent problem and further investigation showed that it was only associated with those bearings with needle rollers in an aluminium cage.

The university's measurements of the stresses inside this type of gearbox caught the imagination of Stephen's colleagues. He was able to submit his final recommendations of reducing the air pressure, re-introducing the original type of bearing and using a more appropriate lubricant.

Since the findings of the exercise had revealed that there was a flaw in the design modification that the manufacturer had introduced, a local meeting was held with their local service engineer who was given a copy of the report and who was also shown the used components that Stephen had been able to examine in the company's central workshop.

The service engineer didn't say very much about the problem, but he did make polite conversation, no doubt in order to get to know Stephen and learn how to play him in future. But an unexpected outcome for Stephen was being invited to see new examples of the gearbox being manufactured. His job was getting better by the minute.

There was little further response from the manufacturer, but the original design of the planet gear bearing was reinstated. Over the next few months, the failure rate dropped from fifty units per month to twenty-five, with an annual saving of sixty times Stephen's salary. He hoped that he'd justified being taken on in this role.

Chapter 7
The huntsman

The following week, there was an announcement to all staff: we've got a new chief engineer.

No one had been aware that the present one was leaving. Communication with him had almost always been by memorandum, but whenever he had been seen in the office, he was focussing on what the team were doing. He always seemed keen to be kept up to speed with current projects, and he encouraged staff to keep pursuing them. He had never been known to criticise anyone, and so people found no problems with telling him about the progress they were making. So, what would the new person be like?

In the office, people were chatting about the news when their line manager came out of his office to bring them all up to date. The chief engineer had moved to an equivalent position in his hometown and it was assumed that he was preparing himself for retirement. Two people had made internal applications for the position, one was Jim but, for whatever reason, an outsider had been chosen. 'Was this job advertised?' was an inevitable question. Yes, it had been, internally and in the press. So, with the exception of Jim and someone else, why had none of the others seen it?

"You must have all been hard at work, heads down. Well done."

Was that a compliment, or disinformation? It didn't particularly matter. The jobs were satisfying, the atmosphere friendly.

When Stephen was alone with Jim, he asked who had been appointed. "Who are we getting, Albert Einstein?"

"Not exactly," was Jim's measured reply. "His name's Eadie. But while you're here, there's some good news for you. I've agreed for the transfer here of one of the quality control people you may remember from your job in the central works. His name's Alec. Does that ring any bells?"

"It does. He and I got on very well. So, why's he coming here?"

"Our outgoing chief engineer was aware that your workload had increased so much that he thought you might need some assistance. It's only a temporary move so far but Alec's manager is fully supportive. He said the experience would be very useful for him."

"That would be great. There's so much to be done that some help would really speed things up and I can't think of anyone better than Alec to do it."

What fantastic news.

*

The following Monday, the new chief engineer was shown round. I've seen him before, thought Stephen, at a vehicle evaluation group meeting hosted by one of the vehicle manufacturers. But while he had remembered the new person, the reverse didn't seem to be true. A handshake and smile, and the chief engineer was moved on by the head of personnel.

The works manager had asked Stephen to look at a modification that his team had made to the exhaust silencer of the main vehicle type in the fleet. It was good. The problem simply arose from one end of the silencer being too close to the road, and in exceptional conditions, it would make contact and the shock would loosen its support brackets. It had been reported to the vehicle manufacturer but to date there had been no response. Well done the works' team.

Another memorandum. There was to be a night out for all staff the following Friday, and the new chief engineer was going to introduce himself formally. All members of the central engineering team had to make a presentation describing what their current workload involved, and the works manager asked Stephen if he wouldn't mind making a full-sized cardboard model of the silencer in question. No problem.

In the hotel, there was plenty of drink, although not provided by the company. Stephen had seen Ian installed at a table at the far end of the room and went over to join him. After several rounds, the atmosphere was very relaxed and enjoyable.

Time for Eadie to introduce himself, but first he asked members of the central team to present their current projects. It was a very lifelike cardboard silencer but by now people were no longer interested in work-related talk. And Eadie was quite dismissive before asking the next person to come up.

"He must be nervous." The voice came from behind Stephen, and so did the reply.

"Let's hope this isn't a sign of things to come."

Eadie then took over. He described his own background and said that he was aware of the current problems in the organisation. "I can do all the jobs that you can do," he said.

"I don't think so," somebody whispered.

The following morning, it was business as usual. The phone rang. It was Ian. "Is it true that you know something about these vehicles with fully automatic transmissions? Twenty of them have been transferred to this depot and fourteen of them are retained for transmission failure. The depot engineer asked to be demoted and his replacement and I were transferred here this week."

"Poor thing," replied Stephen. "Well, I know there's a problem. I've taken the workshop manual home and I've looked at some failed units in the central workshop. What's your main concern?"

"Obviously, we're worried about vehicle availability, and recently we've noticed that, if we change the oil, we tend to lose the transmission within a few days. Yet another vehicle out of service."

"Well," said Stephen, "I assume the first thing to do is stop changing the oil. I'll phone a contact I have in the manufacturer's concessionaire and see if that's a known problem. I'll get back to you as soon as I've spoken to him."

As he had anticipated, the contact was very helpful. "I've seen that before," he said. "I think that your people are greasing the gasket when they replace the oil filter. They shouldn't. The odd way in which the hydraulic circuit is designed in this case allows air to be sucked in from the outside, and when that moves through the oil pump, it reduces the oil pressure throughout the transmission. But there's never any sign of oil leaking out."

"Got you," said Stephen. "Thanks very much."

"That was quick," said Ian. "It sounds a bit odd, but I'll do one myself when the shop steward isn't looking. I'll come back to you."

A few days later, he did. "It seems to be working. Can you come out to the depot and have a look at the other issues?"

"Of course," said Stephen, "but before I do that, could you meet me in the central workshop? I've got to know this unit quite well since you first called me and there are a few things that might interest you."

Ian met him the following day. There were several units that had been stripped down and cleaned before being overhauled.

"Look at this one," said Stephen. "The casing's cracked and that speaks to me of high oil pressure. And look at this cast iron seal holder. It's worn out. Same diagnosis."

"So, what causes that?" asked Ian.

"The early versions of this gearbox had a small oil pump that brought about its own problems: low oil pressure and hence clutch wear. The new units have a larger oil pump that solved the clutch problems but resulted in the higher oil pressures and the problems that they cause."

"But the unit has a pressure relief valve," said Ian.

"That's the dilemma. What are you doing this evening?"

"Why?"

"I could come over to your depot after work and we'll examine one vehicle thoroughly. Does that suit?"

"Make it six o'clock," said Ian. "I'll tell my boss what we're going to do."

*

"I hope this is going to be worth it," said the depot engineer. "By the way, my name's Alan."

"Stephen. Pleased to meet you. I've got pressure gauges here, so we'll soon see."

With the gauges fitted, Stephen asked Ian if he could start the engine. "At idling speed, the pressures are normal," said Stephen. "Now rev it up."

"Look at that!" exclaimed Alan. "Both pressures are going off the scale."

"So, it has been worth it," said Stephen. "And, if Ian wouldn't mind removing the pressure relief valve, we'll check the oil pressures again."

While Ian was busy, the other two helped themselves to a coffee. "So, Alan, what are the other problems with this vehicle type?" asked Stephen.

"Not too many," Alan replied. "The exhaust silencer is troublesome. A few other odds and ends, but if we can fix the gearbox, things will be back to normal."

When Ian had removed the valve, Stephen checked the oil pressures again. "Start the engine, Ian."

The pressure gauges read zero.

"That proves the valve works correctly," said Alan.

"No, it doesn't," said Stephen, before asking Ian to rev up the engine. Again, the gauges climbed off the scale. "What that shows," said Stephen, "is that the valve is functioning correctly but the oil gallery in the transmission case is too small, too restrictive, for the new, high-output oil pump. The manufacturer should have modified the gallery when they increased the oil pump output. I'll raise that with them tomorrow."

They then all climbed on board, and as agreed, Ian drove them a short distance from the depot and back.

The vehicle was sluggish when moving off but otherwise behaved normally.

When they arrived back at the depot, Ian refitted the pressure relief valve. "Case closed," said Stephen. "I'll arrange for all your replacement units from now on to have the oil gallery modified. Just keep an eye on your oil changes and your problems will be over."

It was now nine p.m. and Ian suggested that a pint in a nearby bar might be a pleasant way to end a very successful evening.

"The first round's on me," said Alan.

"I'll get the second one," said Ian.

As usual in these impromptu gatherings, the chat was both good fun and more useful than the average formal meeting. By the end of the evening, Alan and Ian had been given solutions to problems they hadn't yet experienced.

"Thanks for all your help," said Ian.

"I didn't do anything. I just networked to get the problem fixed. Families look after each other. That's what's important," said Stephen.

The following morning, Stephen found a note on his desk. Jason had been looking for him so, before he dealt with his own priorities, he went over to see him.

"This new guy, Eadie," said Jason. "He's been on the phone complaining about the number of my vehicles that had overheating problems yesterday."

"I'm glad he's settling in."

"Well, I'm not. He wants to know what I'm doing about it."

"So, what are you doing about it? It's not exactly a new problem."

"I had nightshift clean the radiators of all the buses involved, but that's not the answer, is it?"

"You're right, it isn't. It's a weakness of this vehicle type, but it's not one of our priorities at present, is it?"

"You can say that, but with Eadie hunting me down every day, it's mine."

"Right, let's do something. As new, the vehicle doesn't have a problem, but the radiator is badly mounted in the engine compartment. It's prone to vibration and the manufacturer has chosen a slightly old-fashioned design. It doesn't have much reserve cooling capacity, and even worse, being rear-mounted, it's prone to blocking with road dirt."

"That's why we clean them."

"Indeed. But one of the problems is that the cooling fins that are soldered onto the radiator tubes are prone to separating due to the salt thrown on the roads in winter. They eventually become detached and cease to be effective. That's a common problem and it's easy to see when it happens. However, it's less easy to see when they are partially detached and less effective than they should be. So, your team might have carried out a thorough cleaning job, but they haven't fully solved the problem."

"So, what do you recommend?"

"I'll follow it up to work towards a final solution, but meanwhile, to get Eadie off your back, make a list of the vehicles most affected and fit new radiator tubes to them."

"There are eighty-three tubes in each radiator. So, where do I get the extra staff to do that?"

"Instead of cleaning the next vehicle, change the tubes. That vehicle won't bother you for a few years, so the time you would have spent cleaning it again, you can use to fit new tubes to the next one on your list. And your materials budget overspend can be justified by improved vehicle availability. Remember, you weren't the one who chose to purchase them."

"I'll do it, but don't forget to find me a permanent solution."

Back at his desk, Stephen's list of priorities was headed by brake noise, but first he had to phone the manufacturer about Alan's gearbox problem. He noted down everything that he was told and was relieved that the problem was slightly less complex than he had feared.

He phoned Ian. "You can relax," he said. "There have been two revisions to this transmission. The first one had too small an oil pump and the resulting low oil pressure resulted in the internal clutches wearing out quite quickly, but all these gearboxes have been upgraded with the larger oil pump. It was one of these that we looked at last night. While these vehicles were still under warranty, the manufacturer replaced the failed units with ones that had received the second upgrade and they should be more or less trouble free. You can tell which type of transmission is in each vehicle by simply looking at the serial number. If you can let me have the serial numbers of each transmission, I can arrange for the at-risk ones to be upgraded in our workshop. Does that sound good?"

"It does indeed," said Ian.

Within a few months, all twenty vehicles were in service and running reliably.

*

Another division of the company was undergoing a major reconstruction and Jim was leading it. Giving the infrastructure a major makeover was a twenty-four-hours-a-day activity, but it was quite a few months into the project before Stephen realised how much time his manager was putting into it. He had always been at his desk during the day but what had been a surprise was finally hearing that he also spent most nights with the team carrying out the work. That seemed to be going beyond the call of duty.

But now that it had come to Stephen's attention, he became more aware of people from that division visiting the office for meetings. When they finally introduced themselves, Stephen felt that he was entering another world. They were as enthusiastic about their project as

Stephen was about his. He wondered if that was true for all people. Were all other people as fortunate as he was?

As everyone involved learned their new routines, perhaps subconsciously, they aligned their tea breaks and found out more about how their colleagues passed their days. There were, of course, many, many similarities.

But Stephen's in-tray continued to fill and require attention. So, back to business. There had been numerous complaints from the public that some of the company's vehicles were making terrible screeching noises around town. Where was that article?

A few months earlier, Jim had placed a magazine on Stephen's desk. It had an interesting article on the mathematics of brake noise, and it had been very thorough but nonetheless easy to follow and luckily, Stephen still remembered some of the theory from his engineering degree. In fact, it had been so interesting that he'd taken it home and read it several times.

When Stephen looked into the problem more thoroughly, he discovered that the problem had been reported to the manufacturer by a number of operators and some feedback had been received. This seemed an ideal moment to contact their local service engineer and see how the issue could be taken to the next level.

But before he did that, Stephen started to use his lunch breaks to walk to nearby sandwich shops and look out for any of his company's vehicles in the area. In fact, he started to listen to all vehicles as they slowed for corners or stopped at traffic lights.

*

The meeting would take place in Stephen's office the following day. The service engineer seemed very keen; no doubt it would earn him a pat on the back from his boss. The manufacturer was experimenting with small friction pads fitted to the open end of the brake drum and Stephen was asked if he could arrange to have them fitted to three vehicles and monitor their performance in service. The further request was that they should be monitored against a control group. That group would quite simply be the other, unmodified vehicles based in the same depot.

This seemed like an interesting project, but the first thing that had occurred to Stephen was that he had recently approved the continuing use of the brake linings that the manufacturer had specified for this vehicle type. Oh, dear. Was he about to find out that he'd made a mistake?

While there would, hopefully, be a successful outcome of the trials, the operating depot where the trials would be based would have to put up with the inconvenience. To offset this, the vehicle manufacturer offered a free set of brake drums for the vehicles involved. They were delivered and fitted, and the trials began.

The fleet numbers of the test vehicles were 1102, 1104 and 1107 and they were allowed to settle in for a few weeks before routine auditing began. There was now time to re-read the paper on the mathematics of the problem.

Taking notes as he worked his way through it, Stephen remembered one of the questions that had been put to him during his interview for this job. How would he address the problem of brake squeal? The problem had obviously been on the radar then, but Stephen had been unaware of that. But his response to the question? Fit dynamic absorbers to the brake shoes.

Filed away in the office were the detailed specifications of the vehicles associated with the problem. He noted that the brake linings fitted to them had a different specification to those fitted to earlier contracts for this type of vehicle. And one of the trials that had been put in place by his predecessor involved a batch of these vehicles in another operating depot. After a bit of searching in a filing cabinet, there was the list of the vehicles involved and the specification of the trial brake linings fitted to all of them. This was getting interesting. His understanding of the theory told him that this new trial involving the manufacturer wouldn't be successful; the forces involved were too great. The noise was produced by the open end of the brake drum and it varied between one thousand cycles per second and two thousand cycles per second, a really high frequency screech. No wonder people complained about it.

He could walk over to Jason's depot and see dynamic absorbers that were in use every day. There was one mounted on the front of the engine crankshaft in every vehicle that they operated. Why couldn't the brake lining material be the key to the vibration problem by allowing the mass of the brake shoe to control the behaviour of the brake drum? After all, the other types of drum-braked vehicles in their fleet made no noise. His next move would be to monitor the behaviour of his predecessor's trial vehicles. Why hadn't he been told when he started this job that brake squeal should be near the top of his list of priorities?

That night in bed, Stephen's mind was still working on the problem. He looked at the alarm clock on the bedside table. It said 11.02. And two minutes later? Yes, it said 11.04. There was no escaping this project.

After lunch the following day, he thought he'd better visit the depot where these trials were taking place. It was a good job he did, since the depot engineer hadn't been monitoring them. He had enough on his plate already without that, but at least Stephen was able to leave him a list of the vehicles involved, and if he phoned back in the morning, he could find out where the vehicles were likely to be. That should allow him to follow as many of them as possible and hopefully hear how quietly or noisily their brakes were performing.

Back at his desk, he found a note stuck to his phone. Would he please contact Jason? Important. Some of his new vehicles were making shuddering noises when the brakes were applied. Stephen looked at his watch. Jason would have gone home. He would contact him first thing in the morning.

*

"Where have you been?" That was 'Good morning' in Jason-speak.

"Have you retained the vehicle with the vibration problem?" asked Stephen.

"I've got one on that pit over there. It's one of these brand-new vehicles and drivers say that they all do it, but only when they're braking."

"I'll be there in one minute." Stephen reached for his jacket. Once there, he said, "Now, could somebody apply the brakes while I have a look from underneath?"

"I'll call someone over," was Jason's response.

It didn't take too long for Stephen to see what the problem was. "Jason, look up here. It's one of the brackets for the brake actuators on the rear axle. One side's fine, but because the differential is offset, the bracket adjacent to it is more complex in shape and it flexes every time the brakes are applied. It will cause a shudder at the rear of the vehicle. I'll contact the manufacturer."

"Thanks, but make it quick. I don't want drivers deciding not to drive them."

Back in the office, Stephen reported the problem to Jim. "Jason's just complained about brake vibration on these new vehicles. I had a look at one just now and the bracket for one of the rear brake actuators is slightly flexible. We could modify it ourselves, but I'll put it on the agenda for the next service meeting."

"Well done," said Jim. "But, while you're here, how is your other project going?"

"The vehicle type in question usually operates perfectly quietly, but in dense traffic, when the brakes heat up, they do get noisy. But we have identified an alternative lining material that avoids the noise problem completely and I've fed all the data back to the manufacturer via their local rep. We should soon hear if they've given it their approval."

"Again, well done, but before you go, Eadie wants you to attend my progress meeting with him tomorrow."

"I didn't think I was part of your project."

"You are now."

Chapter 8
Jealousy and pride

The central workshop was Stephen's next stop.

The foreman called over to him. "You got my message? We've got a vehicle in here that should be in MOT preparation in its operating depot, but they say the bodywork is too corroded for them to be able to repair it themselves. They asked our manager if we could do it for them. OK, we're the body specialists here, but we've already got our own work programme to deal with. Come over here and tell me what you think."

They walked back towards the entrance door to the workshop and the vehicle in question stood out from all the other vehicles under repair. Why had Stephen not noticed it on his way in? The external cladding had been removed and all that could be seen was a brown mass of rusting steel. "A long job?" he asked.

"To do it completely? Over a week, probably two. But I could do without that just now."

"I won't keep you. I'll just have a good look at it and I'll come over and tell you what I found."

And what he saw confirmed the supervisor's concerns. With the outer body panels removed, it was obvious that all the inner panels were heavily corroded, many beyond repair.

This vehicle type was just over six years old but Stephen had never seen this level of corrosion on any other vehicle in the fleet. No doubt all other examples of this vehicle type would be in a similar condition, but that was something he would have to confirm by inspection. The steel could have been better protected during manufacture.

"I've examined it. You're quite right to flag it up. I'll tell the chief engineer what I've seen," said Stephen.

The foreman expressed his thanks, and Stephen went back to the head office. He gave Jim a brief appraisal of what he'd seen and then walked over to see the chief engineer's secretary to get the issue added to the agenda for the next weekly meeting.

The vehicle that he had just been shown was based in Sid's depot so he called him to ask why he thought he couldn't cope with the problem himself.

"If you come over here, I'll show you exactly why we can't cope." Sid sounded serious.

Stephen hoped that he could get a sandwich on the way. It was a twenty-five-minute drive, but well worth the time in order to see what was happening at the coal face. As it turned out, the traffic was worse than usual for that time of day and he didn't get a sandwich. At least the depot had a coffee machine.

Sid told him that the vehicle now in the central workshop was the first one of the twenty examples of that vehicle type in his depot that he had started preparing for its annual MOT test that year. They had all been delivered as new vehicles at the same time, and in retrospect, he realised that he should have spread out the tests through the year in order to avoid this mess.

He had only looked behind the outer body panels of that particular vehicle because it had suffered some light body damage in a traffic accident, but he and his team had been shocked by what they had found.

"Well, in retrospect, I suppose that you should have spread out your MOT presentation dates," Stephen replied, "but nobody could have foreseen this. I've already put it on the agenda but it's probably best that Eadie sees it for himself in order to understand what you're up against."

When the weekly meeting took place, Eadie sat at his desk, reading through the notes while the others sat around the table. He went through each item, making notes where appropriate, and asking for opinions where he felt it necessary. Finally, it was the corrosion item and Stephen described what he had seen. Eadie asked the works manager for his opinion but he said that he couldn't comment until he'd been given more information. The pressure was back on Stephen.

"The problem's quite serious and it might be useful if you see a vehicle for yourself. It might not be possible to justify the repair costs."

Eadie looked at him and said, "I'll meet you at the depot first thing tomorrow."

At least that was something achieved. Back at his desk, Stephen phoned Sid. There would be a vehicle for Eadie to examine.

*

As before, the external cladding had been removed and the stress panels were visible. Solid metal and a fresh coat of underseal stared back.

"I don't see much wrong with that," said Eadie, turning to Stephen. Then he climbed back into his car and drove off.

Stephen couldn't believe what he'd just seen. "What's happened here?" he asked.

"You don't think we were going to show it to Eadie the way it was?" said Sid. "It would have been our fault, wouldn't it?"

"Thanks very much," was Stephen's only answer.

Later that year, all forty vehicles were withdrawn from service and scrapped. Had Eadie discussed it with his friend, the central works manager? If he had, he never said.

*

The board had given approval to purchase one hundred and fifty new vehicles in the next financial year, happily not the same make as those being scrapped. The formal process was initiated by the finance director and then passed to the purchasing manager. The commercial director had made the business case for their purchase, and now engineering had to meet the manufacturer and agree the detailed specification and allow a final price to be quoted.

The specification would, in principle, be the same as that used last year, but any detailed changes thought necessary would now be discussed. The commercial director had not asked for any to be made, so it should be a relatively straightforward task.

However, one of the things that Stephen noted when he had visited the central workshop was the number of early examples of this vehicle that were undergoing significant repairs to the bodywork. Happily, with this vehicle, not a corrosion issue.

Rather than bother the foreman again so soon, he walked over to Jason's depot and asked if they were aware of any issues with that vehicle type.

"They're usually quite reliable but the newer ones with the big windows can suffer a fracture of one of the body pillars. It's always in the same place. Come on and I'll show you." Jason pointed to an area just above one of the windows. How odd, thought Stephen.

"And what do you do when that happens?" Stephen asked.

"We put it into the central workshop. We couldn't take on anything as serious as that."

It was now obvious why the central works didn't want to take on the corrosion problem. Maybe he'd better go back and see what was involved in this kind of job.

The foreman wasn't there when Stephen arrived, so he just looked for one of the vehicles in question. There were already around six hundred of them in the fleet and so the prospect of another one hundred and fifty arriving next year was quite serious. This was the ideal time to put this problem to the top of his list.

"Are you looking for the foreman?" said a voice from inside the vehicle.

"No. In fact I'd rather keep out of his way for a while. I think he associates me with bad news. Could you tell me exactly what you're doing here?"

"This body pillar's fractured just above the window. The pillar's like a top hat in cross section, but do you see up there? The manufacturer's cut off the flanges to allow that horizontal support be to be attached to it. That's where they all break."

"Have you reported this before?"

"We have, but your predecessor couldn't be bothered getting involved."

"Thanks for your time," said Stephen, "I think I understand exactly what's happening."

He didn't, of course. There were lots of joints on the bodywork where the pillars met the supports, but this was the only one that was breaking.

Back in the office, he reported his findings to Jim. "It's not one of our biggest problems," he was told, "but you're right, it has to be followed up before the next order is placed. But, while you're here, we've got a new chief executive."

"What's he like?" asked Stephen.

"Very focussed. A bit too focussed perhaps."

"How do you know?"

"He was the chief engineer when I started here seven years ago."

"And is he qualified for the job?"

"Very much so."

"That's good to hear."

"He interviewed me when I started. He knew what he was talking about. And I was very happy when I received a letter telling me I'd been successful. However, the following evening, there was a knock at the door. He had sent one of his staff members to deliver a workshop manual, no doubt for me to read and memorise that evening. I thought that was a bad start, but he didn't do anything like that again. However, he always wanted to see progress being made, no matter what we were doing."

"So, not too bad an appointment?"

"He's a known quantity, but I'll leave it at that."

Stephen took a cup of coffee back to his desk and did some sketches of what he had seen. He then showed them to Alec. They both agreed that this could be a good project.

Back at home that evening, he looked out the notes from the third year of his engineering degree. The body pillar had a stress raiser in it because of the flanges being removed, but the major unknown here was the flexibility of the chassis. As the vehicle was rear-engined and the fracture was close to the rear axle, it seemed important to pursue the investigation.

The following morning's news was a surprise to everyone. Eadie had been demoted. No one was quite sure what would happen next. A witch-hunt? Little was done in the office as the news was the topic of all conversation.

At lunchtime, with no further news, the canteen was also alive with gossip. Was it simply demotion or had he been sacked? Who would be next? The issue was only resolved in the middle of the afternoon when another memorandum was circulated.

Eadie, Stephen's manager, Jim, and Stephen had new job titles, and Stephen would now report to the commercial manager. Eadie himself would still work with the central team but he would now have no control over the operating depots. It seemed completely stupid, and in the middle of all of that, Stephen's main feeling was that of sympathy for Eadie, despite his constant bullying.

Was the change to bring about some kind of improvement or simply make an open statement that Eadie was unqualified for the job? While, in theory, Stephen had a new line manager, his role remained unchanged. He would continue with his mechanical engineering activity in the organisation, and so on with his current project.

He and Alec now looked for a means of examining and understanding the flexing of the chassis and determining if there was a correlation between that and the body pillar fractures that he had been shown. The theory guided him to look at the design of the chassis itself, specifically towards the rear of the vehicle and an immediate finding was that the chassis crossmember immediately ahead of the engine was not a continuous member. An end was in sight, so they now discussed how best to measure the degree of flexing while the vehicles were in service.

After lunch, Stephen looked at his sketches of the body pillar fractures. If the flanges hadn't been removed, a simple modification to the horizontal support would avoid the problem. He made a detailed drawing of the changes that would be required. It would actually be cheaper for the manufacturer to build to the new specification. A win-win result? The door opened and Stephen lifted his head. It was Alec.

"What do you think of that?" Alec asked. "My new tool for measuring chassis flexing."

It was simply a steel tube with a rod inside it. What was special about that?

"Watch this," said Alec. "If you hold an end of the tube in one hand and the rod in the other, you can increase the length of the tool simply by moving your hands apart. Any change in length can be seen if you look at the calibrations that I've etched onto the rod. So, just tack weld each end of the tool to two different points on the chassis, go for a run round the block, and you can measure the chassis movement."

"That's if you can see it," said Stephen. "What do you do if it's fitted to some point that you can't see?"

"Look closely. Near one end of the rod, I drilled a hole right through it. And look at the tube. I drilled a hole through it as well and then, with a file, I lengthened it into a slot. Put the rod back into the tube, line up the hole with the slot and then tap a pin into the hole."

"I'm beginning to understand."

"Pull the tube out the length of the slot. Click. Push it back in again the full length of the slot. Click. All you now need to do is put a clip around the tube on either side of the pin, tack weld one end of the tool to one point of the chassis, adjust the length of the tool to mid-position and now tack weld the other end to the chassis. Now go for a short drive, and when you come back, the tool will show you how far the chassis has moved out from its normal static position and how far it's moved in."

"You're a genius. That's one of the most intelligent things I've seen in a while. The problem's solved. Or it will be in a few days."

And it was.

Stephen and Alec arranged to visit the manufacturer and examine a chassis before the body had been attached to it. They were both intrigued to see the chassis on its own, and they spent some time taking the chance to examine features that they were not able to see on a completed vehicle. They tried to commit them to memory before starting to examine how it would flex in service.

For this, they had taken with them a hydraulic jack with which they now commenced to lift the outer ends of the chassis crossmembers one by one to a predetermined height from the ground. As each one was lifted, they measured the height of all the others.

The full analysis of the finding would have to wait until they were back in the office, but one finding leapt out. The crossmember immediately ahead of the rear axle was by far the most flexible one.

On a hunch, they then placed the jack at the centre of the rear axle and started to lift it up. They were immediately behind the engine and the fact the chassis had flexed slightly under its weight was not in itself a surprise. What did surprise them, however, was that the chassis flexed quite significantly just ahead of the rear axle. That immediately explained why the body problems existed where they did.

Stephen and Alec just looked at each other and smiled. Time to go back to the office.

*

The following morning, they were busy working at the diagram that would explain their findings when internal mail dropped an envelope into Stephen's in-tray.

"Time for tea?" asked Stephen.

Alec didn't disagree.

The letter was a complete surprise. It was from the human resources department of a competitor and it was an invitation to attend an interview for a technical engineering role. Where had that come from? And then he remembered. The previous engineer had mentioned that he had circulated Stephen's report on gearbox failure when he had attended an industry conference not long before he left.

With Eadie's bullying, and the way in which he'd been able to slow down the progress that Stephen and Jim had been making in addressing problems in the company, he had been thinking whether or not he should move on. Was this destiny calling?

Stephen looked at his cup and it was empty. He must have been so distracted by the letter that he hadn't noticed he had finished it. He and Alec got back to work and soon had a completed diagram that they could use to explain their findings. And that would allow Stephen to draft a letter to the manufacturer in Eadie's name and set out the changes to the specification of next year's vehicles.

The offer to move had been very tempting, but the satisfaction of solving this problem made Stephen think that the job here still offered a great deal of satisfaction. He turned down the offer.

*

There was an initially defensive response to Stephen's letter from the vehicle manufacturer, but the changes were eventually agreed, and it was now time to go through the in-tray again and sort out the latest memoranda and letters.

Not surprisingly, there was a request to set up a formal body repair methodology for the central workshop team, using the findings of the latest project.

"Do you want to follow this up?" Stephen asked Alec.

He would indeed. The last few days had opened up a whole new world for him and he was very keen to see how far he could build on what he had learned.

Next in Stephen's in-tray, a letter regarding the earlier work on brake noise. It was from a manager in the research and development department of the vehicle manufacturer and who was also active in academic circles. Would Stephen be willing to produce a paper on operator experience with vehicle brakes for a conference that was scheduled to take place later that year? That sounded like an offer he couldn't refuse. He went through to see Jim.

"Yes, that seems interesting," Jim replied, "but drop Eadie a note before you reply."

The note got an immediate response from Eadie's secretary. "He would like you to go ahead. He says that he'll make sure that you have all the time you need."

A few days later, Stephen got a phone call advising him of the deadline for submission. He now refreshed his memory about the work that had been carried out in the past, as well as going over the theory of noise creation one more time. Yes, it wasn't the manufacturer's trial that had produced a result; it was the in-house trial of different lining materials.

Over the next few weeks, Stephen's in-tray continued to fill up as quickly as before and he never got the promised free time, but in the evenings after work, he and Jim worked on the paper. They set out to show how braking systems, and the materials used in them, were perceived by vehicle operators.

Like many other projects, it was an opportunity for Stephen to get out of the office and visit the operating depots where staff worked round the clock to ensure that vehicles remained available for business. It didn't take long for the staff on the front line to tell him what problems they faced most frequently. And, although they understood exactly why he was there, they took the opportunity to show him other problems that they felt were hindering them in providing a more reliable service.

He couldn't let that get in the way of getting the paper written, but if he noted these other issues now, it would help him update his own priorities. Any issues of which he had been unaware would be followed up. At the end of the day, he was only there to help make the organisation run more smoothly and so anything he learned should make him more effective in the role.

Interruptions or not, he was learning more about how theory was functioning in practice. One example of that was that a recent evolution in brake shoe design had been dealt with quite differently by two vehicle manufacturers. Each design had a weakness, and that would provide useful information for the paper. He would also put that on the agenda for the regular service meetings held with the vehicle manufacturers.

The paper was completed and sent off on time, and not long after that, he received confirmation that it had been accepted.

The deal seemed to have been that, if Stephen and Jim wrote the paper, Eadie would present it. The reward would be that, after the conference, Eadie would take them both out to dinner.

There was one other demand. Eadie asked them to write a parallel paper, the one that he would actually present. It wouldn't focus on the theory of brake system design, but instead on the density of today's urban traffic, and he asked for a number of slides to be produced of the company's vehicles in service in known high-density areas.

*

The conference apparently went well and there had been wide discussion of all the papers presented, but that was now in the past and it was again business as usual.

Another new vehicle type had recently been launched and the board had approved the purchase of five of them. The commercial director had chosen the depot from which they would operate, and as it was an entirely new design, it would receive round the clock support from the manufacturer in its first few months of operation. The depot staff would then have to be brought up to speed before this support was withdrawn.

The vehicle specification was certainly up to date. Air suspension was now the norm, the chassis design seemed to address the problems experienced with the previous generation of vehicles and the engine was a known quantity. The gearbox was a new design, and again, should avoid the known weaknesses of older types, but of more interest, it incorporated a retarder. This device was designed to help the brakes to slow down the vehicle. The heat generated by doing so would be lost through an oil cooler, but a corresponding benefit would be that the brakes would run cooler, and their linings would last longer.

Yes, this was interesting, but what about dinner?

It eventually arrived.

At the end of the day, Eadie asked, "Are you both ready?" The three of them walked across to an adjacent bar. "A pint?" said Eadie.

He ordered three and a relaxed conversation about work and non-work-related stories took place over the next half-hour.

"Another round?" Jim asked. He went to the bar. I wonder if we're eating here or somewhere else, Stephen thought to himself.

Time flew by as more chat ensued. All three now had empty glasses. "Another round?" said Stephen. Good manners demanded it.

"Yes, why not?" said Eadie.

"Me too," said Jim, before adding, "I fancy a cigar."

"Yes, so do I," said Eadie.

Stephen was a non-smoker and so, at the bar, he ordered three pints and two cigars. The conversation continued, although Stephen felt less involved than earlier.

When the glasses had emptied, Eadie looked at his watch. "Have you seen the time? I've got to go home. See you tomorrow."

*

Next morning, as he and Jim, both rather amused, reflected upon the previous evening's adventure, Stephen said, "Do you know, I think I learned something last night."

Chapter 9
Good night

With the revised specification to the body design now formally approved by the manufacturer, it was time to implement the agreed body modifications in the central workshop and allow vehicles already in the fleet to have the design weakness upgraded.

"I've invited one of our apprentices to join us," said the works manager.

Stephen turned to shake hands.

"Hi, I'm Joe," said the apprentice.

Joe and Stephen were left alone for Stephen to describe the changes that would be made. "We've agreed with the manufacturer that this joint will be redesigned," he explained. "It won't fail in future. So, when you're repairing any vehicles of this type that are brought into the workshop, you can introduce the new design. It's also worth looking at the two floor support brackets."

"They go all the time," Joe butted in.

"If you manufacture replacements with a slight bend in them, they'll cope better with body movement. In fact, Alec has made a cardboard model of the chassis, and when you flex it, it behaves just like the real thing.

I'll let you see it the next time I'm here. Meanwhile, Eadie has signed my letter describing the mods, so they're official."

"Don't mention that name to me," said Joe. "He once called me up to his office for a mauling."

"Did you deserve it?"

"I'd missed a day release class, but I didn't expect to get the bullying I did. You'd think he would have more important things to do than that. But anybody here who's had dealings with him says the same."

"What do they say?"

"They say that after he's been through the place, the handbrake goes on. The pace of work just slows down."

"They're not the only people to say that," Stephen said, reassuring him, "but the show must go on. If you're determined, you'll succeed in spite of him. And I'm sure that applies to anyone who's had dealings with him."

Despite Eadie's failings, Stephen still felt sorry for him. If only he hadn't got this tendency to snap at people, to try to bully them, the place would run much better. He simply seemed to have a huge chip on his shoulder over his lack of education.

But the day-to-day business continued. Responsibility for managing a major project in the other division of the organisation had been formally delegated to Jim. And Eadie had already started to muscle in.

"Where's Eadie today?" Stephen asked.

"I've been told he's off sick," said Jim.

"Nothing trivial, I hope. An interview?"

"I can't tell you. I've been sworn to secrecy. But you'd be amused if I could."

"Then we'd better make progress while we can. I've just had a phone call from the depot engineer about these five test vehicles. There seems to be some body movement."

"Who called you? Colin? Where did he say the problem was? I assume it's above the rear axle."

"No. Surprisingly, the front."

Stephen drove over to the depot where they were based.

"Thanks for coming," said Colin, "I'll show you exactly where the problem is."

Everyone had assumed that these vehicles would be trouble-free. Obviously not.

"Look down there, just where I'm pointing," said Colin.

Nothing disastrous, but it was right that the depot should have flagged it up. Stephen crouched down to take a closer look. "Loose rivets," he said. "Is it possible to remove that access hatch? I'd like to see what's happening behind it."

"Sure. I'll get somebody to do that, but while you're waiting, you can also get a good view of this area from underneath. That's why we put it on an inspection pit as soon as you said you were free to come over."

He led the way, with Stephen in tow. Colin picked up the inspection lamp. "Look," he said. "Do you see that? The front suspension unit is right here, slightly to the inside of the chassis longitudinal, always pushing upwards, and therefore outwards, but the shock absorber is in the other side of the chassis longitudinal and it always opposes the vertical movement of the vehicle."

"I see," replied Stephen. "So, the chassis will flex from side to side as the suspension moves up and down. Time to make use of the tool that Alec designed. And, while your team weld it on, can we have a look through that hatch and see if there's anything else to find?"

The measuring rod was set to its neutral position. Colin's foreman had come over to see what was happening and so the three of them went for a drive around the block. Colin and Stephen looked down through the open hatch while the foreman behind the wheel asked what they could see.

Just as predicted, as the front suspension compressed, the chassis members moved apart, and as it expanded again, the chassis members moved inwards. It hadn't been necessary to drive too far for the problem to be demonstrated quite clearly.

Back in the depot, Stephen measured the degree of chassis flexing that the tool had recorded; each longitudinal chassis member had moved out by seven millimetres and in by three.

The foreman looked at Stephen. "That looks serious, doesn't it?" he asked.

"Not in itself," replied Stephen. "It's not unusual for a chassis to flex, and it's not a problem if it doesn't go too far. The problem here is that the manufacturer attached these body panels to the chassis at its most flexible point. So, one option is simply to leave them attached at the non-moving points and not attach it here. Putting in a supplementary chassis crossmember would be another option. From your point of view, it's nothing like the problem on our other vehicles, and secondly, any repairs like this are the manufacturer's responsibility. Remember, these five vehicles are prototypes. They're learning from your experience."

"I can relax now. Thanks for coming over. And your assistant's invention's quite amazing. He should patent it."

"I'll tell him that."

Back at the office, Stephen passed on Colin's comments. "That invention of yours is even better than I thought. It'll also be able to measure engine movement relative to the chassis on these older vehicles and show us how to redesign the exhaust system and avoid these problems with the manifold coming loose. Meanwhile, the manufacturer of the prototypes is becoming more interested in them now."

"Thanks," said Alec. "I'll bear that in mind. By the way, Eadie's secretary was looking for you while you were away."

Stephen went through to see her. "Mr Eadie wants you to write the maintenance manual for your line manager's project," she told him. "You've to join tomorrow morning's progress meeting at eleven o'clock."

"Thanks," said Stephen. "I'll put that in my diary."

Why had Eadie's secretary, rather than Jim, have to tell him that? Then he remembered that he had been pre-warned. Since he had been demoted, Eadie had been keeping his head down but now he was probably just flexing his muscles where he still could.

Not the best note on which to end a day and Stephen was already regretting his decision to turn down the recent offer of the interview with the other organisation. How had he expected his career to progress? He was an engineer, and year by year, his experience was increasing. But experience in what?

He could identify design weaknesses, although he realised that it was much easier for him than for the people who had designed the vehicles. He saw them in operation day in, day out. This was almost a privilege: access to trials that these people could only dream about. He certainly had the ability to design out product weaknesses, but could he have designed any of those products from scratch?

With experience, no doubt. So, should he perhaps look for a job where he could get such experience? If he was honest with himself, he enjoyed learning. Formal education was one path; so too was doing what he was doing at present, but he was also aware that he would never want to settle into a job where he did the exactly the same thing every day.

With Eadie having brought the place to a halt, moving on really seemed to be his only choice. But where should he go?

One answer came from a surprising source. In his spare time, Stephen was a member of the board of directors of a language school, and while the monthly meetings were enjoyable in themselves, an extra treat was staying behind after each one for a glass of wine and a chat with his fellow members.

One of them told him that she had recently resigned from her job to undertake a business course. Stephen was keen to learn more.

It was a two-year programme condensed into twelve months and it was aimed at people already well into their careers. This was getting better by the minute. Over the next hour or so, she explained how the course was structured, the range of subjects on offer and those that she had chosen.

While his main interest was in road vehicles, Stephen began to wonder why he was so fascinated by her description of business policy, marketing, human resources and accounts and finance. He felt that this had been a kind of wake-up call, a reminder of the fact that he had recently become fascinated by the effect that individual people had on an organisation.

It wasn't all about repairing the infrastructure of a business, although that was certainly important; it was about understanding, and if possible, influencing the role that people played in its day-to day-activities.

Marketing, in particular, caught his attention. As the discipline was described to him, he was suddenly reminded about a thought he had had not too long ago. When he was examining a rather tired vehicle, it suddenly came to him that customers were, at least in part, responsible for the vehicle's sad state and the potential cost of bringing it back to new. Was the answer to get rid of customers?

He couldn't believe that he'd actually thought that. In his own defence, he quickly reassured himself that he hadn't been serious - it had just been a thought that had come into his head – but it did remind him of the need to look before one leaps.

And now, what about human resources? How does an organisation ensure that every necessary function has the right number of people dedicated to it and that they are all fully qualified to play the role that their function demands?

An epiphany moment.

Stephen had been so engrossed that he'd forgotten to queue for his second glass of wine, but in truth, he'd hadn't missed it. Hopefully he would learn more after the next month's meeting.

Another possibility was applying for an MSc in transport engineering. What should he do? Go deeper into his current discipline or change direction and look at the bigger picture of business?

This surely had to be his next big decision. But it didn't compensate for his frustration in the delay in resolving other issues. He couldn't see his current organisation ever getting back to the way it had been when he joined it. And none of the thorough investigations that he had carried out would be repeated. That was very sad.

All the proven benefits of such work seemed now to be irrelevant. The business course that had been described to him in detail now seemed to be the wisest choice to make. He updated his CV and applied, but he didn't tell anyone at work. There was no guarantee that he'd be accepted.

How could one person bring an organisation to a halt? Yes, he had been demoted, but Eadie was still able to decide what projects Stephen could undertake, or not. Now, all Stephen was allowed to do was answer questions that he assumed had been passed down by the board to Eadie in advance of their monthly meetings.

It was very disappointing, but it was also very interesting. Stephen constantly liaised with the coal face, trying to develop solutions to problems that were experienced while people were trying to deliver the service to the customer. The questions he was now being asked implied that the board itself was out of touch with the product that the organisation delivered, and upon which its survival depended.

If the business course were as good as he'd been told, he might be able to take a significant step forward in his career. It might also allow him to better understand how organisations worked and thereby get the answer to this paradox.

In the meantime, his list of priorities was continually altering. Depots were asking him to look at another transmission problem. He was aware that, in terms of vehicle downtime and repair costs, it was important that it was addressed. He had seen a number of units being overhauled in the central workshop and he'd again taken the workshop manual home with him to allow him to better understand the force systems at work inside the unit.

He had learned that his company had always specified these vehicles with an unusually high final drive ratio. He had also learned that other organisations in the same industry had not done so and apparently didn't experience the same failures. That seemed to imply that the solution would be simple. That night at home, he began to create a stress diagram for the unit with all the available ratios and worked on it until it was time for bed.

The following morning, he showed Alec the sketch. "The units all fail here," he said. "The casing splits from this stress raiser down to that one, but of course the forces arise purely from the forces generated by the gears."

Stephen was reaching for his pen when the phone rang. "Hello, yes, it is," he said, answering. "How are you? Yes, I'm sure you can, but you'd better ask him." Stephen covered the speaker with his hand. "It's for you," he said to Alec. "The prototype vehicle people are asking if they could borrow your invention."

His assistant took the call and when he put down the phone, he was shaking his head and smiling. "It's not every day something like that happens," he said. "They want to use the tool to measure the way the chassis is behaving with another customer. Their design team seems to have been very interested in our findings and they want to carry out some tests of their own before developing a modification to the vehicle."

"Your findings, remember," Stephen said. "But that's great news. Teams working together. It doesn't get any better than that."

"It doesn't. If teams of people everywhere worked together to solve problems, there soon wouldn't be any problems left. But that reminds me, Stephen, there's something I was meaning to tell you. I've applied for a job in IT."

"Here?"

"No. Look at that." Stephen was shown a magazine open at the adverts page. "The one at the top. I think I could do it."

"Well, if you do, apply for it. Life's too short to spend it all doing something you don't enjoy. If you do apply, I hope you're successful."

"Thanks. I really appreciate that."

Stephen wondered if he should have told Alec about his wish to move on, but that would probably have to wait. The first issue was that he might not be accepted for the business course. And, of course, if he were accepted for it and he took up the offer, he would have to tell his manager. And, if Alec left at the same time, what would the poor manager do?

By coincidence, it was Jim who suddenly put his head round the door. "Are you coming to your other job?" he asked.

A slightly shaken Stephen smiled before reaching for his briefcase. "I am indeed."

The draft maintenance manual had been in and out of the typing pool since the previous meeting. Stephen was now handed this latest version. Hands reached for coffee cups and then replaced them on the table. There was little sound except for the turning of pages and some scribbling with pens or pencils.

"Any comments?" Eadie asked.

The divisional manager asked everyone to look at section seven, page sixty-eight. He wanted to make a few changes, and it was after all his operation and he would be more affected by these procedures than anyone else around the table.

"But we agreed this at the last meeting." Who else but Eadie?

"I'm aware of that, but since we last met, I've been discussing the exact wording with my team. We couldn't safely carry out these checks during the day, so I'd like it to be put under the heading 'nightshift activities'."

Stephen took note of the changes and waited for further comments. This went on for another two hours but at least there was a break for another coffee, this time with biscuits. On the way back to his own office, he could only think about the application he had made. Acceptance would be gratefully received.

*

The following week, when he arrived home after another annoying day, there was a letter waiting for him: he had been accepted for the business course. He had to read the letter more than once to convince himself he wasn't dreaming. He often switched on the television, simply as a distraction, but not tonight. He went to the fridge and took out a bottle of white wine.

Since Stephen hadn't formally told his manager that he was intending to leave, he was cautious the following morning when he mentioned the letter that he had received. He hoped, however, that the secret of his determination to leave had somehow leaked out and that his news wouldn't be too much of a shock. "I've been accepted for a business course, so I'll be handing in my resignation," he said.

"I'm sorry to see you go," said Jim, "but remember, you'll be welcome back at any time."

That was a bit of an anti-climax, but he was now thinking ahead to the course. Of course, he also couldn't help wondering how Jim would react if his assistant got the job that he'd applied for.

Back at his desk, he began completing all the documentation relating to his current workload when the phone rang. It was Jim. "Are you free for a drink after work tonight?" he asked.

"Yes," Stephen replied. "What's the occasion?"

"Eadie's invited us all out."

"Why?"

"He's leaving."

"Say that again?"

"Eadie's leaving. So, you could have stayed, carried on fixing things, enjoying yourself."

"If only I could. I've paid for the course up front. There's no going back. When did you find out?"

"Two minutes ago. His secretary called me."

"Are we invited for a meal?"

"What do you think? I just thought you'd like to buy your friend a pint."

After work, the evening turned out to be better than Stephen feared. One or two people spoke to Eadie, those sitting beside him, but most of the evening was spent with people describing to their friends all the stupid things that had happened to them over the previous few weeks. No doubt there was a great deal of exaggeration, but nights out were meant to be fun, weren't they?

Stephen's last week in the office was even more hectic than usual. All his current projects had to be set out in a report to Jim. But one thing that he had not anticipated was the farewell party that had been arranged for him. People had contributed to a gift voucher that would allow him to buy whatever he wished.

The event was a low-key affair held in the office just before finishing time on his last Friday. There were toasts to him: coffee, not alcohol, and a round of handshakes before, perhaps not unexpectedly, he was asked to make a speech.

His mind was blank, so he just started to say what he was looking forward to enjoying on the course. He described the reports that had been given to him about the staff he would be meeting and the things that he would be learning, but he quickly found himself thinking how much he had enjoyed his time with his colleagues, at least until Eadie's arrival, and his sudden feeling of regret about leaving when he heard that Eadie was moving on. He stopped at that point, and simply toasted the others and thanked them again for their gift.

Different conversations then began as small groups broke away to talk about what they had been doing that week.

Life would obviously be going on, and Stephen began wondering if he would be missed at all. While these colleagues were based here in head office, they, as he had done, spent much of their time visiting operating depots and the central workshop, and the following Monday, they would no doubt simply be continuing with their current projects.

It was now simply a case of stopping work this evening and starting the course in three days' time.

Chapter 10
Morning greeting

The course was, as he had been told, effectively two years condensed into twelve months. And no doubt that was to make it more accessible to its students who were almost all in mid-career. There were part time and distance-learning options, but the full-time course was the one that Stephen had chosen.

On that first day, the structure of the course was explained. Nine examinations would be taken, and a written thesis then submitted for appraisal. Four foundation classes would immediately be chosen and then examined in February. The core subject was business policy, and its examination would take place in June, along with the four electives that would be chosen in February. The thesis would then be undertaken and submitted for appraisal before graduation in twelve months' time.

Each foundation class was presented by the appropriate tutor and the students chose their first four subjects. Stephen chose marketing, management of human resources, accountancy and finance, and statistics. Let's get started, he thought.

It was odd being a student again, listening to the lecturer and taking notes. While he had been studying for his engineering degree some twenty years earlier, he had been very aware that the standard of teaching was very much higher than that in secondary school. Now, teaching standards here were of a higher level again. Perhaps it was because the subjects here were more focussed.

In theory, that might have been expected to be rather stressful, and that is exactly what Stephen thought when he enrolled, but in fact the pace was no different to that of his typical day at work.

Marketing was the subject that had intrigued him most, and as its lecturer presented the syllabus, Stephen immediately thought back to the direction he seemed to be taking at work, and that embarrassing thought about eliminating customers...

While he had been aware of that, he had given it little thought, but now it was being set out in detail, with references in the appropriate literature being recommended for further reading.

Accountancy and mathematics were also well-taught and interesting and he learned a lot from both, but marketing and human behaviour were the ones that he found most compelling and the ones that he thought he would take the following term if they were also available as electives.

It wasn't long before he'd all but forgotten the last ten years. The course was very intense and fast moving but he was captivated. New information couldn't come along fast enough. Even spending evenings in the library didn't seem an odd thing to be doing. This was amazing.

The classes were fascinating, but so too were the coffee and lunch breaks. His fellow students came from all over the globe and without exception, they too were in mid-career. He learned so much from talking to them: different disciplines, different countries, different lives. Was there a common factor? Not one that was immediately obvious.

"Is anybody sitting there?" said a voice.

Stephen looked up. "No. Come in and join us," he said.

"I'm John, by the way."

"Stephen. What business are you in?"

"Electronics. And you?"

"Transport."

"And what made you decide to take the course, Stephen?"

"An interesting question. I enjoyed my job, but then a new boss joined the organisation. He had nothing to offer. He just brought an end to all the progress we'd been making."

"Was that the only reason for leaving?"

"Interestingly enough, it wasn't. I'd always looked for job satisfaction. I was spending the greater part of my waking life trying to earn enough money to survive, so I wanted to enjoy it, and I enjoyed solving problems.

But, as well as wondering if I could be making better use of my time, I knew someone who took this course last year, and she described it to me in great detail. That was probably what made me decide what to do. So, why are you here?"

"Interestingly enough, it was my company that decided I should take it."

"Not your choice?"

"I'm in middle management, and maybe they thought that the course would be the next step in moving up."

"Do you regret taking it?"

"No, it's interesting. I'm learning a lot, but I'm also looking forward to getting back to work."

Stephen found that an interesting response. They were due back in the lecture theatre in a few minutes, and they would again be listening and taking notes. Stephen would have to leave this question for another time. And talking to more of his fellow students would no doubt help with that. Meanwhile, the course went on.

He had studied statistics as a branch of mathematics in the second year of his engineering course and choosing it as one of the foundation classes had probably been done to avoid the risk of being overstressed. Much of the syllabus was familiar to him, but there were, of course, some new things to learn. What he found most intriguing was a practical exercise that involved selecting at random some pre-numbered items from a container. The findings were amazingly accurate, and somehow, seeing the theory carried out in practice was very reassuring. Small surprises like that took place in all the foundation class subjects, then suddenly, the Christmas break arrived.

Time again to relax, but January would be coming soon, bringing with it another five weeks or so of intensive learning, and of course revision of everything that had been covered so far. Socialising with friends and family made these three weeks of freedom very enjoyable, and in spite of the social whirl, very relaxing. The only danger here would be over-eating.

Even if Stephen had wanted to forget the course during this break, there were many people who were fascinated to learn what he was doing mid-career, and why he was doing it. Their interest seemed to be genuine and he explained what he had studied so far, and what he hoped to learn during the next term. He heard what he was saying and realised that he was describing the course to them in exactly the same way as his friend had described it to him. Had he just recruited next year's intake?

New Year, more drinks and socialising – but now, in January, it was back to work. A number of assessed writing tasks had been given out over the first weeks of the course, and now they were returned to the students with grades and comments from the tutors. They would be useful in deciding where to focus during this revision. And now there were just four more weeks of lectures, four more weeks of learning, before the examinations were due, so the homework now also included revision. The pace had increased again.

*

It was now February, and the exam timetable was published. Stephen had one day between each of them. Was that planned, or just a coincidence due to the subjects he had selected? No time to worry about that, just revise, revise, revise. And, when his first examination took place, he felt more relaxed than he had expected.

Everyone had been told to wait until being told to turn over their paper, and he simply waited calmly until permission was given. Like many of the other students around him, he had placed his wristwatch on the desk in front of him in order to ensure that he paced himself correctly. But the stress? Work had typically been more stressful – not every day, but often, and usually when being pestered for information for board papers. He was going to enjoy this.

*

With the first part of the course completed, he chose marketing as one of his electives. And, since human resources had also been a fascinating foundation class disclosing the theory behind human behaviour, he also took that to the next level. Commercial law and economics also appealed. Maybe he would learn how governments could work towards making poor people better off.

Students were encouraged to carry out further reading of published documents relevant to the subjects they had chosen to study, and this wasn't hard to do. The university library had more sources of information than Stephen could have devoured in a lifetime. So, he would be there when he was not in the lecture theatre.

If, as he had been told, a business is that which exists to make money, then the economy was also a subject in need of close scrutiny. Would he choose the economy as the subject for his course thesis? Perhaps, but for now, his priority was soaking up the findings of as much research as possible.

There were also more assessed homework tasks, and he took them even more seriously than those of the previous term.

However, he was also aware that he was settling further into this new world of learning. And just how far could he go? He had dealt with the term 'infinity' many times, but he had never fully understood what it meant. Was he now about to learn?

He learned what he could about economics from the lectures, as well as from further reading, but he decided that his priority was still marketing. The subject was becoming clearer as the lectures drilled progressively deeper into the subject, and Stephen decided that he would use marketing as the topic for his course thesis.

Meanwhile, he simply attended the lectures of his four electives, as well as those of the core subject, business policy. In a few weeks' time, there would be an Easter break, but probably, just as at Christmas, most of that would be spent revising. There was a general sense that something important would soon be happening: the final examinations.

Coffee breaks and lunch breaks of course continued, as they had in the first term, as did conversations with fellow students, but the topics discussed were now more serious than before. No longer were they about getting to know about each other, and each other's past, they were now about how much everyone had learned, how well they would do in their examinations, and what they might achieve in future.

As he had discovered during the previous term, there were some people who would simply be moving to the next stage in their present career path, but there were others who were rather unsure of what the future would hold for them. And many of them admitted that that was a distraction.

Stephen, however, was simply focussed on passing the exams, and then finding out who his tutor would be for the marketing thesis. It was the tutor who would agree the exact topic.

In the final few weeks, Stephen began to wonder if the lecturers in all the subjects were giving clues about the questions that they would be setting, but he soon dismissed that as neurosis. This was not the time for losing hold of reality.

As with the first term, the exam timetable was published, and again, Stephen found no problem with it. There had been a lot to take in, but somehow everything seemed to fit together. What was the wording he most remembered? The common thread. That was it.

As he read his notes, Stephen found that he could almost repeat them word for word. This must be how actors feel as they get ready for their first performance. He wasn't brave enough to appear on stage in front of a live audience, but he was sure that he would have no problem responding to written questions, with time to change the word order of his responses if necessary.

He took a deep breath. He was ready.

*

After the sprint, there was the welcome break of a few weeks' summer holiday. Time to let the brain cool down but also refresh his memory about all the things that he had learned and see if any topic stood out sufficiently for him to want to pursue it as his thesis.

His initial assumption was that it would be about advertising: hoardings that he walked past daily in the streets, or happy people presenting some product or service on television. That was certainly there, but the full range of disciplines that it covered was enormous. And somehow, he was now reminded of a series of photographs he had seen in a newspaper weekend magazine.

They were of the planet Earth, and they had been taken from a spacecraft as it made its way back from the moon. As the journey progressed, the Earth grew from a small sphere, lost in a dark background, to a holiday postcard.

The first image was of a dark and cold background with a small blue Earth, partly covered in cloud. In the next image, the Earth occupied the majority of the page but some darkness was still visible behind it. Then there was still some cloud, but the blue sea was surrounded by green and beige land masses. Closer still, and there was a continent, again mainly green, but now with darker areas.

The next photograph was immediately recognisable; it was effectively a map of a city. He had seen images like that before. And one last photograph. It showed an area of a township, houses and gardens, one of which had a swimming pool.

These images had fascinated him at the time but now, perhaps after his life experiences had taught him to think differently, they reappeared in his mind. His engineering training had taught him about understanding the construction of materials at the atomic level. People could blend different mixes of materials – types of steel, for example, in order to obtain properties appropriate for their application.

His engineering course had also taught him how failure of a part could begin at the atomic level, and advance unseen, until the point of catastrophic failure. This was problem solving. Problems are identified in the macroscopic and solved in the microscopic. That's exactly how the photos from space were encouraging him to think. He was effectively carrying an imaginary microscope that he could use to see and solve problems in their particular context.

Having studied engineering, a relatively narrow subject but very deep in detail, and now with this course, much wider in subject matter, and obviously less deep in detail, Stephen suddenly had a vision of knowledge available to mankind.

There was a lot of knowledge out there, but not everybody had direct access to it. But probably every subject on the planet had its own experts. Stephen imagined this resource as a large cube, as wide as it was long and as it was tall.

It was covered in square concrete slabs, and each slab was an academic subject. The area stretched out as far as the eye could see: the list of subjects for study was endless. No one person could study everything, but Stephen was glad to know that all these subjects existed. And, in each subject, its specialists could drill down and obtain the solutions to all its problems.

This was a time for reflecting, but also to pursue marketing and learn how to put its disciplines into context in all the situations he could bring to mind. Now, with no formal classes to attend, Stephen was free to plan his visits to the library or meet up with fellow students.

Everyone was now much more relaxed than before, but they now had to concentrate on their theses. They knew roughly what they wanted to do, but the next step was to get agreement on exactly what their research would include. When Stephen met up with his tutor, he was told that the university was considering a new course for people working in the discipline.

It would be offered on a part-time or distance-learning basis and the university wished to learn what the potential demand for such a subject might be. Interesting.

Stephen would have to meet his tutor on a weekly basis to keep her updated with the progress that he was making, and the final version would be required to be submitted in two months' time to allow it to be assessed. Graduation would be some three weeks after that. And, so far, the exam results had not been announced.

One morning, quite unexpectedly, he met Eadie in the street. What was he doing back here? "We've just bought our company," said Eadie. "If you've got the time, come up and have a look around."

That was the last thing that Stephen had on his mind, but he agreed. He had probably been caught off guard. It would be interesting to see where Eadie had ended up.

The company that he was talking about was one that Stephen had visited earlier in his career, simply to exchange experiences of operating a specific type of vehicle, and how each organisation approached its maintenance. How would it be operating now? "I'll be busy for the next three months," said Stephen, "but after I've graduated, I could give you a call and see when would be convenient."

That was agreed. Stephen had been going to the library, but instead he went to the coffee lounge and thought about what he should do. Was it a wise decision to have agreed to catch up with Eadie again? After all, Eadie was the reason that Stephen had left the industry to go off in this new direction.

Some fellow students were sitting in small groups, too busy chatting to notice Stephen's arrival. That suited him perfectly.

He had enjoyed his job, until Eadie had arrived; a bully who knew less about the business than Stephen and his colleagues. So why did he say that he would accept Eadie's offer? Out of politeness? Or had the satisfaction that he had taken from his role in the industry been sufficient for him to be interested in another organisation with the same challenges that he knew well?

The coffee was cold. Back to the library.

Stephen was designing a questionnaire to be put to the marketing industry to try and determine what potential demand might be for the proposed course. Having received the approved of his tutor, this was sent out. While waiting for the initial response, assuming that there would be one, it was time to set out the methodology of the survey.

Fortunately, there were many examples of similar theses in the library and he found it very useful to read them and try to get into the mind of the author: what had been the initial assumptions made, what had been the methodology used in the research? In some ways, it was little different to the reports he had written at work, setting out the findings of his investigation into problems and the recommendations that he had made. Here, of course, he would be required to concentrate heavily on the theory behind the work and show how it had been used.

When the responses to his survey began to appear, the pace quickened. Where appropriate, interviews were arranged to look further into the feedback that had been given. Then it was time to produce the final version of his work and submit it for assessment.

With that work competed, all that remained to do was wait patiently for the final results of the course to be announced.

The main question now was deciding what to do with everything that he had learned. He was grateful he had learned that the discipline of marketing existed; he wouldn't make the mistake of undervaluing customers again. Should he try to move further into marketing? That was appealing, but he felt that he had learned as much about it as he needed. However, the idea of taking his studies further very much appealed to him.

He had seen money in use, he had earned money, and he had used it to purchase food, clothing and entertainment. But where did money come from before people were able to start circulating it in the economy?

He made an appointment to see one of his lecturers and seek advice on how to pursue a doctorate in economics. He couldn't afford to do that on a full-time basis, but the course he had just completed could be done on a part-time basis, so why not a doctorate?

Before the meeting took place, Stephen had been uncertain of how he might approach the subject, but during it, ideas flowed into his mind. And when it did take place, the lecturer was very encouraging and suggested that he should give more thought to exactly what he wanted to study before making a formal approach to the university.

He now often met up with fellow students for a coffee and a chat about what opportunities there were in the world for all of them. Some had already returned to work, but for the small number of people in the same situation as Stephen, these chats were very informative.

Interestingly, no one talked about careers in the city, and Stephen found that slightly disappointing. Some people were simply hoping that they could move up to board level in an organisation similar to the one that they had left in order to join the course.

They talked about increased job satisfaction, but reading between the lines, Stephen believed that they were simply looking for an increased income. Nothing wrong with that. For him, however, money was not the aim. It had always been, and still remained, job satisfaction. It was as simple as that.

He could no doubt choose a business where he would obtain this satisfaction, but would any such business choose him? He had been reading newspaper advertisements for the last few weeks and there was certainly a great deal of opportunity out there.

The adverts seemed to be as much about saying that the organisations were magnificent as they were in describing the type of employee that they were seeking. At least, that's how Stephen read them. But they did, of course, include job descriptions.

Not all of them fitted his education and experience. Not all of them were close to home. Another coffee? And then he remembered his promise to Eadie.

Chapter 11
Where to?

His work was accepted, and a few weeks later, he graduated. He phoned Eadie's secretary. She put him through and somewhat surprisingly, he was asked if he could spend a few weeks looking at a specific issue. It was, of course, an environment with which he was familiar, even if he had abandoned it to pursue his business course.

Different layout, different people, but the same activities that he knew inside out. And, yes, he had visited the same organisation many years earlier when it was under different ownership. It was similar to the business that Stephen had been in, but much, much smaller and that visit had simply been made in order to share experiences. It had been a well-run organisation then, so he was intrigued to see what changes, if any, had been made.

When he arrived, he was told about the recent buyout of the organisation. It seemed that a good deal had been done, and the management team apparently felt confident about the improvements they could make.

Eadie then took him down to the operations department. He wasn't introduced to any individual, but

Eadie explained who Stephen was and said that he'd be spending a few weeks looking at vehicle cleaning. He was then taken to meet the engineering director and Eadie left them to decide how they would go about the project.

"Do you know this industry?" Stephen was asked.

An odd question. He had assumed that Eadie would have explained to his team what the project was and who was going to carry it out.

"Yes," he said. "I was working with one of your competitors when Eadie joined us as chief engineer eight years ago."

"Ah," was the only reaction.

"I think there are some vehicles I can look at?" said Stephen.

"Yes, I'll show you around the premises."

On his previous visit, he hadn't been shown the complete site, and it was larger than he had expected. He was now shown a relatively young vehicle that had just returned to the depot and it confirmed that there was indeed a problem. It was filthy. However, he was quite surprised by a walk to the back of the site in order to view a much older vehicle that had been marked for disposal. It was much cleaner than the younger one, both inside and out.

The cleaning process itself was similar to the one he knew from his previous organisation. As each vehicle returned from service, it was parked by the driver who then signed off, and it remained in the queue to be refuelled, driven through the mechanical vehicle wash and then parked. And it would remain there for service the following day unless it was on the list for planned servicing or repair that evening.

The members of the nightshift cleaning team each had a list of vehicles that they were to clean out, and they walked around the site looking for them one by one.

But that one question remained. Why were the older vehicles cleaner than the younger ones? Stephen agreed to return that evening and meet the nightshift manager. He was very friendly and he too walked Stephen around the site, following the path that the vehicles would take after they had returned from service. And, as the evening wore on, Stephen could see that vehicles tended to return in groups at infrequent intervals.

The queue for refuelling initially grew and then began to shrink steadily throughout the night.

The nightly cleaning process initially seemed to be relaxed, but there was a sense that an underlying tension reflected the need for all vehicles to be dealt with before they were again ready for service.

The following day, the scheduling team explained how they allocated vehicles for business. Older ones were given lighter duties and tended, therefore, to leave the depot later and come back earlier. The younger vehicles were more heavily used, but as Stephen had found out, they received the same daily cleaning attention as the older ones.

The other observation, of course, had been that the cleaning team spent a high proportion of their time walking around looking for the vehicles on their list. This reduced the time that they were able to devote to each vehicle and so the cleaning process would be compromised.

With the pattern of scheduled return times, Stephen now set out a table of vehicles due to arrive back at the depot during each ten-minute period of the night. This was compared with the number of vehicles fuelled and parked and so the size of the queue could be predicted for any given time.

The time to fuel and park these two groups did vary, but not significantly. In order to manage the queue – and avoid it spilling back out of the depot onto the street – the number of people involved in fuelling them had been determined through experience and divided into a backshift team and a nightshift team.

More thorough cleans were carried out during the day at weekly and four-weekly frequencies. These activities only dealt with a small number of vehicles each day and the process was therefore more efficient as the amount of walking time had been reduced.

Before setting out a theoretical plan, Stephen looked for a means of making the nightshift process more efficient, and he also looked for an improved method, rather than the need to make the cleaners work faster. His target was the time wasted by walking from vehicle to vehicle, and he looked for a method of avoiding this. The next challenge would be the provision of improved equipment and facilities.

The layout of the depot was such that, having returned from service at the end of its working day, each vehicle was moved from the parking area through the fuelling island, the automatic vehicle wash and then back to a specific parking bay in clockwise circle. Observation suggested that this typically took around fifteen minutes.

The cleaners' facilities were based in a long shed beyond the vehicle wash and it seemed to be an ideal location for the nightly activity.

If the process could be located there, it would allow more cleaning time to be spent on each vehicle and more equipment and materials, including running water, could be made available. His training in method study meant that he naturally turned to documenting and integrating the refuelling and nightly cleaning cycles.

He had also noticed a tyre store that was situated close to the exit from the vehicle wash and which had the potential to overlook both the fuelling and cleaning activities if it were converted into an office.

The solution to the problem was becoming very obvious. The next move would simply be to integrate the fuelling and cleaning activities into one process, and he knew typical times that were taken to complete each cycle.

He therefore turned his attention to the number of vehicles in the queue. This would be managed by choosing the number of fuellers and cleaners on a backshift when older vehicles tended to return from duty and then those on nightshift, when the emphasis on cleaning needed to increase.

The method that he set out would simply ask the fuelling team to collect vehicles from the parking area as they had always done, drive them to the fuelling station, top up the tanks, drive them through the vehicle wash, turn right into the long shed and now, step out of the vehicle and into the previous one, and then continue the clockwise drive back to the outdoor parking area.

While the vehicles in the fuelling cycle each now spent fifteen minutes in what would now be the cleaning area, the nightshift cleaners no longer needed a list of those that they had to process. They simply stepped on board a vehicle that had just been delivered to them and now had the full fifteen minutes to clean it, simply because their previous walking about time had been saved.

In addition, located indoors for the first time, their working conditions would be improved, and they would have access to litter bins and hot and cold running water.

Stephen set out a report using multiple activity charts, one of the work study techniques he had been taught, and they included the relationship between vehicle, fueller and cleaner throughout the night. The report included not only the findings and recommended process, but the theory behind them in order to allow the system to be evolved, if necessary, in the future.

He was not present to see the new system introduced, but he was later told that it had gone like clockwork.

Apparently, people had been very sceptical about it working, but it had been raining on the evening that it was introduced, and that was perhaps one reason that the cleaners had been very pleased with their new indoor workstation.

The project had been interesting. However, of more importance to him, it had been satisfying; he had produced a solution to a problem. But finding a permanent job was now the pressing issue.

Reading newspaper advertisements was reassuring; there were lots of jobs out there, but of course not all of them matched his training and experience to date. However, by chance, he met someone who suggested that he approach a local electronics firm that was looking for someone with a work study background.

The job would eventually become that of production manager but initially, it would involve working with a firm of management consultants who had been employed to introduce just-in-time manufacturing. This was usually referred to as JIT. He had been taught about that, but it would be interesting to see it in real life and get a better understanding of what was involved.

He applied and was invited for an interview by the managing director. After a brief chat, he was accepted and given a starting date, when he would meet the production manager.

The firm was a subcontractor to larger organisations in the electronics industry and it manufactured wiring harnesses and circuit boards to the clients' specifications. Meeting agreed delivery dates was important.

The job was to be part of the team that turned orders into products by buying in the necessary materials and setting out the different stages of assembly to ensure that the agreed delivery date was met.

Interestingly, the management team was made up mainly of men, although there were one or two women. However, the people on the shop floor were almost exclusively female, and some of them were quite young. Was this the first job they had found after school, and would they move on as soon as they could?

Stephen had certainly seen wiring harnesses before, but the finished products didn't necessarily give a full understanding of how they were made. He was now about to learn.

The total time was, say, fifty minutes to manufacture a particular loom and this had been determined by good old-fashioned work measurement with a stopwatch. The process had been divided into four basic stages.

Firstly, it would be set out on a board with the wires of each branch tied together. The second stage involved snipping the harness off the board and passing it on to the operator who would cut and loosen the rubber insulation at the end of each wire. The third stage was removing the loosened insulation, and then attaching the terminals.

The final stage, blocking, was clipping the terminals into the connectors as set out in the drawing for that harness. Job done. Or almost.

After each stage had been completed, the batch would queue for the next one, and that could take several days. Assuming that the order was for twenty harnesses and each one would take fifty minutes to manufacture, that might imply a total time of one thousand minutes or sixteen hours and forty minutes: just over two days. Yet, when the average product was tracked through the plant, the total time in manufacture was around three weeks. Surely that could be improved.

It would have to be. After the manufacturing process had been completed, each harness queued for inspection to ensure that it complied fully with the manufacturing instructions. If not, it queued for the defect to be put right before being inspected again. This could not only be improved, but it had to be improved. Phone calls from customers chasing up orders were being received every day.

There was more to the problem than this. The company was being paid for the planned labour time and parts used in the order, but because of glitches in the manufacturing process, it was almost routinely putting more of both into each part. Was it profitable? If Stephen had understood the problem during his first few days with the company, he assumed that he wasn't alone. This would be why the consultants were there.

As the weeks went by, Stephen got to know his colleagues, during tea breaks or at lunch in the canteen. They were all very friendly, but it wasn't long before he discovered that they all regarded the place as a sweatshop.

One day, he was taken down to the basement by an inspector and there he saw a frighteningly large quantity of abandoned products.

"If the boss knew what was here, he'd go mad. When these harnesses reached quality control, there were so many faults that it was decided to start again rather than try to re-work them."

More haste, less speed. Looking around, Stephen felt a certain amount of sympathy for the boss. What had this cost the company? Why hadn't the boss noticed the problem through the accounts? Yes, maybe he had, and that would be why this move to JIT manufacturing was now taking place.

Stephen's current role was to produce job times for new products, however the majority of the work in plant was fulfilling repeat orders for products for which the job times had been produced by his predecessor. That left time for him to spend with the consultancy team and learn what changes were being made. It was fairly complex, but it was so logical that it was easy to follow.

Stephen was initially based in the main office with eight other colleagues, but he was then moved to the quieter side room to join the consultants. There were four of them in the team, but on most days only one or two were present. Stephen was now effectively one of them.

They had spent their initial time with the company listing all the products that were currently on order, along with listing the staff numbers and making a detailed inventory of all the tooling and equipment.

With most of that work now completed, they were designing just-in-time cells for the top twenty products by weekly volume. And that is now what they described to Stephen.

Sitting in that little room with them, he was immediately aware of the calmness with which they went about their work. That was almost the exact opposite of the atmosphere in the main office where there was an underlying tension about who would next receive a phone-call and how irate the caller would be.

There was none of that stress here. The team leader simply explained why the consultancy had been employed. It had been a government initiative to encourage companies in the industry to use a subsidy to improve their efficiency with a benefit both to that industry and its customers. The team leader himself had specialised in introducing this process to different industries for the greater part of his career and his enthusiasm for it was obvious. That in itself was very reassuring. Stephen leant forward to pay more attention to what was about to be said.

"What we're doing is introducing a system that will produce a perfect product without any time delay. If we take the last part number that you were working on, the job time is fifty minutes, yes? Then this system will produce a perfect product in fifty minutes. However, if we put eight operators in the team, we'll produce the first perfect product after fifty minutes and the remaining nineteen will arrive every six and a quarter minutes: a batch of twenty in just under three hours instead of three weeks. And you won't be paying for remedial labour or the use of extra parts."

That was almost unbelievable, so Stephen asked the team leader for clarification. "For this particular product, the four stages are of different lengths. The fifty minutes are made up of eighteen, ten, fifteen and seven. So how do you divide that into eight?"

"A good question," was the reply. "You do that literally. Fifty divided by eight is six minutes and fifteen seconds. You take the original time study and make each new stage last that time. So, if your original first stage was eighteen minutes long, you now give it to three operators."

"How accurate do you need to be when dividing up the original job time?" Stephen asked.

"Another good question. The original times are only indicative. How accurate do you think the original time studies were? The aim here is simply to strike a balance between the assumed time for each section and the stage of the manufacturing process you're dealing with. We just want the operators to take more or less the same time for the process that they've been allocated. And before you ask, there's no need to achieve the overall original time here. It's a guide, that's all. But what you're going to see here is a dramatic improvement in the overall efficiency of the process. And you'll find that no operator works more slowly than any of the others. That's something you couldn't guarantee in the old system."

Quite a lot to take in. For Stephen, it was just a specific example of job design and that in itself had captivated him.

The next few weeks were spent converting the original time studies into the revised format and quite quickly the layout of the factory floorspace began to change.

When Stephen had first joined the company, there were workstations everywhere. The whole place simply looked very untidy, and the fact that there were also two walkways through the shop floor didn't really help. There were tables everywhere, mostly covered with partly completed products, and the rest of the floorspace was taken up with large cardboard boxes with produce queuing for the next stage in their manufacture.

Now, as the JIT cells were set up one by one, the tables and machines started migrating to the far end of the factory where the stores area was located. The transformation was completed by the progressive disappearance of work-in-progress.

Equally apparent was the disappearance of faulty products being re-worked. There was no need for that now. As predicted, the inspectors simply sat at one corner of their workstation, and if they found a problem with a completed product, the line was stopped until the problem was described and addressed. Then the line started again. Sometimes Duncan, the machine setter, was required. Perhaps a crimping machine required to be adjusted. Sometimes, it was simply necessary to point out to one of the operators that a wire had been plugged into the wrong position of a terminal block.

But, as soon as the detected problem had been corrected, the cell got moving again. And, yes, instead of minutes of manufacture taking weeks, products could be delivered to customers the following day.

The manufacturing costs were now fully under control. There were no telephone calls from angry customers, there was no stress in the team. Why couldn't this have happened sooner? That was what intrigued Stephen. Evolution was normal, and as here, it usually came in small quantum jumps. Surely method study should be universal.

The consultancy team had now left, no doubt to make life less stressful for another client, and as time went by, this new way of working totally replaced the previous one. Chaos had been replaced by tranquillity.

This, perhaps, should have made Stephen less anxious to leave what had been a stressful job, but it didn't. He had been part of an improvement process, and he had found that very satisfying. He had learned something new, and he had always enjoyed doing that. He wanted a new challenge, but perhaps it was too soon to make another move.

Summer was arriving, and that in itself was cheering. He had made friends in this organisation, and that too was cheering, but he wanted to try something new. He would just have to be patient.

Chapter 12
Wandering

One day, out of the blue came an advertisement for a position with one of the big-six consultancies. It was the job description that had caught his eye; they were looking for someone to work in JIT manufacturing. He found the opportunity impossible to ignore.

He applied, and within a week he received a letter; he had been invited for an interview. The consultancy was based almost two hundred miles from Stephen's home, so it would obviously be important that he was making the right decision. However, he had found the new discipline of JIT manufacturing so captivating, and the idea of working for one of the big six was also so compelling, that he contacted the practice and made an appointment.

When the big day came, he was impressed by the office. The reception area was very well laid out, and the staff were professional and welcoming. As he looked around, he began to think that his impression was exactly what an organisation such as this would try to make on a new employee or, of more importance, a new client.

The interview was a one-to-one, and his interviewer was very relaxed. That helped Stephen remain more relaxed than he had expected to be, and it helped him answer all the questions in a logical fashion. When he was asked if he had any questions, he had none. He would regret that later.

The drive home was relaxing. It was almost as if he was returning from holiday, and at work the following day, he felt exactly as if he had done just that.

What had he missed? Anything? No, the new routine of the JIT cells was now quite normal for everyone. The random tea breaks that had been normal when people worked on their own schedule were now a thing of the past. Teams formed round each batch of the product next due for delivery, and a few hours later, it was complete and ready for delivery. As soon as the quality inspector had declared the batch problem free, those in the cell disappeared, some going outside for a cigarette, others to the coffee machine. They had all adapted to this new routine, and although they were all now controlled more closely than before, none of them appeared to find this to be stressful.

Stephen assumed that part of that came from the fact that the need to re-work faulty parts had all but disappeared, and the implied criticism that went with that had also disappeared. Amazing.

Then Stephen received a letter inviting him for a second interview with the consultancy. That too was amazing. He booked another day off.

The second interview was again a one-to-one, this time with one of the partners. Again, it went well. Stephen answered all the question that were put to him, and interestingly it was shorter than the first one. It seemed that the partner was simply seeing if he agreed with its findings.

Within a week, Stephen received another letter. He had been successful. He handed in his resignation to the engineering manager and then he heard that another colleague was leaving. Why was that? He found out that it was genuinely a coincidence. The colleague was simply moving to a larger organisation in the electronics industry, and he was organising a farewell party, a night out.

Then Stephen found out that the coincidence went even further. He and his colleague were leaving on the very same day, and the night out was scheduled for their last Friday. A function suite was hired in a local hotel and Stephen booked a room there. Driving home at the end of the night would not be a possibility.

These last few weeks were over in no time. It was now Friday. Work carried on as normal that day; as people prepared to go home, the engineering manager came up to Stephen, shook hands and wished him well, but the company owner who had interviewed him was nowhere to be seen. Later, the word was that he felt betrayed.

"See you later," called two of the chargehands, waving over as they left. It would no doubt be a good evening.

And it was. People arrived for drinks at the bar before the meal was served. They all knew each other from work, of course, but their interaction here was to a new level. The drink hadn't had time to take effect, so there must have been some other reason for it. Just being away from the managed work-routine?

The managing director had appointed Stephen in a simple, straightforward manner, but interestingly, the engineering manager whom he had next met had somehow implied that the place was a bit of a sweatshop. Stephen had not initially been aware of that; he had simply been trying to understand what was happening around him in order to fit in as quickly as he could. But now, having stepped away from the company, he could finally see that it had been.

These people deserved better than that, and hopefully the step-change in the work process would allow them all to better enjoy their jobs. In fact, the job design would guarantee it. That was the secret to everything.

The night had been very enjoyable, but Stephen now had two days to prepare for the new challenge. He would be staying in a hotel until he was able to move home, but he first needed to settle in.

*

The team leader who had first interviewed him now invited him into his office and described the projects currently being undertaken by his partner's team. Interestingly, because Stephen had not yet re-located, he was told that he would initially be joining a healthcare project in his hometown. That wasn't what he had expected, but he did like the idea of having more time to go house-hunting.

"I'll take you through to meet Rick, who's leading this project. He'll bring you up to speed," said the team leader.

Another attractive office; small but with a good view. "You're Stephen," said Rick. "I heard that you'll be working on our healthcare project. I see from your CV that you've spent two years working in the O and M team of your local health board. You're just the man we're looking for. Oh, just before we start, would you like a coffee?"

Music to Stephen's ears. "Yes please. Milk, but no sugar."

Rick went out to fetch it, and Stephen had another look out of the window. Nice day, nice city centre.

"There we are," said Rick. "I'll just take you through what we're doing."

The explanation went on for about an hour, but Stephen didn't notice the time passing. The project was interesting, and in an environment he knew well.

The approach taken by the practice was good old-fashioned work study. Its intended outcome was to track the treatment of each patient following their initial diagnostic code, and thereby help management create a more effective process that both improved patient treatment and reduced its cost. A very worthwhile project, but not what he had applied to do. However, he could drive home that evening and join the other members of the team on-site the following day.

*

Stephen's area would be laboratory medicine. He would use a questionnaire prepared by Rick and use it to obtain feedback from the client. Among the people to be interviewed were two former colleagues. What a small world.

The interviews with each of them took place a few weeks apart but he had looked forward to seeing them both again and indeed they were very friendly when they greeted him. However, when the formal part of the meeting began, both were equally reserved in their responses to the questions. He had initially been intrigued by this but it suddenly reminded him of when he turned up in his first transport job as a fresh-faced graduate, being looked up and down in a rather dismissive fashion. This time, the look wasn't dismissive, but it still said the same thing: what gives outsiders the right to tell us what to do in our own area of expertise? Stephen wasn't a total outsider; he had worked with them for two years, but he did represent an outside body, one that intended to interfere in their daily routine.

Yes, that was a perfectly understandable response, but hopefully the final recommendations would be for a system that they believed was workable and offered demonstrable improvement over the current system.

His role in this project meant that he also visited other departments in the same health board, asking similar questions and handing the results to Eric, the project manager. An unexpected outcome was that Stephen was able to send in his weekly timesheet with one hundred percent of his time chargeable to the client. Apparently, that wouldn't always be the case.

When Stephen's role in this exercise was over, he was based at head office, and this should have allowed him to devote some time to house-hunting, but learning what his next assignment would be came as a shock.

He hadn't been told during the interview, but his new employer had obtained three major contracts for healthcare projects, and they were almost identical.

From the consultancy's point of view, this made perfect sense. The significant cost of developing the software could be spread over the three contracts, making each of them more attractive to the client. And Stephen understood that completely, but it was the last thing that he wanted to hear.

What about the advertisement he had seen? It had very clearly stated that the consultancy was looking for someone with experience in just-in-time manufacturing.

So why was nobody now mentioning that? Should he ask? Perhaps not. But he now knew that this would not be his new career, so the choice would be to move again, or sit out the remaining eighteen months. He associated moving every two years or so with incompetent careerists who moved on before being found out.

These eighteen months would, however, allow him to see how universal the long-established work study techniques were, and seeing them in a different environment would no doubt teach him something new.

He would effectively be repeating the first exercise, but now in a health board close to head office. He would also be based there, but the idea of selling up and relocating was now out of the question. He would rent a property, stay there during the week and travel home at weekends.

*

Time for the second assignment. The buildings were different, the people were different, but the questions were the same. However, he didn't know any of the interviewees, and that allowed him to distance himself from the project. That probably made him more objective – not necessarily a bad thing.

Stephen's involvement was over a five-week period, shorter than the previous project. He and his colleagues went through their findings with the team leader, who then handled follow-up interviews, and when the questionnaires were available in their final version, they were given to the IT people at head office who then keyed in the data to the software that they had developed. It was at that stage that Stephen's role was over, and he waited to learn what he was to do next.

It was a surprise. He hadn't realised it at the time, but he was one of a number of new-starts, and he would be joining them on an internal training course on how to deal with clients face-to-face.

Stephen had always viewed himself as more of a back-room boy, gathering data and analysing it, but this was certainly a good opportunity to learn how to act in front of new clients and make a good first impression. The course itself was only two days in length and it took place in a local hotel, with all participants staying overnight and therefore spending the evening socialising with each other.

During some of the presentations that each individual had to make, they were asked to behave in a rather stupid fashion. At the time, that proved rather difficult to do, but afterwards, Stephen was fascinated to find that his self-confidence had improved significantly, and no doubt he would in future find himself more confident when making presentations to clients. And, as the course was over two days, there was time to talk to his fellow students and find out more about them: what they did before, what they were doing now, and what they hoped to do next. The after-dinner drinks in the bar helped with that. Stephen suspected that he was not alone in regretting his move here, but with the tutor there, there was a limit to what could be said.

He would now be more likely to make the clients feel more reassured. Yes, the course had been short in length, but it had been worthwhile. Back at head office, Stephen was introduced to another team leader. No more healthcare, but neither was it JIT. He was now to be trained in quality control systems and would be dealing with a new client base. Geoff, his new boss was very pleasant, and also enthusiastic about the projects in which he was involved.

This time, the clients were all smaller organisations and Stephen felt that he would be able to build up a closer working relationship with them, and indeed, that usually turned out to be the case.

He was later involved in one more healthcare project but setting up quality systems was what he now did. He would just have to hang on as best he could.

*

Over the next few months, as he got to know some colleagues better, he would meet up with them from time to time for an after-work drink.

There were also office nights out, meals, or visits to bowling alleys. Good fun. But again, what intrigued him most was learning how many people didn't like their job and were trying to find employment elsewhere.

One morning, while Stephen was typing up a report in the office, Peter, one of his new friends, came over to him and asked him if he wanted a coffee. Stephen seldom said no to that. And, as they stood by the machine, Peter said that he had recently noticed a colleague writing a letter of application to another organisation, and interestingly, not another consultancy.

"How did you see that?" asked Stephen, quite intrigued.

"I'd just arrived back in the office, and there was only one workstation free, so I went over and put my case down, before taking off my coat. It was while I was standing behind him that what he was doing caught my attention. I stood as long as I dared, and then I went over to the cloakroom. On the way back, I had another look before sitting down at my computer."

"That might have been a one-off."

"It might have been, but it wasn't. Whenever possible over the next few weeks, I tried to have a quick look at what everybody was up to, and he isn't the only one. I found four different people, mainly from the new intake."

Stephen found this news quite reassuring. He certainly wasn't alone. But that should really not have come as a surprise. He had often heard that this was a known pattern. When people joined new organisations, some found the job totally satisfying and stayed, while others didn't, and left. He was in the second group.

*

Luckily, the summer holiday break soon arrived, and that allowed Stephen to book a holiday abroad. In what was a totally different environment, he quickly forgot about the disappointment of the job and was able to relax for the first time in months.

Yes, life could be enjoyable. And he even looked forward to going back to work; in another eighteen, fifteen, months he would be able to move on.

*

Back in the office to learn what his next assignment would be, Stephen was pleasantly surprised to be met by Geoff. Another engineering project.

He was even more pleasantly surprised when the company in question was one that re-manufactured automotive components. They wanted to be quality-assessed in order to seek to expand their customer base and his contact was the retired father of one of the two owners.

While Geoff had taken him through the requirements that the customer would have to meet, Stephen felt that his knowledge of the automotive world would allow him to bring something to the party.

His contact was very friendly, as were all the other members of staff whom he met, and every process that was being carried out was familiar to him, although some suggestions for improvements immediately came to mind. But Geoff had made very clear to him what his role was here: it was to set out the activities of the client in accordance with the requirements of quality management systems, no more than that.

And that is exactly what Stephen did. He noted everything that the company did in the re-manufacturing process and noted the inspection criteria that they had set for themselves. He then set out that information in the format required by the relevant British Standard document.

Geoff used the term 'delivery' when describing to Stephen the service that the organisation gave to its clients. Stephen could only think of a maternity hospital.

Since he would only see his clients in this discipline once per week over ten weeks, it meant that he would require to be dealing with at least three at the same time in order to keep his timesheet acceptably full. Ten weeks would be almost three months, so five times that would take him up to his two-year minimum stay. He was able to relax again and concentrate on delivering quality systems to the clients.

Some people simply wanted to get help in becoming better organised, but the majority were seeking to meet the requirements of their customers, in particular local authorities where there were often many requirements to be met in order to bid for contracts. And when he learned that Stephen found himself pulled in to work closely with the client and ensure that their operational processes were appropriately designed and documented in order to maximise their chance of obtaining future work.

These feelings made him reflect on the fact that human beings readily bond with someone who has been a total stranger until the point where they discover that they have something in common with each other. An innate response.

Time passed more quickly than he had anticipated, and it was finally time to move on. But where? Another consultancy, but this time one that did have an engineering focus. After more browsing through newspapers, he found an advertisement for a consultancy that he knew of. They had done some work for the transport organisation that he had joined over twelve years earlier, although it was over by the time that he joined. But the best thing about it was that it was in his hometown. That would solve two problems. And he could phone Eadie for a reference. It was as simple as that. Not to work with him, of course, but to get out of this place as quickly as possible.

Chapter 13
Weathervane

The first time Stephen tried to phone, Eadie was on holiday. But on the second occasion, he was caught by surprise.

"When can you start?" asked Eadie.

Not what he had expected to hear. What should he do? With no time to think, he accepted. He was invited to the head office where he could talk through what his role would be and what he would be paid.

"In my consultancy role, I was charged out at a daily rate," he said.

"We're not paying you that sort of money," Eadie said, grunting.

It was finally agreed that Stephen should keep his consultancy salary and he would join the team in the company's first major acquisition the following day.

*

Stephen reported at the front desk and the receptionist phoned through to the engineering director. What sort of response would he get? A look of disdain? A grudging acceptance. The receptionist had been very friendly, and when the engineering director came through to greet him, so was he. "Good morning. I'm Tony. I heard you were joining us. Come on through to my office and I'll describe the company to you."

There was music playing quietly in the background, and there were a few hellos as they walked through the main office. "Excuse me a minute. I've got a letter to sign," said Tony.

While Tony was doing that, Stephen took in his surroundings. The environment felt very comfortable. He hadn't had the opportunity to speak to anyone but it already seemed that he fitted in.

"Sorry about that," said Tony.

"Not at all," replied Stephen. "Seems like a friendly place."

"It is. I think you'll enjoy your time here. Did you manage to find us without any trouble?"

"Yes, I did. I think I drove in the exit gate, but I'm parked just outside reception. It seems quite calm here. Everything running smoothly?"

"Anything but. I've been here for about six months – from the time the company was bought. A number of people were made redundant, probably just to bring the staff-to-vehicle ratio down to the industry norms, but it's obviously made things more difficult. The company was run down before it was sold, probably to make it look more profitable. They'd cut back on expenditure, including vehicle maintenance, and now we're paying the price."

"I can imagine, but it's just a matter of getting back on your feet, isn't it?"

"Hopefully. I'll take you round all our depots this week and you can see things for yourself, but we can start at the main depot next door if you want."

"Yes. Let's go."

Back through the main office, and again, despite Tony's concerns, he got the impression that people there were happy at work, working hard, and hopefully finding the job satisfying.

Tony opened a door and they were in the large central workshop – vehicles everywhere and people working on them. The first thing that became apparent was the variety of vehicle types. Different parts of the business would require different types of vehicles, but the range that he saw here went far beyond that. The decision to buy them would have been made by the previous owners. Why? In the hope that they'd be wined and dined by the manufacturer each time they placed an order?

Would the company be able to hold in stock the full range of fast-moving spare parts that such a wide range of vehicle types would require? Would the maintenance staff be trained thoroughly in all vehicle types? Would the drivers be fully familiar with them all? But, for the moment, he said nothing.

The next door took them into the main depot that had ninety-two vehicles allocated to it. Again, its workshop was full of vehicles with people working on them. It seemed busier than Stephen had expected, so he asked Tony how many vehicles were currently unavailable for business. They were currently eight short every day.

And the other five depots? They were all smaller than this one, but the problems were similar. Not good. The company was losing money, and it was easy to see why. In this depot, twice as many vehicles as he'd expected were unavailable for service. Lost income was therefore a major problem, even before the high operating costs were considered. It was vital to get as many vehicles as possible back in service, but permanently; quick, short-lived repairs that he sensed were being carried out would have to be stopped.

After a sandwich lunch, Stephen was introduced to a number of Tony's senior colleagues. Only one person, the central workshop manager, looked him up and down suspiciously.

Stephen was immediately reminded of the first time he had met Ian, almost fifteen years earlier. He would obviously have to choose his first words with care. Maybe he and Tony should go back through to the main depot and start the ball rolling by having a word with the depot engineer.

"Who does your oil and filter changes and your chassis greasing at present?" Stephen asked.

"We've no time for that. We're just fitting replacement parts to get vehicles back on the road."

"But, if you're not carrying out regular preventative maintenance, almost every component will have a shorter life than normal."

"You're quite right, but we get threatened from above if we're not seen to be putting vehicles back into service as quickly as possible."

"What do you mean 'from above'? Tony?"

"No, from the folk above him. I expect he'll be getting it in the neck as well." So, they weren't as happy as he'd first thought.

As Stephen examined the retained vehicles in turn, it was apparent that some of them would be under repair for a few days. Some could, of course, be returned to service more quickly.

"We can't rush them," Stephen said to the depot engineer. "Let your team work on them until we're all confident that they could run until the next planned inspection."

"And when somebody asks me why I'm doing that?" asked the depot engineer.

"If they do, you can refer them to me, and I'll ask them what approach they would recommend, and why. But to be honest, I don't think it'll come to that. The first thing to do is get people on to the ones that can be put back into service more easily. So, where's your list of planned inspections?"

"We don't have one anymore. If a vehicle's been off the road for a while, we inspect it before we put it back on the road but that's it, I'm afraid."

A check of the depot's records showed the planned inspection programme was scarcely relevant because of the uncertainty of vehicle availability.

"I'll re-write the programme," said Stephen, "and we then hang other planned activities, oil changes, et cetera, on top of it. You won't see any improvement immediately, but in about six weeks, you'll find things starting to get back to normal."

"Guaranteed?"

"Absolutely."

Stephen pointed to a vehicle from which the engine had been removed and asked the depot engineer to explain its history. He explained that the job was held up by a shortage of spare parts. "That's one of our biggest problems," he continued.

Apart from visiting the other operating depots to meet the staff there, the rest of the week was spent rewriting the main depot's inspection programme and investigating the parts procurement system.

At the end of the week, Stephen and Tony were drafting a paper for the next board meeting when the door of the office opened. It was Eadie. What was he doing so far from the head office?

"How's it going?" he asked.

Stephen looked up and replied, "Very well."

"I don't think it's going very well," Eadie snapped back.

The conversation continued, but Stephen was scarcely aware of what was being said. His first instinct was to walk out after saying to Eadie, 'You fix it, if you can. You've had long enough', but he bit his tongue. He and Tony were already well underway with the process of turning the company around.

"What did you think of that?" Tony asked when Eadie had gone.

"A bully," said Stephen. "You just have to learn to ignore him as best you can and get things done in spite of him. Certainly, that's what people used to say the last time I worked with him. But, while I remember, one of the things he asked me to look at when he and I first spoke about me coming here was the rear axles of your latest vehicle type."

"That's right, we've had a couple of catastrophic failures."

"It's a known problem; it's easily avoided, and the parts are cheap. We'll go to the stores office and order them up on Monday."

One effect of the support in getting vehicles back into service would be the improved morale at depot level. And two weeks later, activity was already starting to speed up: there was light at the end of the tunnel. From now on, no matter what problems were found, no one was blamed.

This in itself encouraged people to report problems that formerly they would probably have hidden. And as they were raised, they were addressed. Stephen had experienced most of them before and he knew that they usually had a simple, well-documented solution.

However, the problem with parts availability was another issue entirely. When either an operating depot or the central workshop required a replacement part for a vehicle, they requested it from the purchasing team in the central office and they, in turn, placed an order with the supplier.

One of the problems arose because the delivery address given was that of the depot that had made the request. When the part was delivered, the depot was no doubt grateful to receive it, but no one informed the central purchasing team.

Supplier invoices were received at the centre, but since the central team were unaware that the parts had been delivered, they did not pay the supplier. A 'no goods received' note meant that the supplier had not been paid and had therefore placed the company on stop. Stephen therefore began taking a list of the most outstanding invoices out to the depots to get certain parts' lines on stream again, but the real answer would be to set up a central store. But before that was done, spare parts would come in through a common point where supplier invoices could be matched to orders and processed. Internal transport would then deliver the parts to the depots.

*

The hub reduction gears for the rear axles were delivered to the central workshop, and the manager arranged for one vehicle to be upgraded. The three relevant depot engineers were invited to visit the workshop in order to see what was involved.

"It's a quick and cheap repair that will get a vehicle back on the road," said Stephen, "and it will guarantee that you'll avoid the catastrophic failures that you've seen in the past. It also ensures that you can forget about this problem for the next two or three years."

Everyone nodded in agreement. They seemed to be slightly less stressed now.

Stephen and Tony felt that they deserved a coffee after that. It was time to roll out the revised servicing and inspection schedule in the other depots.

"We seem to be going somewhere," said Stephen. "and I suppose the next move is to tell the regulatory agencies where we've come from and how we intend to go forward."

The engineering director went to see his boss, the managing director, someone whom Stephen had met some four years earlier at head office. He agreed that Stephen should put together a presentation and said he would put it in his diary when the engineering director had been given a date.

Considering how run down the fleet had been, the presentation went well. The company was thanked for approaching the agency before it felt the need to approach the company. Its representatives seemed reassured by the recovery plan presented to them.

Spare parts were now available when required but a report from a depot of a premature gearbox failure could not be ignored. The supplier was contacted.

"Driver abuse," was their response. "No warranty – buy another one."

"Rubbish," Stephen said to Tony. "That type of transmission was my first project as a rookie. What they claim is impossible."

The unit was lying with the supplier when Tony and Stephen visited them.

"Look at that," they were told. "That gear's worn out."

"No," said Stephen, "it doesn't wear at that speed, but if the re-manufacture has not been carried out correctly, the lining can fracture and that's probably what's happened here. It's long lasting, but very brittle."

He rolled up his sleeve and reached through the oil to fish out a piece of the lining material from the depths of the gearbox, broken but unworn.

Silence.

"We appreciate your support," said Stephen, "and we want to stay with you, but I suggest you look at your re-manufacturing processes.

"If you remember when we first met, about fourteen years ago, the organisation I was with then was having another problem with this gearbox type. Do you remember? It wasn't the friction material fracturing and falling off, it was the metal brake band itself fracturing. I looked into the problem, and once I understood the failure pattern that we were experiencing, I arranged to visit the manufacturer with one of your colleagues and discuss the problems with them.

"It was very useful. They made a few simple changes and the average life of these gearboxes in our operation doubled. I know that it's no longer in production, but I can set out a few checks for your current re-manufacturer to make and the problem will disappear."

"Yes, I remember the problems you mention. And the brake lining in this gearbox shouldn't have fractured, so I'll arrange for you to have a replacement supplied free of charge."

"Thanks," said Stephen.

Tony had said nothing while all of this was being discussed, but his relief at this piece of good news was obvious.

"What next?" said Stephen as he and Tony made their way back to the office.

The next surprise occurred the following day. Thomas, the finance director and Eadie's number two, had come down to see the managing director and took a few moments to see Stephen.

"You know that salary you agreed with Eadie," he began. "I don't think the people here would like that. I suggest that we give you two thirds of that."

I don't think that they'd approve of your salary or Eadie's, Stephen thought to himself. This was three months after Stephen had started with the organisation and he had so far received absolutely nothing in payment.

I have a verbal contract with Eadie, Stephen thought, but he said nothing. He had no wish to stay in this tacky little character's company any longer than necessary. Again, his first reaction was to walk out. He said nothing, but went back through to the engineering director's office and asked, "Where were we?"

There was more work to do on the younger vehicles. The rear axles were no longer a problem but the suspension system locating them to the chassis now had to be dealt with. A correct repair took the greater part of a day, but vehicle availability was now no longer an issue. It was time to reduce the workload demanded by these vehicles by replacing rapid repairs at high frequency with a longer repair at two-yearly intervals.

Again, Stephen remembered being involved with the same problems in the past and he knew that there was a manufacturer's bulletin that set out the process of setting up the suspension correctly and thereby avoiding the problem. The bulletin was dug out of Tony's archive and copies given to the relevant depot engineers when they were invited to visit the central workshop and have the problem explained.

"With the vehicle at normal ride height, you jack up the rear of the suspension bogie to this height. In this position, the two upper suspension links should not be under load, so undo one and adjust them as necessary and then refit them. With the tie rods correctly adjusted, you'll avoid the rear bump stops shocking the bodywork immediately above them – yet another reason to do this correctly.

"One last point. In my experience, the rubber bushes on the lower links have a five-year service life but the upper ones only last about two years. When the rubber bush wears out, the tie rod starts to act like a sliding hammer and punches a hole in the cross member. It's worth replacing the bushes every second MOT and you'll have no more trouble."

Again, the central workshop manager arranged for the work to be carried out on the test vehicle and show the depots what was involved.

"I'm on holiday next week," Stephen said to Tony, "but do you remember the manufacturer's bulletin on the rear brake mechanism? I've rounded up the necessary parts and the workshop will fit them to the test vehicle so now, instead of a major overhaul every two years, you'll never have to rework them again."

Tony agreed. "Certainly, leaving them as they are is really time consuming. This will be a real improvement. Enjoy your break."

*

On his return, Stephen's first port of call was the workshop manager's office. "What did the depot think of the mod?" he asked.

"They didn't see it. While you were away, Eadie arrived and said, 'What's that vehicle still doing there'? I told him it was your test vehicle and he threw one of his tantrums. 'Get it back in service'!"

"Well, I suppose we should be grateful that he stayed away long enough for us to make some improvements," was all that Stephen could say.

"And that's not the only thing he did. Have you noticed anything different about the office?"

Stephen looked around for a moment, before saying, "There's no music playing. Don't tell me he told you all to switch that off as well."

"He did. And everybody's a bit down because of it."

"Has he never heard of the wartime 'Music While You Work' on the radio, designed by experts to keep morale high while people worked for their country?"

Just another example of Eadie's bullying behaviour. Behaviour that lowered morale, reduced people's enthusiasm for the job and seemed to confirm his complete lack of understanding of how organisations operated and how they should be managed. Was it simply some testosterone-driven response that he couldn't control, or was it a deep resentment of people who could solve problems that he could not?

Again, Stephen's first instinct was to think of leaving, and he rebuked himself for being stupid enough to have accepted Eadie's offer to join the group. But again, the satisfaction that he'd received over the last ten months or so eventually calmed him down and he reflected upon where things currently were. And the satisfaction was genuine, something he could take home and reflect upon. He was able to make use of his education and experience to date, and they had both been worthwhile.

They had allowed him to contribute to the significant improvement in the company's performance, and in particular the improvements to vehicle reliability meant that the business was meeting budgeted levels. They were moving from loss to profit, so what was the next step to take?

Now was probably the right time to set up the central store. There was a vacant building in the main depot. It was in good condition, no water leaks, and it was sufficiently large for all the materials that they would wish to keep in stock. The only point of concern had been providing an overhead power line from the main building, but despite the distance, that was achieved without any problems.

The three weeks that it took to repaint the interior of the building and move spare racking from the depots went past in no time. The parts foreman was moved from a tiny office in the main building to this new location and his delight was obvious to everyone.

He was now totally responsible for his own area of the company and he was able to operate it in the manner that his experience had taught him.

Stephen went over to see how he was settling in and was delighted to be shown round and given a detailed description of where supplier deliveries would be made, where the parts would be stored and how deliveries would be made to depots.

Deliveries of new materials from suppliers were now made, without exception, to the central store, and of course since the central store now issued and delivered the materials to the depots, supplier invoices were now paid on time. Everybody was happy.

Vehicles were now being inspected and maintained to a central programme and MOT preparation and presentation were now added to it. That in turn allowed Stephen to produce a vehicle repaint programme and synchronise it with the MOT programme itself. If a vehicle was to be repainted, it made sense to paint it ahead of the MOT test rather than after it, and thereby reassure the testers that a major improvement to the fleet was being made.

With all these changes in place, there seemed little to do now except watch the condition of the fleet continue to improve, and also for Tony to see the financial position of the company improve at each successive board meeting. The company had been operating at a significant loss when Stephen had joined it and now, eight months later, the loss had been replaced by double that value in profit. That probably explained why there was now less interference from head office.

What to do next? Continue the improvement, of course. That was Stephen's instinct and it seemed to be true for everyone else. Even during the difficult times, there had still been a strong team spirit throughout the company, and even though he hadn't witnessed it, he sensed that people were once again the big, happy family they had apparently been in previous years.

The next step came out of the blue. One morning, the managing director looked round the door of the office where the workshop manager was showing his current workload to Tony and Stephen.

"I thought I'd find you here, Stephen. I'd like you to help me set up a management away-day. The business has found its feet again and I want to arrange a session where I can bring all the management up to date and tell them what our next steps will be. I'm using an external consultant, and I want you to meet him and help him make all the necessary arrangements."

That was a surprise – a very pleasant one.

"I'll leave you in peace just now," he continued. "Just come over to my office about three o'clock. OK?"

"Yes. I'll be there."

*

The MD explained to Stephen that the main board was satisfied that this company was now operating successfully, and it was time to withdraw his involvement and bring the management team together and let them get back to their normal day-to-day activities.

But it was no surprise when he was told that Eadie wanted him back at head office to take on another project. New challenges were always interesting, but was it wrong to want to enjoy the fruits of one that had been concluded? Was it selfish to want to enjoy the satisfaction that could be obtained from a project that had been completed? Perhaps.

*

The group AGM had been arranged for the following day. Stephen and Tony travelled together, and on the journey, they were able to reflect upon what they had achieved over the last eleven months. They agreed that it had been satisfying and that the time had simply flown by.

At the meeting itself, Eadie presented the performance of the main company and the new acquisition. Tony whispered to Stephen that Eadie looked much less confident than usual. Stephen nodded; he had noticed that as well. Was he feeling out of his depth? Stephen had never seen him like that.

Of course, that made the rest of the meeting more interesting for both of them and they focussed on every word of everyone who made a presentation. Yes, apart from Eadie, the presentations were very professional, but they lacked content, totally.

Certainly, it was the main board that advised the employees of the direction that the group would be taking, but having met all its members, it was apparent to Stephen that none of them could have managed any aspect of the business; they were all simply going along with Eadie's demands. And he was simply driven by some need to be seen as top dog. His determination, not ability, seem to be taking the place somewhere. Whether it would be a good place or a bad place remained to be seen.

It had been a fascinating day.

*

Some weeks later, Stephen was taken aside by Eadie.
"That company I mentioned to you, I'd like you to take a look at it now. It's a recent acquisition and it's not performing as it should. I think that its MD's simply run out of ideas."

Yes, there was a law of diminishing returns. Learning curves also level out, so it was probably time to move on. He would move at the beginning of the month.

How long would this project last? Another eleven months? Stephen would have preferred some stability in his career. Surely, he couldn't go running around in circles forever.

Chapter 14
Benumbed

The company had been bought some two years earlier. It was a vehicle parts dealership and its intended role was to continue trading commercially in the wider market but now also to manage all the stock used by the organisation's main depot in keeping its vehicles on the road and available for business.

One of the advantages in buying the company was that its premises and stock-holding costs in the main depot would be paid for by the income from its external trading. That alone would be a saving for the core business, and if that goal could be achieved, this model would be replicated across other companies in the group.

Further benefit would be obtained from the company selling parts to the core business at tight profit margins and so help to reduce operating costs. So, what was the task here?

Thomas took Stephen to his office and went into more detail about the day-to-day operation of the company. It had four branches across the country, and it sold to external customers. Its head office and main depot were now on the same site as those of the group.

The company was not yet computerised and that was the first thing that interested Stephen. Why not?

The company was also an agent for a main brand of brake lining materials, and on this site, it had a workshop where it could reline brake shoes if the customer so required. The group's main depot now also used it.

The end of the current financial year would be in about six weeks' time, and it was suggested to Stephen that he should get himself up to speed in order to become directly involved in it. That also sounded interesting.

Thomas then explained how the current stockholding system worked. "If there are three examples of a given item in stock, you will see that written on the stock card. Now, if you order another four examples of the same part, and on receipt from the supplier, you book them into stock, you update the stock card and three now becomes seven. And if you then issue two items from stock, you update the stock card and amend the total in stock to read five."

Heady stuff thought Stephen. I don't know if I'll be able to keep up with this.

The phone rang and Thomas took the call. "I'll see you later," he mouthed to Stephen and pointed to the door, implying he should leave.

What to do now? He took himself over to the workshop of the main organisation to see if he could catch up with any of the people he'd met during his cleaning project.

He glanced into the supervisor's office and immediately recognised Sandy, the charge-hand. Stephen tapped on the window. A blank expression quickly turned into a broad smile and a hand signalled him to go in. "What are you doing here?" Sandy asked.

"I'm not quite sure yet. But what are you doing?" Stephen replied.

"Oh, I'm just reading through the inspection sheets of this morning's five vehicles. Not too much work to do. No, wait a minute, have you ever come across a problem with brake vibration before?"

"With these older vehicles?" Stephen asked, pointing to one of them. "Well, yes, I have. Why do you ask?"

"It's a new problem here. It's difficult to be certain when it started but I'm sure it was after this new acquisition started relining our brake shoes."

"I'll follow that up and let you know what I find."

Eadie had said that Thomas would introduce Stephen to the managing director of the new company but the phone call had got in way of that. Maybe this was the ideal moment to go back over to the office and introduce himself.

The managing director was very friendly and asked Stephen about his background. He simply replied that he liked working with motor vehicles and that seemed to satisfy his host. He also said that he had just learned that the company now relined vehicle brake shoes for the main organisation.

"Yes, we do. We're an agent for a major brake lining manufacturer so we've got a state-of-the-art workshop for relining shoes for our external customers. We now also do it for the main organisation. Is there a problem?"

"Not at all. It just came up in conversation, but I wouldn't mind having a look at it if that's possible."

"I'm preparing a board paper just now, so I'll take you through to meet my local manager. He'll show you round the office and introduce you to the workshop team."

The manager spoke and moved quickly. Did he always do that or was he just trying to look busy? He and his colleague booked all stock items in and out and that was a full-time job for both of them. Stephen was fully aware of parts departments and had seen them in action on and off for the last seventeen years, but again he wondered why this one was not computerised. The accountant in this company worked upstairs, and he had a computer, so why not here? "If you've seen enough here, I'll take you over to the workshop."

"Please," said Stephen.

It was quite large. It was tidy and it appeared to have been repainted quite recently. A batch of brake-shoes was being re-lined when he arrived. The process was rather noisy and the operator was wearing ear defenders. In a small room, someone else was sand blasting a batch of used brake shoes that had had the old linings removed. Both people seemed to know what they were doing.

On a work bench, behind the riveting machine, was a batch of about twenty shoes waiting to have their worn linings removed and something clicked in Stephen's head. He went back across to Sandy's office.

"How do you carry out brake relines?" he asked.

"What do you mean?"

"Do you reline a vehicle's brakes one wheel at a time?"

"Yes. What's wrong with that?"

"Nothing at all. It's what I've been used to seeing all the time in this industry. But you remove both brake shoes, and until recently, you would reline the same shoes before mounting them back on the vehicle. Since the new company began relining your shoes, they do it in batches; that makes it more effective for them to use their sandblaster. And the result of that is that the shoes that you refit are not necessarily the same ones that you removed; they're no longer a matched pair."

"What are you getting at?"

"About twelve years ago, I was investigating a similar problem and one of the things I found was that this type of vehicle had rollers fitted to the shoes, but the design wasn't ideal. The two rollers and their spindle were made out of one piece of metal, and when the rollers rotated, so too did the spindle. That progressively wore into the slot in the shoe, but if you kept the shoes as a matched pair, there was no great problem. But here, if you fit a well-worn shoe with a less worn one, only one will touch the drum when the brakes are applied. If you continue to operate the vehicle for a few weeks, the brake problem will go away, but it can be avoided altogether."

"Well done. How did you work that out?"

"I've just seen the problem before. That's all."

*

Stephen was now getting up to speed, well aware of the systems used in the dealership, but he wanted to follow up the purchase of some old units that he had found during a walkabout the previous day. They had not been purchased from the original manufacturer and they would therefore not be accepted by the manufacturer as a credit against the new unit surcharge. They were likely to have been overvalued in the company's accounts.

He reported to Eadie's office the following morning. "I heard you were following up the brake vibration problem."

News travelled fast around here.

"Yes. The lining material is OK," said Stephen. "The problem lies with the brake shoes themselves and it only affects first-generation vehicles with shoes that have roller cam followers. When Sandy's team are relining vehicle brakes, they do it one wheel at a time and so the brakes shoes are never separated. He knows that he now needs to match re-lined shoes before refitting them."

He said nothing about his suspicions of the stock being over-valued, so what to do now? He wanted to follow up the apparent use of non-original equipment parts, something the company's MD had undertaken not to do, so he walked back over to see Sandy. "What's this vehicle doing here?" he asked.

"MOT preparation," said Sandy.

"That's maybe just what I'm looking for."

Stephen went underneath and picked up a hand lamp. The chassis had just been steam-cleaned and all components were clearly visible, and any parts that had just been replaced in preparation for the annual test were quite apparent.

He moved slowly around, examining the chassis to see if any appropriate parts had been replaced and yes, there was one. "Where are the parts that have been removed from this vehicle?"

Sandy pointed to a pallet. Yes, there was the old component. Stephen lifted it out and went back to the office. And when he checked the records for this part, there had been only one in stock and that was now fitted to the vehicle.

He knocked on Thomas's door. He was free, but he obviously wasn't pleased when he was shown the evidence of non-genuine, over-priced parts. That would make him look bad. "We'll discuss that later," he said.

So be it. Meanwhile, a more worrying finding was that many used parts held in stock were over-valued. Quite a number of vehicle spare parts carried a surcharge when purchased from the manufacturer and the invoice would show this alongside the cost of the part. If a retailer bought such a part in order to sell it on, the customer would pay the cost of the part along with a mark-on plus the surcharge. When the customer handed back the used part, he would be given a credit for the surcharge but of course, if he had returned the old part at the time of purchase, the surcharge would not have been passed on. It was simply a system used by the manufacturer to ensure that they got back their old parts. Quite straightforward.

The problem here, however, was that a number of such used parts in stock had not been new parts when purchased; they had been re-manufactured. As they were not from the original equipment supplier, they did not carry a surcharge. But, in the company's accounts, a surcharge had been applied to each one of them. Quite simply, the stock was over-valued. Is that why the MD had been keen to get the group to buy his company at book value? What was his intention? To trade through the over-valued stock and then, when the actual value reached the book value, offer to buy it back?

Stephen was scheduled to meet Eadie the following morning and give him an update. Yes, buying such a company made perfect sense. It would provide low-cost parts for the company's vehicles and avoid any stockholding costs by making profits from selling to other organisations. Just change suppliers back to original equipment manufacturers and write down the overvaluation in the current stock. Easy. And a further benefit was that the reliability of the fleet would be improved and maintenance costs would slightly reduce.

What was the next project? Hopefully going back to continue with the last one.

That wasn't to be. He was to take over the running of this company by replacing the MD and addressing the issues that he'd identified. The quick fix was simply to change a number of suppliers and write down some stock but that wasn't an option with which Eadie agreed. The stock profile would simply be improved by trading through it. How long would that take? Months? Years?

Stephen's home was a three-hour drive from here, so a daily commute was out of the question and so his first thought was the sooner it was fixed the better. He would have to stay here each week until the problem was resolved.

However, that turned out to be less stressful than he feared. One of the salesmen in the company was a car enthusiast and a member of a local car club. It held monthly meetings and the next one was a quiz night. This was more like it.

The daily activity for one team of this company was to supply parts to the core business while the other was buying and selling automotive components for the outside market. As well as retaining existing customers, it would speed up the recovery process if the sales team could increase the market share. Stephen certainly encouraged them to do that, but he wondered how he could best help until he gained a fuller understanding of the business.

Meanwhile, maybe he could see if there was anything he could do to help Sandy. Resolving the brake vibration problem had certainly helped the parts business develop a closer relationship with the main operation. Was there anything more he could do?

The weeks went by more quickly as he became more comfortable in his new surroundings. How long had he spent on his last project? Eleven months. And how long had he been here? Eleven months already, and still no end in sight. Surely that wasn't possible.

It was still a matter of changing the stock profile to top brand names as the lesser-known brands were sold to external customers and it would probably take another year before that task had been completed. That would be twenty-three months but would probably feel like forty-six.

In the back of his mind was another question. What could the unique selling proposition of this company be? What would it take to make it better than any competitor in the sector? Offering advice on selecting vehicle components? Would it be possible to ask the relevant manufacturers' sales representatives to give his sales team a talk about the characteristics of their products? Why not?

One morning, there was a phone call from Eadie's secretary. A meeting was to be held in the boardroom the next day, and Stephen had to be there.

When the next day came, the main board was present as well as other senior managers. The meeting had simply been called to update everyone on the state of the organisation. It was Eadie who spoke. "We've convinced ourselves that we can turn companies around."

Stephen nearly fell out of his chair. 'Which one of you can turn companies around?' he wanted to ask. It wouldn't have been polite to do it there and then, and so he wondered if he should have a word with Eadie when the meeting was over. He felt that would also be rather impolite and so he did nothing, but the thought remained with him, for a long, long time.

Back at his desk, he continued with the business plan. The concept of the company was certainly a good one. It was not the organisation's core business, but the provision of spare parts at discounted prices was an important benefit. In addition, this benefit could be offered to other group companies, reducing their costs while improving the finances of this one.

When the plan had been completed, Stephen submitted it to Eadie but there was no immediate response.

The priority, therefore, remained trading through the stock to get it back to the value in line with the price initially paid for the company and that was how the time would pass. Yawn.

*

A note from Eadie's secretary. The annual general meeting was to be held the following week. At least that would be a break in the monotony of the daily routine. Stephen then remembered he had attended the previous year's meeting with Tony. How was he doing? He dialled his number.

"Hello. Tony speaking."

"Good morning. It's me. How are things?"

"Well, you're a blast from the past. Things are going really well here. We've just been working away, and now that we're back in profit, there's no pressure from anyone. And we're now able to concentrate on all the details that we couldn't before. How are things with you?"

"I'm bored out of my mind. I like doing new things, but things that aren't totally outside my experience, not sitting at a desk doing the same thing every day. It's almost a form of torture. But the reason I called is to ask if you'll be at the AGM next week."

"I will indeed. We can meet up outside to make sure we get seats together."

"I look forward to that."

The format was much like that of the previous year. The hall was almost full and all the main directors, including Tony's boss, were on the platform, Eadie at the centre.

There were general statements about the group, and it had grown through several acquisitions that had been made during the last year. That sounded good.

There were some points of interest to Stephen and Tony, and although they had not said anything to each other, what they were both waiting for were the results of Tony's company to be read out and compared to the parent company as they had been the previous year.

They both knew that those for Tony's company had now surpassed those of the parent company and they were waiting for Eadie to announce them. What was said?

Nothing.

Stephen and Tony, with broad smiles, turned to each other and said quietly, "Got him."

That was the best part of the day.

*

Back in the daily routine, Stephen wondered when he would get feedback about his business plan. There was no immediate response, but a few weeks later it became apparent that the company was to be put up for sale.

That wasn't much of a surprise, but what he had not anticipated was being called to Eadie's office and asked to leave. "You've become an embarrassment to me," he was told.

Stephen's immediate thought was 'You don't need me to embarrass you. You do that yourself,' but as usual, he said nothing.

What had brought that about? It was a shock, but it was also a relief. Almost three boring years simply watching the clock tick.

Stephen was tempted to ask Eadie why he had not paid him the agreed salary, especially when, in both companies, he had solved problems that no one on the board had succeeded in doing. He didn't ask; again, he was too polite. But at least he had learned a great deal about business in this last project.

He left. Willingly. The time that he had wasted there was a reminder that he should do something more satisfying in life. And as the days went by, he was reminded of how short life was. It was important to make the most of it.

Chapter 15
Last hope

I'm free. Those were the first words to come into Stephen's mind. There was a world out there. He had family, he had friends and could have sensible conversations with them all. He was free and could do what he wanted, rather than what he had been asked to do.

He had identified what was wrong with the company, but why had he felt obliged to stay with it? Because he had promised that he would, that he would help Eadie tidy up a stupid mistake, an easily avoided mistake? Three years of his life wasted. He would never get them back, but the question now was what to do next.

Catching up with an old school friend revealed that he didn't enjoy his job either, but then, neither did he detest it. Stephen was reminded that it was possible to avoid becoming too involved in a job.

"But does that not affect your performance, how much you contribute to your organisation?" he couldn't help asking.

"Well, yes, I suppose it does, but you have to survive. People go to work because they have to; they go to work to earn money. If you enjoy it, even better, but you still have to go. Your problem was that you took it too seriously."

"But is that not the key issue?" Stephen responded. "Shouldn't jobs be designed to make people enjoy them, and as a consequence, give their all?"

"But that can work against you. Contributing to the organisation is one thing, but what if any senior colleagues are put out by you solving issues they can't?"

"That's a special case. Some senior people certainly do behave like that, but not all of them. The hope is that the action of encouraging people to work in a more conscientious fashion would imply that those doing so should be pleased with the outcome, not annoyed by it. But I take your point. If some senior managers do behave like that, they should be identified for the harm that they're doing to the organisation, and dealt with accordingly."

"Yes, you could be right. But I think that people behave more like other animal species, and by that, I mean instinctive behaviour. They're genetically programmed to behave in particular way. Human babies cry out all the time if they're not happy about something and that usually gets them the attention they're seeking. But in some animal types, babies seem to be programmed to remain silent in times of danger. Just one squeak could alert a predator.

"Animals often seem to have mating seasons driven by the time of year, hot and cold weather, availability of food.

"In humans, you get things like road rage. People can get enraged if some other person drives into the part of the road that they considered their own. I used to think that was bad behaviour but I now regard it as natural behaviour. The driver's reaction would probably be a squirt of adrenalin but what they then did would very much depend upon how they'd been brought up."

Stephen was quite intrigued by this statement and he had begun to slip into an internal discussion about human behaviour when his friend asked, "Are you still with me?"

Yes, he was. He could finish these thoughts later. "Sorry," he said. "What you said about people's relationships in large groups was so true, but I'm trying to work out what to do in a much smaller group."

"How small?"

"Just one, me. Or two, if you're interested in doing something new. Are you?"

"Well, I'm considering early retirement, so I may be. Tell me more."

Stephen took a deep breath.

"This could be a long story. I was wondering how I could make use of my training and experience to try and create a perfect business. Some start-up costs will be inevitable but they'll have to be limited."

"You're not going into car manufacturing?"

"I was thinking of going into retailing, selling things that other people have made. That saves me the cost of making them, avoiding investment in manufacturing costs. And also avoiding development costs."

"Sounds good, but won't there be some equivalent risks in retailing?"

"All activities have risks but those in retailing are much less significant."

"And to put that into terms that I can understand?"

"Simply that I'd sell other peoples' products. I'll invest in a website and source and sell popular goods. I've got another friend who's interested in the idea, and they've got the free time as well."

"How would you know if those goods would be popular?"

"It's easy to identify products that are popular. You only need some to get started, and if their popularity drops off, if they go out of fashion, for example, you move to those that still are popular. I did my course thesis in marketing research. Remember?"

"Let's do it."

Stephen had already decided to start by importing and selling up-market food from France and exporting goods in the other direction. That would minimise the effect of currencies fluctuating. He would also visit potential suppliers in France and see what they might see as a unique selling proposition for their products, while also having a holiday there. He hadn't had one of those for a while.

The ultimate goal would be to increase the product range beyond food, almost infinitely, and thereafter simply respond to consumer demand rather than choosing a particular product range to offer to the market. And the first product range would be used simply to pay for the software necessary for online sales.

The next step was to lease a retail outlet. The software to allow the ultimate goal to be achieved would be unaffordable at this stage in the project, but a local IT specialist, a friend of a friend, said that he could develop the software as quickly as Stephen asked. And another requirement, obtaining a licence to sell alcohol, was also easily met.

This was a new environment for Stephen, and he recognised that. He was slightly out of his depth, but not totally. It took eight months to get to that stage, but as soon as the retail unit had been set up, it was trading actively over the counter. Christmas was approaching and customer response to the product range was very reassuring.

"Where have you been all my life?" one lady asked. Stephen wasn't quite sure how to interpret that.

The layout and decoration of the premises themselves had been inspired by a shop in Paris and the first range of stock to be held had been chosen after visiting a trade show, also in Paris.

A local printer had produced business cards for Stephen and his partners before the Paris trip and he was sufficiently interested in the project to suggest that he could later produce up-market brochures if that was of interest. It was.

The first brochure was designed and printed and there was even a slot on television for the fledgling company. Stephen was now beginning to take it more seriously.

He updated his business plan, but one of his early thoughts, driving backwards and forwards to France to collect produce, had been forgotten. A fun idea initially, but totally impractical. Established transport networks would be used for all aspects of the business.

His training in marketing had certainly not been a waste of time – quite the opposite. He'd heard it time and again, but it was true. The customer is always right. And this seemed to be confirmed when two regular customers suggested that they would like to invest in the business. He felt that was a reminder that growth could be rapid if external finance was used but he was not convinced that the business was sufficiently robust to encourage other people to invest in it. But it was nonetheless good to know that that was an option.

Growth was slow but steady and the first year ended up ahead of budget. The next stage would be to widen the range of products and to pay for the software for online sales.

There was a brief setback when Stephen's school friend suddenly announced that he was no longer interested in the business. A pity that he hadn't been more honest when he was first asked if he wanted to participate, but a replacement was soon found and that problem was forgotten. The only issue was that the replacement had to be paid, but the level of sales meant that that was not a problem. They were getting somewhere.

Stephen couldn't see it at the time, but his interest was in creating the business, not necessarily taking it forward. Another offer to invest in the business was turned down. This time it had been from the printer. The money, any amount, would have helped to accelerate the creation of the infrastructure, but the responsibility of respecting the trust placed in him would still have been a distraction. That's simply how he was.

There was, however, no doubt in his mind that the direction he was taking was the correct one. No business could be in a safer place and the potential for growth was limitless. What was the next step?

The subjects selected in his business course had included accounts and finance along with commercial law, but marketing remained the discipline that had most fascinated him. Could he still remember enough about it to put it to use?

The memory of a holiday spent on the island of Harris in the Outer Hebrides slowly came back to him. He had visited the community set up by the philanthropist Viscount Leverhulme, who had apparently later said, "Half the money I spend on advertising is wasted; the trouble is I don't know which half." A search online named several other people to whom the same phrase was attributed, but no matter who had invented it, there was a degree of truth in it. Caveat vendor.

But was it a universal truth? Not exactly. It was apparent that television advertisements now were very targeted, and successfully so, but the tale was still one of caution.

The software could also be taken to the next stage. An internet website was set up and the first online sale was a remarkable moment for all three of them, albeit not the original three. The world truly was their oyster, in the metaphoric sense, at least.

What next? It was a phone message. From Thomas. That was really unexpected. Would Stephen be willing to meet up with Alan, the same Alan in the same company where he and Stephen had worked for so many years? Eadie's group had now acquired that company, and as with the first major acquisition, there seemed to be a lot of work to do. It was a six-month contract.

If they really felt that they needed Stephen's help, the call would be quite flattering, but if he had truly been an embarrassment to Eadie, what was behind it? Had Eadie discovered that Stephen hadn't in fact been an embarrassment to him, or had he simply wondered if Stephen might have sued him for unfair dismissal?

What should he do? He had moved on and after a difficult ten months, his new career had started to take off. But the money would be useful, of that there was no denying. Stephen phoned Alan.

*

The following Monday they met up in Alan's office on the ground floor. Eadie had appointed Alan engineering director, so should he not be upstairs in the directors' suite?

Over a coffee, they caught up with what they had both being doing since they last met. For Alan, the last few years had also been stressful. His boss had been difficult to work with and had introduced some controversial changes to the way their vehicles were maintained. He had then moved on, leaving Alan and his colleagues to try and clean up the mess he'd created. The more the situation was described, the more Stephen could see how serious the situation now was. They would need as many hands to man the pumps as they could find. Was that simply why he'd been invited back?

It was also interesting to learn that many of his former colleagues were still there, but equally it was not surprising to learn that many others had either left or retired. Alan himself was probably nearing retirement age.

Stephen asked if Alan wouldn't mind if he met up with as many of his former colleagues as he could. That wouldn't be a problem. And, while many of them were based in the operating depots, four or five of them were here in the head office.

Alan led him through to another room and there were three of them plus two younger people who presumably were new to the company. Broad smiles and comments such as 'where have you been' from those he recognised started more long conversations.

The people hadn't all changed but the mood that hung around the room was totally different to that of the company as Stephen remembered it. Morale was low and everyone seemed to be in some kind of survival mode. But the thing that was immediately apparent was how much they had disliked the engineering director. They were all glad that he had gone, but they seemed uncertain that things could ever get back to the way they had been. That wasn't good.

Back with Alan, Stephen learned that rather than purchase new vehicles, his predecessor had purchased second-hand ones. And to make matters worse, they included many different makes and models. As they weren't new, they didn't have any manufacturer's warranty cover, and due to the variety of them, an insufficient supply of spare parts was held in stock. The last issue was that maintenance staff were not familiar with them and that made fault diagnosis difficult. What a mess.

"I should perhaps visit the depots tomorrow," Stephen suggested. "Would you come with me?"

Alan said that it might be better if Stephen went on his own. The largest depot was adjacent to the head office, and perhaps not surprisingly, never had too many operational issues in the past. Its engineering manager was Jason, a name Stephen remembered from the past, but the following morning, he took Alan's advice and went straight to the second-largest one.

Driving to it, Stephen felt that he had never been away, and when he arrived at the entrance gate, it was exactly as it had been when he last saw it. Inside, however, things began to look a little different. There were more vehicles in the workshop than before. And, as Alan had said, there were more vehicle types than before.

Stephen parked his car, got out and began counting them. Four, five, six, seven, eight, nine. That was three times as many as before. How could people keep up with that change?

He went over to the foreman's office and looked in. At least something hadn't changed. "I heard you were on your way," said the foreman. "Alan just called me."

"I thought he might," said Stephen. "How are things?"

"A bloody nightmare."

"In what way?"

"Vehicles unfit for service. No time and no spares to get them back on the road. Are you here to close us down?"

"That would probably be the humane thing to do, but I'm here to help you get back on your feet."

"It'll take more than you."

The foreman was right. This was an even bigger mess than the last major acquisition. It would take much longer here to get things back to normal. "I couldn't help you on my own, Stephen said. "That's not why I'm here. I'm just a fresh pair of eyes sent here to work out what help you need to get your workload down and get the place back to normal. Dealing with replacement parts is one thing, but, as I said, the target is to see what help you need to get your workload down. I've seen it done before, and no matter how bad things seem here, they can be fixed. Who's your depot engineer now? Alan didn't say."

"It's Bill."

"Good. I remember him. Is he still upstairs?"

"No. He moved his office over to the other side of the workshop. See, over there in the corner."

"Thanks. I'll go over and have a word with him."

"Good luck. He hardly speaks to us anymore."

The walk took Stephen across the workshop where all the inspection pits had a vehicle in some sort of disrepair. People were walking backwards and forward between them and the spare parts counter and even more were queuing there. That in itself confirmed that there was a problem, but of more concern was how little obvious enthusiasm there was.

They all seemed to have switched off. Again, the mood here reminded him of the first major acquisition. Therefore, it could be cured.

He knocked on the door. There was no answer, so he gently opened the door and looked inside. There was Bill, sitting at his desk, reading through vehicle inspection sheets, but Stephen's first impression was how old he looked. That was a shock. "Good morning," Stephen said.

Bill looked at him blankly.

"It's Stephen. How long is it since we last met up? Eleven years?"

"Where have you come from? I thought you'd left."

"I had. And now I'm back, at least for a few months. How are you doing?"

"I'm not. As soon as I can get out of here, the better."

Not much point in keeping this conversation going. "I was in the foreman's office and he told me you were over here. Good to see you again."

"You, too."

Stephen closed the door quietly on the way out.

*

Back in Alan's office, Stephen described what he had seen. "Morale's really low, but that will only be a problem until some improvements are made. The number of different vehicle types you're being asked to look after is ridiculous, and the problem related to that is the need to improve access to fast-moving spare parts. The first thing I'll do is make up a list of all the vehicles in the fleet and set it out by vehicle type and age. If some vehicle types are approaching the end of their normal service life, you could maybe dispose of them."

"But we're struggling to meet customer demand as it is."

"I know you are, but I can identify the families of younger vehicle types that are currently unavailable for business, for whatever reason, and then arrange to do whatever it takes to make them available again. That means that we'll make a very quick improvement in overall vehicle availability. But the other thing that I noticed when I was visiting the depot was the chaotic inspection and servicing activity. I couldn't believe that I was looking at what I would call a self-inflicted wound."

"That's another problem we inherited from the outgoing engineering director, the guy I'm supposed to be replacing. As he tightened up spending, no doubt with the board's approval, our maintenance workload just went up and up."

"And he would be aware of that, I suppose?"

"He certainly was."

"But were the other members of the board aware of the problems that he was building up?"

"I doubt it."

"That's rather worrying. I knew your MD very well before I left here for my business course. He was in finance at the time and he was as sharp as a razor. So, the question is, did he and the other members of the board realise how much of a mess the ED was creating and didn't care since all they wanted to do was sell the place for a profit and retire? Or, more likely, did they trust the ED and assume that his actions would not put the company at risk? In the end, it really doesn't matter what they thought. His actions have put it at risk and you and all the other people still here are having to deal with his legacy and will have to do so for some considerable time."

"I won't be staying around," Alan replied. "I'm retiring at the end of the month, so you can get on with it. You like fixing things, don't you?"

"I like making things better, and fixing problems is certainly part of that, but it isn't very satisfying having to fix the same problems again and again. We had to deal with similar problems when you and I worked here years ago, although nothing on this scale. And more recently, Eadie asked me to help out in his first major acquisition; just like the way this place is now, but on a smaller scale. So, this place can be fixed.

"But just explain the mess that I found in Bill's depot. There's no planned inspection and maintenance programme. Why not?"

"Again, it was my predecessor's idea. Some vehicles were out of service for so long that they were effectively missing their two-weekly inspection and planned maintenance schedules, so he came up with the idea of inspecting them only when they were repaired and ready to go back into service and then two-weekly thereafter."

"To cut down the inspection and servicing workload?"

"Exactly."

"But that must be really complicated for the depot management to work out. Where do they get the time?"

"They don't do it. They probably couldn't do it. It's too complicated. It's done here and an update is e-mailed to them every day."

"You're joking?"

"No. Andy in the next office to mine does it. It's his full-time job. Just go through and he'll explain exactly what he does."

"I assume it's the same Andy I worked with in quality control?"

"It is, but don't spend too much time reminiscing. Just get him to explain what he does with the inspection and servicing schedules. I'm sure it'll be fascinating, but the sooner it can be stopped the better."

*

Over the next two weeks, Alan agreed to withdraw eight of the oldest vehicles from Bill's depot from service and Stephen persuaded Bill to phase out Andy's flexible inspection and maintenance programme.

The schedule for the youngest and heathiest vehicles was set out on a wall chart in the foreman's office and they moved immediately to planned maintenance rather than failure maintenance. It seemed such an obvious thing to do that the folk there wondered why they hadn't done that earlier.

This was keeping Stephen busy, and he was enjoying it. But, what about his own business? It was trundling along by itself and Stephen was only involved with it at weekends.

What should he do? Further develop his own organisation to make money, or carry on here doing what he'd always enjoyed? He would have to decide.

Chapter 16
Becalmed

Progress continued. Bill saw it, his staff saw it and Alan saw it. However, it was the staff who were responding most enthusiastically to the improving situation. Morale was also improving, and they were becoming more proactive in the day-to-day management of the situation.

However, neither Bill nor Alan seemed to be interested in what was happening, and perhaps not surprisingly, Bill announced that he was going to retire. A few weeks later he left without saying a formal goodbye. Sad, but not a surprise.

Stephen was now spending most of his time at the depot, making notes of all the issues that needed to be addressed and then following them up, often with the purchasing manager, Felix, whom he also remembered from his previous time with the company.

This flurry of activity had occupied him so much that he had forgotten that Alan would also be retiring. And it would be as soon as the following Friday.

Behind the scenes, a new depot engineer had been appointed to replace Bill, and Eadie had apparently told Alan who would replace him. And, in this small world,

Stephen wasn't surprised to learn that he had met this replacement, Jack, a number of years earlier at an industry conference. He knew the business and was both energetic and enthusiastic. He would be starting on the Monday after Alan left. He wasn't being given very long to settle in, but it was possible that Eadie had already brought him up to speed.

When Alan's last day arrived, he spent it making his farewells to everyone but he asked Stephen if the two of them should go for a drink afterwards. They did, and it was a very enjoyable evening.

They began their conversation with the time they had first met, when Stephen had helped Alan deal with the issue of getting a number of vehicles with an unreliable transmission back into service. At the time, Stephen had not realised how close Alan was to Eadie, but over the last few weeks, he had learned that they were very close indeed and probably had been for some time. He decided to tease Alan and see what kind of reaction he got. "Do you remember the gearbox problems that you and Ian had? Sixteen vehicles in your depot unavailable for service because of them. And the work we had to do to get them back on the road."

"I do. In fact, I'll never forget them."

"I remember you telling me at the time that Eadie had operated some vehicles of the same type in his previous company. They were just as unreliable, and they were spread over two or three operating depots. To make sure they weren't just parked up and ignored, he moved them all into one depot and forced the poor engineer there to get on with it. What would you have thought if he'd done that to you? Not exactly a supportive gesture. You would have been stressed out, wouldn't you?"

Alan's silence was very loud indeed. What brought about that degree of loyalty to someone who'd have sold him down the river at the drop of a hat?

They both took another mouthful from their drinks before the conversation picked up again. This time Alan described how Eadie had taken part in the management buyout of the company he had moved to at the same time as Stephen had left for his business course. It was interesting to hear Alan's take on how it had been set up.

Things then moved back to the present situation.

"The current MD here hasn't a clue," said Alan. "He wanted me to start making all our vehicles look nice and up-market. Paint them all nice colours. Never mind about the number of engines that need replacing. He probably doesn't know that vehicles have engines."

"All packaging and no content?" Stephen suggested.

"Him, or the vehicles?"

"Both. I had a school friend who acted like an idiot most of the time, but when he wanted to be taken seriously, he just lowered the tone of his voice. Is the MD like that?"

"No. He's just so confident that he gives instructions all the time. He listens to what people say, but then simply tells them what he wants them to do. And, of course, it's usually something stupid. It's all superficial. All about appearance."

"Certainly, appearance is important for customers. Just like an interview. They say that you've only got thirty seconds to make a good impression. But an artist can't paint on a decayed canvas, can he? Nor can this place carry on the way it is."

"That would depend upon how bright he was. This guy certainly hasn't realised the seriousness of the situation we're in. I know you haven't met him yet, but I'm sure you soon will. I wonder if Eadie told him you were starting here. Maybe not. Anyway, drink up. I'm off into the sunset. Good luck with the rest of your career."

The following Monday, Stephen was back in the office. The rumour machine confirmed that Jack had indeed started and Andy had been asked to drive him around and introduce him to all the depot engineers.

With the second largest depot now showing early signs of recovery, Stephen set off for the third largest to see what was happening there. The first impression was somewhat of a surprise. The car park was full of new Mercedes and BMWs. Stephen's own car was now seven years old.

The foreman's office was no surprise. It was unchanged since Stephen's visit to help Sid with his corrosion problems twelve years earlier. Well, there was one change; Sid had moved on, but here at the desk was his replacement, issuing job cards to his technicians like there was no tomorrow. He nodded to Stephen but gave the impression that he didn't want to be disturbed. That wasn't necessarily a bad thing.

For the moment, he could be left to survive on a day-by-day basis. The immediate need was to make note of the twelve mid-life vehicles that Andy had said were awaiting major repairs before being presented for their annual MOT inspection and going back into service.

Stephen went upstairs to the depot engineer's office and took out the records of the twelve vehicles involved. The inspection sheets revealed that the work necessary to return them to MOT standard was significant, and he could understand why the depot engineer had decided to set them aside.

Four of them were a type he knew well. They were the same model that he had dealt with when he was helping out at the group's first major acquisition five years earlier.

He therefore produced a diagram setting out the preparation of all twelve vehicles for MOT inspection over the next six weeks. They would be done two at a time, ensuring that each vehicle with a high workload would be paired with one with a lighter workload.

The next question was who would be willing to carry out this project.

The following morning, Stephen took himself to the central workshop and explained to the foreman what required to be done. This workshop was there to carry out major vehicle refurbishment or cases of major accident damage, not day-to-day depot work, so Stephen didn't expect this to be an easy sell. It wasn't, but the foreman knew that making vehicles available for earning money was a priority. And so, he agreed.

Stephen made a quick call to the depot engineer and he could almost hear the sigh of relief on the other end of the line. The project would start the following week.

Stephen then made an appointment with Jack's secretary to catch up with him when he got back to the office. It was late in the afternoon before that happened, but after a few pleasantries, they sat down to discuss the plan to get these twelve vehicles back into service. While Jack was familiarising himself with the proposed timescale, the door opened and the MD looked in to say good night. Jack took the opportunity to explain the plan to him and the MD smiled both at him and at Stephen before leaving. That was the first time that Stephen had seen him. Would it also be the last?

It was time to go home.

"From what I can see, your idea looks quite good, Stephen," said Jack. "Just go ahead with it. But can you come in and see me first thing tomorrow? I've got another project for you and Andy."

Jack wanted to take the re-introduction of planned preventative maintenance to the next stage. He wanted wall charts to be set out for each depot on a monthly basis, with each vehicle and its planned inspection and servicing programme clearly identified in order to smooth out the workload.

Since Andy had been the person responsible for managing the previous, chaotic system as best he could, Jack suggested that he and Stephen produce the new charts, depot by depot, introduce the depot engineers to the new programme and then monitor it to make sure that there were no teething problems.

Depots would simply follow this chart and mark up each activity when it had been carried out. That would make it straightforward for them to get back on track and for anyone visiting them to see what progress had been made. That only took about a week, and now everyone was able to focus on this simple plan. When everyone was up to speed, it would be transferred to the computer database.

The most interesting part of this task was the reaction of all the depot engineers. Every one of them had accepted it without any complaints. They seemed to be relieved that some form of normality was being restored, but also that it was a collective effort. No longer would they be blamed for the failings of the system that had been thrust upon them.

As always, it was seeing morale improve that Stephen had found the most satisfying part of this exercise, and it further improved when news got out that the local MD had been replaced. While Stephen had been involved in preparing the maintenance charts in the central office, he had become aware of somebody new working quietly in a corner.

He had never spoken to them and they had been too busy to enquire about who he was. Yes, it had been the replacement MD getting himself up to speed before the incumbent was shown the door.

Nothing that was happening now seemed any more than common sense. Back at the office for his next meeting with Jack, Stephen's only question was, how had things been allowed to get into such a mess to begin with?

He knocked on the door and Jack looked up. "Come in," he said. "We're up to date on the maintenance programme now so I've been asked if you could give Felix a hand with the stock-check. It's going to be quite a task."

"Is he expecting me?"

"Yes. Just go through."

Stephen knocked on the door before opening it. Felix looked up and smiled. "Hello, stranger."

"A stock-check?" Stephen asked.

"I'm afraid so. The biggest one yet. It was Derek, my boss, who asked Jack if you'd be free. I think he'd heard that, when you were first here, you worked with purchasing in approving annual contracts. But before we talk about that, where have you been?"

"Here and there. But yes. I did work with annual contracts. We were lucky then that the purchasing manager was always intent on getting the lowest price but also asked for engineering approval to ensure that everything was fully fit for purpose. Are you saying we're doing that again?"

"No, not yet. We're just trying to sort through all the spare parts that we have. This company was putting itself up for sale, so the directors simply wanted it to look very profitable. They bought second-hand vehicles and cheap spare parts."

Stephen likened that to holding your breath in order to save oxygen. That wouldn't be sustainable for very long. "So, how can I help?" he asked.

"I've got a couple of my staff isolating redundant parts. Spares that were for some vehicle types that are no longer in the fleet. If these vehicle types relate to vehicles still in service in other operating companies, we could transfer them. That is, if those companies were willing to take them. If they aren't, I have a supplier who would be willing to make me an offer for them. That would save us having to write them off completely. It won't be easy, but I'd appreciate you helping my people with that."

"Yes, that would be fine. I've been concentrating on getting the engineering workload down but it didn't take me long to work out that you had fifty-two different vehicle types in the fleet."

"Spot on."

"Some vehicle types were getting towards the end of their lives, and before he retired, Alan did agree to dispose of a few of them. I devised a re-work programme for another group of them, but when I showed it to Jack, he said he'd prefer to take them out of service rather than waste time and money on them. That would reduce the spare vehicle capacity, but free up resources to lift the standards of the rest of the fleet. It would also remove three more vehicle types from the fleet and that immediately ring-fences a further list of parts to get rid of. Tedious, but not difficult."

"Good news," said Felix. "But you can see that we're stuck here until the main board allows us to start writing down some of this redundant stock."

"They probably won't do that until we can improve vehicle availability and get income up again. That's what we'll all have to focus on. It won't be quick, and the improvement might not be apparent to outsiders looking in, but at least we'll get some satisfaction from seeing things move in the right direction.

"Do you know, said Stephen, this reminds me of a graph I saw when I was studying engineering. It was called a steam table. Imagine a line on a chart, starting off at the bottom left, then moving upwards and to the right. That's the water heating up as time passes. The chart suddenly levels out at boiling point, just moving horizontally to the right as the water progressively turns to steam. Then it starts moving upward and to the right again when all the water has been turned to vapour."

Felix was intrigued. "It's a graph of what?"

"Latent heat. The energy that's involved in a change of state, water to vapour. It's also a graph of what's happening to us at present. We're putting in lots of effort but people looking in from the outside won't necessarily see any improvements."

"I'll take your word for that."

Stephen sketched out the graph on his things-to-do-today sheet, and then he pointed to the horizontal part of the graph. "We're here at present. But soon, we'll be taking off."

"Yes, I like that. I might do a similar sketch and keep it on my desk. I'll keep looking at it until were out of this lull. Anyway, back to the data input. I'll catch you later."

The group was now about to put its spare parts purchasing out to tender, and the first stage was for each operating company to produce lists of all the part numbers that they used, along with the annual quantity of each. They then forwarded these lists to the operating company that had been selected to deal with that specific product group.

Dealing with this was much more tedious for each operating company than putting out the tender documents for their own parts usage, but the benefit to the group was the economy of scale. Larger quantities should attract lower unit costs.

*

There was brief respite for Felix's team until all the supplier quotations had been received. Then the noise of keyboards once again took over the office, but after a few days, a recommendation was ready to be submitted to the main board. If the recommended supplier for the parts group delegated to Felix was given approval, they would soon be providing bespoke parts catalogues for every depot. Yet another step on the road to recovery.

The new managing director introduced weekly meetings for the central team and he used these to ensure that everyone was kept up to date with any changes that might affect them. He also answered any questions that arose from those briefings.

*

Little seemed to happen over the next twelve months, except for Stephen being offered a permanent position. He was still with this company five days a week and working on his at the weekends. There was gentle progress with each, but he didn't feel that he was going in any specific direction.

One day, there was a surprising piece of news. Jack was moving to a divisional role. He was very close to Eadie, so had his appointment here simply been designed to let him get up to speed with the group before being moved to his intended role? Whether or not that was a good thing would depend upon who was replacing him.

Stephen was surprised, and pleased, when it turned out to be someone with whom he had worked seven years earlier. It was Sandy, the engineering supervisor who had identified a brake problem and worked with Stephen to resolve it, and he would be visiting that Friday before taking up his role the following week.

No one else in the meeting seemed to know who Sandy was, so it would be some good news to share afterwards. And over the next few days, the majority of questions coming from depot engineers were how well Stephen knew Sandy.

News gets out. But now, what would Sandy's role be? The company where Stephen and Sandy had first met had always been well-run. Sandy would in all probability never have experienced many of the problems that everyone here had recently lived through, but that was not necessarily a bad thing.

Things were much better now, if not exactly back to normal, so his role would simply be to ensure that good working practices were in place. From his point of view, that was a role that he understood well and in which he had many years of experience. The company was still far from perfect, but morale was now good, and hopefully he would feel at home quite quickly.

*

Felix appeared at Stephen's desk. "I've just met your pal, our new engineering director."

"And?"

"He seems quite approachable."

"He is, and he's come up through the ranks, so he'll quickly learn exactly where we are at present. But, talking of that, where is he?"

"He was speaking to the finance director, but when she introduced me to him, he told me he'll be coming along to see you."

"Well, hang around. I'm sure you'll enjoy hearing some old adventure stories."

That's exactly what Felix did, only he went to the coffee machine first. "I should have asked if you wanted one was well. Do you?"

Stephen was about to reply when Sandy appeared. "Hello again, Felix. I see that you know Stephen. He and I go back a long way."

Sandy and Stephen reached out hands simultaneously. "But, Sandy," said Stephen, "Felix and I also go back a long way. How long? Twenty years?" Stephen started the conversation. "It's great to see you, Sandy. Are you aware of what lies ahead?"

"Not yet. Please don't tell me. I'll find out soon enough. But it's great to see you again. I kept the role I had when we first met until about three years ago. Then I got a divisional manager's position. It was interesting to be able to see people performing a similar role to mine in a different situation. Before I made any comments, I tried to imagine what I would have done under the same circumstances. I learned a lot from that. Why were they doing what they did? Were they free to make their own decisions, or had they been backed into a corner?"

"You never stop learning, do you?" said Felix. "In an ideal world, people should only have to make decisions in situations where their experience is relevant. But what do you think of the situation we're in at present?"

"This company? It's been run into the ground, but things seem to be moving in the right direction now. And I feel that I can turn to Stephen, and you, if there's anything that needs to be explained, but I know the business and I'm familiar with most of the vehicle types you operate. Yes, I'm looking forward to the challenge. Anyway, if you excuse me, I've got a train to catch but I'll see you both again on Monday."

When Sandy had gone, Stephen asked Felix what his first impressions were.

"Good," he said. "But, while I'm here, one of our colleagues is leaving and a number of us are going over to the pub for a drink with her after work. Would like to join us?"

"Sounds like a good idea," said Stephen. "Yes, I'd love to."

The rest of the day was spent filling spreadsheets with quotations from suppliers for the second group purchasing contract that they had been given. Most of the staff in the office were involved and they were kept busy until the end of the day.

"Are you ready?" Stephen looked up and it was Felix and another colleague.

"I'll just log off," he said. "Nearly there."

"Do you remember Joe?" asked Felix.

Stephen looked up and slowly, he began to smile. "Yes, I do. How are you? We worked on vehicle bodywork problems, didn't we?"

"Yes. A long time ago. Anyway, are we going over the road?"

The three of them left the office, Stephen and Joe recalling the outcome of that project. "A number of the vehicles requiring that modification have been taken out of service and replaced with new ones, but those that we modified and are still in service are showing no problems. It was an interesting project, Stephen."

"So, what are you doing now?"

"Planned vehicle repaints, mainly, but the work's still very enjoyable. Satisfying is probably the right word."

"I'm glad to hear it."

The pub was already busy when they got there, and the lady who was leaving was at the bar and buying drinks for all the team. Many people were already seated and engaged in conversation, most of which seemed to be causing smiles and laughter.

Stephen sat down with Felix and Joe and they tried to start a conversation of their own, but the activity around them made that almost impossible.

The overall impression was that of a bunch of people who were all very happy in each other's company, and that was something that Stephen had not seen for many years.

It was great to be back with a good group of people, almost an extended family. He felt that he had come home.

Chapter 17
The treasure seeker

Monday morning. What would the new week bring? The e-mails would be a good place to start. Thomas had retired. No surprise there. He had just been interested in the money. He'd probably be sitting at home counting his shares. So, who was replacing him? Taylor. What did it say? He had been in some kind of trainee role in another industry. At least he was educated.

That was the only news, so Stephen went back to the list of priorities that Sandy had given him. The new vehicles in the latest batch allocated to the company were being reported by drivers for struggling around town. He had seen some on the road from time to time but hadn't been aware of any issues. Luckily some were operating out of Jason's depot so Stephen left his desk and walked over to see him.

"Why are you here?" asked Jason. Nice to feel wanted.

"Someone at the centre specified the wrong gearbox for the new vehicle intake," Stephen explained. "Fine for the open road, but not so good round town. The only thing the manufacturer can do is reprogramme the gearshift points. It'll be a compromise. And it will probably shorten the gearbox life."

Jason wasn't impressed. "You mean shorten it at my expense."

"Yes, I probably do." Stephen went back to his desk.

The next e-mail was more interesting. Sandy had called a meeting in his office that afternoon. He was inviting his team of managers to discuss how they would best share out the workload to ensure that all current issues were addressed as quickly as possible. Stephen had been invited to join them.

What could he contribute? He had already revised the list of all the vehicle types currently making up the fleet. He had also set out that list by vehicle type and age and he had visited all the depots to see how the staff were coping with them.

Vehicle availability was now much improved and that meant that some older and expensive-to-maintain types could be withdrawn from service. That in itself did not solve the problem of budget overspend, but it set the company in the right direction. Joe was given the task of refurbishing some mid-life vehicles.

The following two days went very quickly: phone calls, e-mails and brief meetings. Then news got around that Taylor was visiting the company the following week. Not necessarily to meet everyone, but certainly the board of directors.

When he was ready for a coffee, Stephen went to the machine and then along to Sandy's office and asked, "Has he said what he intends to discuss, or is this just a social call?"

"A bit of both. He says that he wants to meet us all face to face and ask us if we've got any particular concerns at present. But he said that he wants to hold separate meetings with the operations directors and with the engineering directors. I've to prepare a paper for that and be ready to present it."

"At least something seems to be about to happen."

Stephen had his now-cooling coffee with Felix. A twenty-minute lunch break would be better than none.

"Look at this." Felix turned his screen to let Stephen read it. Another new appointment. The group engineering director was being replaced. Was he retiring to count his money? And again, where was the replacement coming from? And who had chosen him, and why? Would Taylor have had any input in this appointment? Unlikely. He wouldn't know anyone. The guy's name was Harold, and he was from a similar, but still significantly different, industry.

Felix turned the screen back and continued to read. "It's from the board. They say we're lucky to have Harold with us. He comes with a wealth of experience."

Stephen looked quizzically at him. "Experience in what?"

"Wait a minute." Felix read through the e-mail before turning the screen towards Stephen again. "Only about thirty-three percent relevant to us."

Stephen said nothing until he'd read it all the way through. "A good estimate. He'll have very little to offer but I've got a bad feeling about his appointment. I think he'll do us more harm than good. And what's even more worrying is that Sandy will report to Harold, and Harold will report to Taylor. One inappropriate person in a hierarchy could be handled by going around them tactfully, but when you've got two, one adjacent to the other, that's almost impossible."

"You couldn't make it up, could you?" said Felix. "Apart from Eadie, there's now nobody at the top with experience in this industry. So, why did they choose him?"

"Maybe he's well paid, and that might be an excuse for them to give themselves a pay rise."

Stephen went back to his desk. The coffee hadn't been very good, but he did feel slightly more awake than earlier. There was a note on his desk. Would he go back along and see Sandy. Another emergency?

"Would you be free for us to sit down together over the weekend and draft something for the presentation to Taylor?" Sandy asked him.

"Sounds fun. What about Sunday morning?" Stephen replied.

"That's in the diary." Sandy looked pleased. "I've got two meetings with him next week. He'll be here on the Wednesday and then, on the Friday, all engineering directors have to go down south to his office and make their presentations. But, while you're here, make sure you don't leave your desk next Wednesday. Put that in your diary. Whenever I can, I'll try to lead him through to the main office so you can get a good look at him."

"I look forward to it."

Harold was beginning to make his presence felt. He too would be visiting next week, but that would be Thursday. More immediately, he apparently intended to introduce benchmarking to see how vehicle maintenance staff were spending their time.

What was going on here? Stephen read the e-mail again. Yes, Harold was intending to compare the activities in the organisation with those in his previous one. But they were so different that any comparison would be meaningless. If he were the minister for sport, would he replace football with tennis because he could make a ninety-one percent saving in labour costs?

The week ended with a reminder e-mail from Sandy that he and Stephen would be meeting up on Sunday.

*

Breakfast was earlier than usual that day.

"You're early," said Sandy.

"I can't wait to get started," said Stephen. "What type of report is he looking for?"

Sandy logged onto Taylor's e-mail. "He's asking what we see as our main problems at present, but he's not specific."

"I wouldn't expect any specific questions. He doesn't know enough about the business. He's probably only asking about the perceived problems and their solutions so that he can report back to Eadie and say that he's on top of things."

Stephen sketched out a list of the main issues and possible solutions and laid it on the desk in front of Sandy. "Is that a good start?" he asked.

"As you can imagine, I'm being hounded all the time about overspend. Next comes vehicle ability."

The two of them each started with a fresh sheet of paper and set out the main problems in descending order of importance.

The company had cut back on spending before it had been bought, so there had been a lot of catching up to do when it was taken over, but most of the necessary action had now been taken.

There was no need to look for more customers, and even if that had been an issue, it wouldn't have been Sandy's responsibility. The need was simply to deal with the fleet of vehicles that they had inherited and continue to make them more reliable and reduce their running costs.

The report should therefore simply set out the present situation as succinctly as possible and attempt to convince him that the proposed approach was the correct one under the circumstances.

The main board was still obsessed with reducing staff numbers, but that was probably simply because they saw it as an easy way of reducing costs. And they'd probably convinced themselves that they were right because they had looked at technician-to-vehicle ratios that were the norms found across the industry. The problem with that was that the current situation was still not yet normal.

"This reminds me of something I said to Eadie just after he joined us," said Stephen.

Sandy looked up. "Well, what did you say?"

"I was telling him that there was an optimum speed for dealing with a problem: not too quickly, not too slowly. Look before you leap if you like. Imagine your car is parked at the side of the road. It's got springs, so it can be made to bounce up and down."

"And?" said Sandy.

"But it's also got things called shock absorbers, or dampers. They look like bicycle pumps, one end attached to the car, the other to the wheel."

"I'm aware of that."

"Therefore, if the shock absorbers are very powerful, and you press the car down, it will take a few seconds to rise back up to its normal position. But, if they're very weak, the car will continue to oscillate up and down for a few seconds."

"And the point of this story?"

"The point is that, if the shock absorber settings are just right, the car will get back to its normal, static position in the shortest time. It was something learned when I was studying engineering. It was called critical damping. But that thought remained with me for years. It seemed relevant when solving problems. Solve them as quickly as you can, but not too quickly. Make sure you have understood the problem before you take action or you could make things even worse."

"What did Eadie make of that?"

"Nothing. But, to me, it was one of life's epiphany moments."

"But why mention that now?"

"Because it should be in your report to Taylor. To make sure he doesn't jump to some stupid conclusion just to impress the board."

"Point taken, but just get back to your writing."

They both did and about three hours later, they had completed it.

"I think Taylor would appreciate the final sentence in Latin," said Stephen. "*Festinate lente*, hasten slowly."

"He'll think I'm mad, but why not," said Sandy. "He'll be sizing us all up, but I'll be looking to see what his reaction is. I'll let you know when I get back from the meeting."

*

It was Monday again. The first e-mail confirmed that Harold would be visiting on Thursday morning and Clerk had invited Stephen to attend.

What else? Sandy had asked Stephen to investigate a fire that had taken place on one of the younger vehicles in the fleet. It was now in the central workshop and he picked up his notepad and pen and went down to see Joe.

"It's over there," said Joe. "Sandy said you'd be down to take a look at it. The manufacturer's team was in at the end of last week. They stayed about an hour but they didn't say much before they left."

"I wouldn't expect them to say much to us, but they've no doubt put in their report to their own folk," said Stephen.

"When can we start putting it together again?"

"No idea. Sandy no doubt wants our take on what happened before he follows it up. He'll forward our report to Jack."

"I'll leave you to it then. Good luck."

Joe went back to his office and Stephen began to look around the engine compartment. Everything was covered in soot and it wasn't immediately apparent what components were likely to have been involved.

One thing however was already known about this vehicle type. The exhaust tailpipe was vulnerable to hitting the kerb, and as a consequence, fracturing its support brackets.

Stephen reached in and pulled on the exhaust downpipe just beyond the turbocharger. It moved. Significantly. In service, there would be a flow of hot gas from the fracture.

Looking at the components nearby, the relief valve on the air system was where his eyes settled. If the relief valve had released some oily air through the hot exhaust gas, that could have been the cause of the fire. He would investigate that further. He went back to the office and sent an interim report to Sandy.

He then picked up his jacket and drove off to the depot where the burnt-out vehicle had been based, in order to examine an undamaged example. And when he arrived, he went to the coffee machine before going up to the depot engineer's office.

"You still take two sugars?" Stephen said as he entered.

Colin looked up. "You've got a good memory for someone your age. Thanks for the coffee. But what have you been up to? I hear you're happy to be back."

"Very happy. I enjoyed what I learned while I was away, but I think this is where I belong."

"And now it's the fire?"

"I had a look at it this morning, but I also wanted to look at an undamaged vehicle just to be clear in my mind about how different components sit in relation to each other."

"I'll come down with you. I need to get some fresh air."

Colin led the way over to a vehicle that was in the workshop for an oil change. "These vehicles are usually very reliable," he said. "The only thing we've noticed about them is the occasional snorting noise they make when they're in service."

"And where exactly does the noise come from?"

"The engine compartment. Quite high up."

"The pressure relief valve? Because the air pipes are partially blocked by carbon?"

"How did you know?"

"Just from looking at the other vehicle. It seemed the only possibility. That in combination with the fractured exhaust pipe. Let's have a look at this one while we're here."

Colin brought Stephen a lamp from the workbench. This vehicle was immaculate by comparison with the other one. All components in the engine compartment were clean and identifiable. Stephen pointed to the pressure relief valve.

"There, that discharges directly towards the exhaust pipe leaving the turbocharger. Just here is where the pipe had fractured on the other vehicle, but this pipe is as new."

"So, no worries here?"

"Well, the exhaust is problem free, but it could be that the air system is discharging towards the pipe. Would you mind starting the engine and holding it at full speed?"

Colin went behind the wheel and Stephen listened. "You can switch it off now," he said. "I've heard all I needed. I can put this in my final report to Sandy."

*

On Wednesday, the office was more active than usual. Stephen's first e-mail was a reminder from Sandy that Stephen should stay at his desk. Yes, Taylor was visiting, and this was Stephen's chance to get a glimpse of him. The queue of e-mails on his computer would stop him getting bored as he waited for the big moment.

When Sandy walked into the main office with someone in tow, the wait had been worthwhile. At his side was Taylor, well dressed and nodding politely. When someone noticed Sandy, they waved him to come over. "Excuse me for a moment," said Sandy.

"Of course," Taylor replied.

Stephen watched. What would happen next?

Taylor turned his back to the group and took out his phone. "Yes, I was wondering how I get access to the first-class lounge at the airport. No, not just for today. Is there a permanent arrangement?"

Could he not have done that at some other time? Was he not interested in the other services based here in the main office? Obviously not.

As soon as Sandy was free again, he smiled at Taylor and asked, "Have you seen enough?"

Sandy pointed to the door and Taylor set off. Just before he left the office, Sandy looked over in Stephen's direction and winked.

That had been more fun than Stephen had expected, but he was soon again engrossed in his e-mails. And after lunch, they were finally under control.

Tomorrow was Harold's visit. Would it be even more enjoyable than Taylor's?

Stephen wondered how he should set out his report. Unless he chose his words carefully, different people might be able to make their own interpretation of its findings. His focus should probably be on the design characteristics of the vehicle.

When Thursday arrived, of course, his first e-mail was a reminder that he had to be present at the meeting with Harold. That would be interesting. Another expert to tell them everything that they'd learned over the years was wrong.

Stephen went over to Felix's door and was waved in. "Morning, Stephen. I've just seen Sandy and he's getting ready for the meeting with Harold and so am I. Are you going too?"

"Yes, but why? Will I learn anything? Maybe just how little I'm paid."

The meeting didn't totally disappoint. Everybody could have been doing something more useful than listening to another bluffer but they all noted how confident a lack of knowledge can make people feel.

From what Harold could see, the company was over-staffed and the operating depots were out of date. He'd deal with that.

Stephen and Felix left together. Their only exchange was raised eyebrows. One more day to go and they could sit down and try to make sense of the current situation. Neither of them could remember anything quite as ridiculous.

Friday's tasks were dealt with on autopilot and it was soon five pm. Joe phoned. "See you across the road in half an hour?"

Felix arrived at Stephen's desk. "Let's go. We can tell Joe what happened at yesterday's meeting."

"That shouldn't take long, should it?" said Stephen.

They crossed the road and went in. Felix ordered their drinks, and it wasn't long before Joe joined them. "Well, what happened? Don't keep me in suspense."

"Take that," said Felix. "You might need it. Nothing meaningful was said, but I was reading between the lines. Harold and Taylor – neither from this industry – one reports to the other, one will want to make a name for himself, and one has said we're overstaffed. I think we're in for a bumpy ride."

And that was how the week ended.

With Saturday free, Stephen's business now demanded his time. Mail orders were increasing, with local ones being delivered by hand and long-distance ones sent by post. The only new issue was a reminder that the rental contract for the premises was soon due for renewal. That was something that would have to be given consideration. What direction should he choose? Stay with his own business, continue to develop it, sell it or close it down?

It was a difficult discussion with his partner. Both of them had full-time jobs elsewhere, but both of them had invested much time and money in the business.

Reordering stock was a weekly activity, and that was a distraction for them both that weekend, but they both agreed that they would close it down when the lease ran out. They both felt very sad about it, but the decision had been made.

Stephen couldn't imagine what his partner's emotions were, nor did he feel that he should ask, but for him, the business had almost been like an exercise from his business course. How do you set up a large business from scratch? Like that. He had answered the question. What was the next one?

The other factor that was a major influence for Stephen was his passion for motor vehicles. If he had had his own way in life, he would have worked for a car manufacturer. He would have used his life-long passion, his engineering training and his business training to contribute to the construction of cheap, reliable, easily re-cyclable and economic vehicles; he would have taken a great deal of satisfaction from that.

Instead, he got satisfaction in life from learning and from solving problems. He didn't need expensive cars or flashy possessions to allow him to take satisfaction from impressing others. He lived inside his head.

On Monday morning, he immediately went to Sandy's office and asked him how well the meeting with Taylor had gone.

"It was as bad as everybody thought it would be. He was polite, but it was obvious that all we were there for was to teach him what he should already have known. But the thing that shocked us all was when he said, 'get your nose in the trough, this won't last forever'."

"Spare me. At least he was honest. He's only here for the money and he's implying that everybody else should be thinking the same way?"

"That's the impression we've always had about these new, six-figure-salary people. I take it nobody's going to help him. Just hope that he's found out quickly and sacked."

Back at his desk, Stephen checked his e-mails. Mainly chat between depots about how they were coping with challenges and advising each other of solutions they had found. What made the greatest impression on him was how they worked together, supporting each other.

That was a reminder that he should arrange to visit all the depots that week, on Sandy's behalf, and see what was happening at the coal face. The improvements that had been introduced before Alan had retired and taken to the next stage by Jack were now under threat from Harold's ridiculous cost-cutting drive, one that the young Taylor seemed to be determined to support.

While things were now going relatively well, Harold's ban on replacing people who had left, whether through retirement or simply from moving on, was now suggesting that things might now be going backwards again. Not what anyone wanted to hear.

"It's Friday. Have you remembered that Joe and I go for a drink after work and put the world to rights? You're joining us, I take it?" Stephen had not remembered, and Felix appearing at his side had been a surprise. He was in the middle of writing a report for Sandy, describing what had so far been achieved and what still required to be done.

He looked at his watch. "When do we go?" he asked. "In fifteen minutes?"

"Nearly right. Fourteen. Joe will see us over there."

"I'd really meant to visit all the depots this week, starting with Jason's. I'll put him in my diary for Monday."

*

"We'll sit over there," said Felix. Stephen and Joe followed Felix to the far side of the bar. It would be quieter there.

"So, Stephen, you're glad to be back? Sorry you ever went away?"

"Yes, I am glad to be back, very glad," said Stephen. "Back among old friends and doing a job I enjoy. But I've got a terrible feeling that things are starting to go bad again, but in a different way to last time."

Felix signalled to the barman before asking "What do you mean?"

"Before the company was last purchased again."

"You mean by Eadie?"

"Yes. It was starved of spending to make it look more profitable and valuable, and while not good, that was almost understandable, and the damage could be undone. But what's started to happen now is much worse, believe me."

"I do."

"And so do I," Joe added.

Part Three
Maturity

Chapter 18
Illusion

Friday morning, and Stephen and Joe had both brought a cake to celebrate Felix's birthday. And at eleven o'clock they both arrived at his office. Joe tapped gently on the door and Felix looked up and invited them in. "I'll get the coffees," he said.

Joe and Stephen were signing a folded sheet of A4 paper on which they had scribbled Happy Birthday. "Thanks for the cake, you two, but how are you going to fix the company?"

*

Stephen, in particular, was frustrated, although now less concerned than before. He knew what had been done in the past in order to turn companies when the group was being created, so there was no reason for this not to happen again.

One day later that week, he noticed Clerk walk past his desk on the way back to his office, and someone new was with him. He had seen photographs of this person before and the informal organisation had already decided that Eadie would be retiring and his replacement had been selected. Could this be him?

Stephen went back to the latest e-mail in his inbox. Lockhart's incessant questions about progress with projects were only delaying their completion. The timing and pattern of questions suggested that he was preparing his board papers and was desperate to claim credit for anything that was working well.

"Give him the wrong answer," whispered Felix who had come down to the machine for a coffee.

"Can't," said Stephen tetchily, "but he can misrepresent things if he wants to. While you're here, did you notice that fellow with Clerk?"

"You mean Eadie's replacement?"

"Are you guessing, or have you heard something?"

"Just guessing, but it is a bit suspicious. Some rumours come and go, but this one's been going around for a while."

Something else to think about, but Stephen went back to his screen. This latest e-mail related to a problem with the rear axle of a new vehicle type and it had been reported by the engineering director in another operating company.

One vehicle had suffered a problem with a rear hub bearing. The vehicle in question had been returned to one of the manufacturer's agents, but not before it had been examined in detail by the depot engineer. The fact that the parts in question were showing signs of corrosion had been a surprise, hence the e-mail that had been sent to Lockhart.

As soon as Stephen had read the details of the reported problem, he went over to see Jason.

"Would you let me know when someone could change the oil in the rear axle of one of these vehicles?" Stephen asked.

"Why?" said Jason.

"Someone's reported a problem and I've had a look at the specification of it and the earlier model. There are some obvious changes to the design and they may be related to the problem being described."

"That's all I need. If there is a problem, you'd better find it and fix it."

Nobody could blame Jason for taking things seriously, and it wasn't surprising that he immediately went over to a member of his team and asked him to do what Stephen required.

The main difference between the rear axle of the two vehicle types was that the newer one had a cross-sectional area that was now significantly reduced, probably to save weight. Would that be relevant?

Now, thirty minutes later, Stephen was writing his interim report on the issue and including a copy to the engineer who had first reported it. Yes, the problem had arisen from the modifications, but it could be avoided by any one of a number of relatively simple changes. To confirm what these would be, he would have to examine an axle in more detail and so he arranged to travel the following day to see the axle in question at the manufacturer's agent.

By coincidence, one of the manufacturer's service engineers was there, somebody Stephen had known and worked with on and off for a number of years. They got on well, and working together, they had resolved a number of issues in the past.

Stephen was quite clear what he had seen. In this case, the problem had resulted from breathing and oil flow problems brought about by the changes introduced by the manufacturer in order to save weight. The modification would therefore also have to come from the manufacturer.

Although they were dealing with facts, and they both had obtained photographic evidence, the service engineer made no comment on the possible origins of the bearing failure on this vehicle, and Stephen did not ask him to do so. That was probably something that experience had taught both of them.

On the way back home by train, Stephen sent an e-mail to Lockhart, bringing him up to date with what had been found and then he began writing his final report and recommendations.

Two e-mails jumped out the following morning. Stephen had hoped that the axle he'd just viewed would have been repaired by the manufacturer as a goodwill gesture, but Lockhart had asked the operating company to pay for it. Although he had initially been quite confrontational with vehicle manufacturers, he now seemed to have changed tack completely. Pathetic.

The second e-mail was more intriguing. Millar had written to Lockhart, asking if Stephen could get involved in a review of vehicle interior cleaning by contacting the manager whom Eadie had recently met. That was a blast from the past.

As the day drew to a close, Felix came over to see how Stephen was getting on. "Look at that!" said Stephen. "I designed a procedure for that over twenty years ago, and now it's back on the agenda."

Felix leant over and read the e-mail. "Why did Lockhart ask you?" he asked. "He wouldn't have known?"

"It must have filtered down from Eadie via Millar. Why didn't Eadie simply give my report to Millar?"

"He must have lost it. So much for the tales about him being well organised. Anyway, I'm off home now. Think twice before you reply."

Stephen sent the manager an e-mail and she replied and arranged for them to meet up at an operating company not too far from where Stephen was based. Apparently, Eadie had met her in another division, and in that business, the only option was to bring vehicles to a cleaning station and for Stephen, that confirmed Eadie's involvement. Why couldn't she simply set out an equivalent methodology applicable to this division?

The meeting would take place the following week with the manager, Caroline, in order for them to view a current process in action. They would all then move on to head office where Eadie had apparently noticed a fall in standards over the last few months.

Stephen understood immediately what was going on, but he was intrigued to know why his original system was no longer in use back at head office. Who had changed it? And, after the problems were discovered, why hadn't they simply changed it back to the way he had left it?

The following Wednesday, he met up with Caroline and two local managers from the opco in question. All four introduced themselves.

One of the managers said, "There's a vehicle in the cleaning bay just now and we can go over there and see what's happening."

It was a mid-life vehicle, so it wouldn't be blemish-free. On seeing the team arrive, the two cleaners then began the process, both working furiously. They looked out briefly and smiled from time to time. They also looked genuinely happy, but Stephen's first reaction was that they shouldn't have to work at such a speed.

Did they think that they, rather than the process, were being judged? He remembered cleaning a vehicle himself in order to understand what it felt like, and he couldn't have kept up that pace for long. What they were looking at was a planned fortnightly clean in a cleaning station, but not the daily sweep-out. That would also have to be addressed if the whole process was to be reviewed.

"What do you think?" Caroline asked.

"Good workers," was all Stephen could think to say.

"They are," replied Caroline, "but we've seen everything here that we need to. The four of us should meet up at head office tomorrow and Friday. I'll book us into a hotel and we can look at the dayshift and nightshift cleaning procedures there. When we've finished, I'll bring Millar up to speed. I'll see you all in the morning."

After a three-hour train journey, the following day, Stephen was in reception.

"I'll let her know you're here." The receptionist smiled at him and he thought she looked familiar, but he couldn't be sure.

He simply smiled back and said, "Thank you,"

Caroline didn't come immediately and that gave him the opportunity to look around. The reception area had changed dramatically since he was last here. A new image? For whom? The company, or Eadie?

"Hello," said Caroline. "You made it."

"Yes. I was admiring all the changes."

Caroline hadn't been here before, so she just carried on. "I've just been telling the other two about what I've planned for these two days. We'll look around the site just now and familiarise ourselves with the layout of everything, including where the vehicles move for refuelling and going through the automatic vehicle wash."

When Stephen had carried out his cleaning project here, the nightshift refuelling team collected vehicles from the parking area and drove them to the fuelling islands and then through the automatic vehicle wash that was located immediately after them. With the system that he had introduced, he had used the next shed for the interior cleaning process. But somebody had relocated the automatic vehicle wash and installed it here inside it. That was to some extent understandable. If the original unit had to remain functional until the new one had been installed and put into service, it made sense that they could not both have had exactly the same location, but should the people involved not have considered the consequences of doing what they did?

As it was, the vehicle interior cleaning process had fallen apart and Eadie hadn't noticed. Well, he had eventually, when it was too late. Stephen said nothing. He just let Caroline carry on. "Oh, and before I forget, Millar gave me the job descriptions for the nightly and daily cleaning schedules, so I suggest we go back to the hotel for an early dinner and meet back here about eight o'clock this evening and follow each schedule through. The nightshift foreman knows we'll be there."

Nobody had felt very hungry, but they knew that they'd better eat something since it was obviously going to be a long night. Conversation avoided business and limited itself to weather forecasts and holiday plans.

Back at the depot, Caroline led the way. She introduced the visitors to the foreman and asked him to get his fuelling team to carry on as normal.

The team climbed into the vehicles in the front parking area and drove them to a fuelling island to refill the tanks. With that complete, they drove them through the automatic wash and parked them for going back into service.

In Caroline's business, the vehicles were parked up purely for interior cleaning after all other maintenance activities had been carried out. She now tried to work out how to give the cleaning team an equivalent degree of access to vehicles in this environment.

The backshift activity was now up to speed, and vehicles were coming in the entrance gate and being parked by the drivers returning from duty. They got out and went to the office to sign off for the day.

The procedure then was that the vehicles waited in a queue until one of the refuelling team topped up the fuel tank before driving through the automatic vehicle wash. They had a list of the vehicles which would be required to be taken to the workshop for planned maintenance. Those that did not were simply parked up for the following day's business.

While all this activity was going on, Caroline led her team around the site, unsuccessfully trying to identify a point in the cycle at which she could allow the interior cleaning team to get access to the vehicles for the time they needed for their tasks.

Before they left to go home the following afternoon, Millar asked if they could bring him up to date with what had been achieved over the last two days. Caroline responded immediately, saying what she had done the previous evening. None the wiser, Millar looked at Stephen who mischievously produced from his case a plan view of the site that he had produced back at the hotel.

A similar diagram had been one of the appendices to the original report that he had produced for Eadie.

"I've never seen it presented like that," said Millar.

Caroline glared.

A nod from Millar, silence from her. Stephen took the train home.

*

The following morning, he sipped his coffee while reading through his e-mails. Half-way down the list was one from Felix. He had forwarded an announcement that Eadie was retiring and anyone who wished would be welcome to join him for a drink in a bar not too far from the head office. Yes, a bit further down was the date and the address of the venue. Felix's only comment had been 'What do you think of that?' For his part, Stephen was now convinced that the visitor he had seen was Eadie's replacement.

However, it was difficult to know what to make of the news. Eadie had been far from perfect, but he had been a known quantity. If he'd stayed, everybody would just have carried on in an environment with which they were familiar, doing their best to keep the business functioning, while also hoping that it would dawn on Eadie that the entire board that he had appointed was hopeless.

But was Eadie, in fact, well aware that his appointees had no direct experience of this business? Stephen hadn't considered that before. Had he simply appointed supposed 'experts', trying to make himself look responsible, while also deliberately ensuring that none of them knew more about the business and showed up his complete lack of education?

The main problem for the business now was that there was no succession plan. Eadie had simply surrounded himself with yes-men. So, who chose the new guy? And how quickly would he learn how this business functioned?

An e-mail appeared. From Lockhart. Would Stephen phone someone regarding a problem with road wheel attachment?

It was a name Stephen knew although he had never met the individual in question. A brief conversation with him put the problem in context, and Stephen went through to the secretaries to book a sleeper train for that evening.

It wasn't a well-known problem but some years earlier he had done some work on the design and maintenance of roadwheels and their attachments.

There was nothing complicated about it. Should he tell Lockhart about his experience? No, he thought that he'd better confirm exactly what the problem was before saying anything. He also suspected that if he shared any of this experience, Lockhart would immediately pass it on to someone else as his own. Another reason for saying nothing.

He was met at the station by the person with whom he'd spoken and taken to the nearby depot, and on the journey there, he was told the story so far. Some vehicles had been allocated there for a new contract, but the maintenance team had reported finding loose wheel nuts. There was no report of it having been found by the previous operating depot; perhaps they had been too scared to report it.

It was arranged that Stephen and his host would watch a roadwheel being removed, inspected and correctly refitted before being taken on a short test run.

Everything was carried out correctly and the journey simply became twenty minutes of chatting and enjoying the scenery.

Back in the depot was the moment of truth. All wheel nuts were found to be loose. There was a problem; a real one. Stephen asked if one wheel-nut could be tightened far beyond the manufacturer's recommended setting. Yes. The wheel studs stretched. They were sub-standard. "I've seen this before," he said. "Some parts had been purchased from a non-approved supplier and they behaved in exactly the same way." His host looked concerned, and Stephen continued with his explanation. "Do you remember hearing about a problem many years ago involving a vehicle where a very similar problem was found? In that case, it was just after the introduction of tubeless tyres. There were the first wheel rims manufactured in one piece, instead of two simpler ones held together by a circlip. To make it easier for them to manufacture the new design, the manufacturer chose to use a softer steel. Is that ringing any bells?"

"Yes, Stephen," replied his host, "now that you mention it, I do remember it. It was more or less a one-off problem. As soon as the operator reported it, the manufacturer withdrew all the early wheels and changed the specification."

"As you say, that was a one off, but a few years ago, I experienced the same symptoms on a number of vehicles, but this time it was due to poor quality wheel studs. They were purchased from a non-approved supplier and they stretched when the wheel nuts were set to the correct torque when fitting. We identified all the faulty parts and quarantined them. We then ensured that the replacement parts were purchased from an approved supplier and the problem went away immediately. In this case, the solution is just as simple. I'd recommend replacing all the wheel studs."

"We don't have any in stock."

"That's not necessarily a problem. I recognise them from one of our obsolete vehicle types. We've got some of these studs in stock. Excuse me while I make a call."

Felix confirmed that he had some redundant stock and simply asked if he could be given an order number for the parts and he would arrange for them to be transferred.

It seemed like the problem was sorted. Stephen said his goodbyes and was given a run back into town. It would be a while before his train but he could relax over dinner and read through all the new e-mails in the inbox. And, with the solution found, he should probably update Lockhart.

*

The next morning passed fairly quietly. Felix was still waiting for the order number and Stephen was occupied with two more of Lockhart's daft projects. However, no acknowledgement of Stephen's e-mail the night before.

He was surprised when Felix arrived at his desk. "Fancy lunch?" asked Felix.

"That time already? I hadn't noticed. I was just going to have a coffee and some crisps."

"Come on. Let's get some fresh air. You can spend too long in here."

Stephen logged off, stood up and put on his jacket. "Where to?"

"Just up to the end of the road. The exercise will do us good. And we can pop into the sandwich shop on the way back."

"Lead on."

Even just getting out the main gates into the street made them both feel more relaxed.

"What's that over there?" asked Stephen. "These road works."

"Do you mean pavement works?" Felix corrected him.

"Yes. Let's go and have a look."

The pavement had been dug up, and the trench was over two hundred yards long. Stephen peered down and at the bottom was a cast iron pipe, very corroded and with a number of holes all along its length. Were they replacing it? He looked back up the road and there was a trailer with a giant roll of flexible blue pipe on it. No. They were going to line it and save the cost of a complete replacement.

But how? Stephen asked the foreman and he explained that they were going to send a rope down through the iron pipe and then pull the plastic one through it. It had the same diameter as the cast iron original but that would reduce as it was pulled through. As soon as they stopped pulling, it would recover its original diameter and become a tight fit in the original. Stephen was fascinated but Felix just wanted to walk and take in some fresh air.

"Come on," said Felix. "It'll be no time before we'll have to be back in the office."

"Did you see what they were doing?" asked Stephen. "They're pulling that pipe through to avoid having to replace the original one. While they're pulling it through, it reduces in diameter, making it easier to pull."

"Yes, I heard him say that."

"But if they had tried to push it, it would simply have bulged out and got jammed. It wouldn't have moved."

"So?"

"That's exactly how people behave. If you push them, they resist, but if you pull them, they respond. If you say you'll help them address their concerns, and then thank them for their efforts, they become unstoppable."

"I know that Joe often talks about the negative effects of bullying from management. In my experience, that only comes about because those in our senior management don't understand the job. And they also haven't been properly trained to manage."

"I've just experienced something," said Stephen.

"What do you call it? An epiphany moment?"

"That's exactly what I call it."

A fresh sandwich and a coffee later, they were both back at their desks, reading through the new e-mails and prioritising them. Some were just for information and some were requests for assistance. Stephen, however, had also received some new mad ideas from Lockhart. And some of these were simply some historical problems that had been encountered and dealt with many years earlier.

Rather than ask, Lockhart simply blundered in, not realising that while they may be new to him, they weren't to the more experienced members of the organisation. But that did raise a fundamental problem. Why had he been promoted? Did the board not remember that he had arrived a couple of years earlier with an irrelevant background? How had he performed in his first post with the organisation? He certainly still had a lot to learn before being promoted to the position he now held.

The mid-afternoon walk over to the coffee machine allowed people to stretch their legs and get their blood circulation moving again. It also allowed their eyes to recover from staring at their computer screens. It did help.

Then back to work. Stephen's next e-mail was a new project for the central team. Another seabird. Would this never end? The only pleasure here was reading between the lines. He picked up the phone. "Felix, it's Stephen. I've just remembered about the wheel studs that you set aside. Did you ever get an order number for them?"

"No, not a word. And I found that surprising since you told me they were desperate to get the vehicles in question ready for a new contract. I sent them one more e-mail and then I just gave up."

"I'm sorry that I put you to so much trouble. I thought that we'd been able to help them. And it would have got some redundant parts out of our stockholding. We'll probably never find out how it ended. By the way, while you're still on the line, are we going for our pint this afternoon?"

"Funny that you should mention that. Joe was up here earlier looking for some help getting parts for a vehicle that Jason's desperate to get back into service. He looked a bit down, and when I asked him if he'd be going, he just shrugged and said even thinking about the place was depressing him these days. He said he'd just give it a miss. To be honest, I think that I agree with him. There is nothing good to discuss now. What do you think?"

"I was looking forward to talking to two people who understand the business and would chat about what they'd achieved that week and what they were planning to do the following week." Stephen found that rather sad. "Is that it? The end of an era?"

Felix laughed. "I think it's more like the end of everything. Nobody cares what happens now."

Felix was probably right. Nobody Stephen had spoken to recently seemed to be enthused about anything they were doing. And not just in this opco. Right across the division, people were now simply turning up, doing what they had to do and waiting for the next stupid announcement from head office.

"I'll see you on Monday, Felix."

"Unless I win the lottery."

Chapter 19
Courage

Another intake of new vehicles with a serious defect, one with which Stephen was very familiar, one that could have been avoided at the specification stage.

"Are you taking this seriously?" Jason asked Stephen as he delegated a full day's work to one of his mechanics. "It should have been years, if ever, before we had to do that."

There was no point in staying in the depot today. Jason was too focussed on trying to make vehicles available for business. Stephen went back to the main office.

"Why have you moved desk?" asked Felix.

"Overhearing these purchasing phone conferences was driving me insane. And I said as much before I moved."

"Did it have any effect?"

"Not one bit. Just some polite, patronising response, as if to say, 'what do you know about purchasing procedures'?"

"An exaggeration?"

"I'm afraid not. I was tempted to give my usual response in return. 'I'm not interested in purchasing procedures; I'm only interested in what they achieve, their outcome'."

"Why didn't you?"

"Because there was no point."

"Yes, everybody has to obey established procedures, but surely it's only common sense to ensure that their actions are appropriate to the business that they're in. I was certainly taught how to play a responsible role in my environment."

"You're right, but the board should have given a clearer remit."

"You're blaming the board again?"

"I am. It's their job to see that the organisation beneath them is functioning correctly. Otherwise, they shouldn't be there. Don't pretend that you'd say something different."

Felix went back to his office. At least he knew where to find Stephen now.

The next e-mail on Stephen's list indirectly concerned the problem that he and Jason had just discussed. Lockhart had asked his team for items to add to the agenda for the next manufacturer meeting that was scheduled for the following week.

The air compressor on the latest delivery of new vehicles was mounted in a poor location. Being effectively air-cooled, it would now run at a higher temperature than before, hence the carbon blockages that Jason was finding in the air pipework. There was a fully water-cooled alternative available, but obviously no one had thought to specify it before placing the order.

An associated problem was the design of the engine air filter, but that was less serious. Would now be the ideal time to deal with both of them?

Stephen went back over to see Jason and ask if he could take some photographs of the blocked air pipes; he would include them with his agenda points.

"And what is it you were saying about the air filter?" Jason asked.

"You can see that the plastic housing is cylindrical, designed around the filter itself," said Stephen. "Quite elegant, easy to access for filter changes. But the problem is that the engine and the air system share it. The filter effectively acts as a resistance to the air being drawn in, and the suction developed by the engine's turbocharger means that the engine always wins in its fight for air. The air system's compressor comes a poor second.

"There's a partial vacuum at the compressor inlet and that results in oil being sucked into the air system. That's not ideal, but we've lived with it for a number of years. It's the overheating of the compressor in this case that causes the carbon formation that you're having to deal with."

"So, what are you going to do about it?"

"It's not in my hands. But I'll report it, hence the photos."

"And, apart from a water-cooled compressor, what else is needed?"

"Do you remember when compressors had their own small air filters? People often forgot to change them when they were replacing the engine air filter, hence the current design. But the use of turbochargers means that the engine and compressor should not be sharing a filter. The ideal solution would be an air filter housing that was egg-shaped in cross section and contained two separate interior chambers."

"Why?"

"Let me finish. You could then have two filters inside it, one for the engine and the smaller one for the compressor, and being in separate compartments, there would be no conflict. And anyone changing the engine filter couldn't forget the other one."

"When do I get that?"

"As I said, not my decision."

Stephen's dilemma now was how many issues to raise in his agenda points. He mentioned the water-cooled compressor but he felt that mentioning the air filter modification might be going a bit too far.

A new e-mail announced that the new group purchasing director, Alistair's boss, had somehow duped the board into approving his recommendation to have replica spare parts replace a large number of vehicle components. According to him, they would be cheaper and better. And, yes, the board had given him their approval.

Stephen went through to see Felix. "What do you think about this re-sourcing of vehicle spares?" he asked.

"I'm just reading up about it. I knew you wouldn't be best pleased." Felix scrolled down. "We've employed a specialist company to guide us through the project."

"What does he mean, a 'specialist company'? As far as I'm aware, no one's ever done anything as stupid as this before, so how could they be specialists?"

"I'm just reading what's on the screen."

Stephen went back to his desk.

The draft agenda for the following week's manufacturer meeting was on his screen. Anything missing?

There were twelve items, and the water-cooled compressor issue was near the top of the list. Stephen would leave it at that. He simply spent the rest of the day compiling information for each agenda point.

The following morning, there was an e-mail even worse than the last one. Lockhart had decided to muscle in on the project, no doubt in the belief that he would be praised to the heavens for the benefits he assumed it would bring. The central team had to attend a meeting in his office in two days' time when he would set out the project in detail. Could things get any worse?

A second e-mail now called for the team to work towards producing a report on historical vehicle fires, along with an analysis of how they had arisen and a list of recommendations aimed at ensuring that they would not recur in future.

Each member of the team had to focus on one aspect of the issue and liaise with the others in order to ensure the production of a first draft.

That took two days, but at least they were all sufficiently focussed on this latest task to avoid thinking about the spare parts project.

Wednesday wasn't a productive day. When the team arrived at his office, Lockhart wasted no time in setting out the project on a white board. "This is what I'm doing," he said. "Every part that comes into the company will be booked into the new central store, and from there, it will be issued to the depot that had requested it. If it fails prematurely in service, it will be returned to the central store where it will be examined, and if necessary, redesigned. Soon, everything that we buy will be better than ever before, perfect."

What did he mean redesigned? Stress calculations, choice of materials? And would the supplier have to sign off the revised specification? The whole idea got worse the more Stephen thought about it.

The other members of the team were probably equally dismissive, but they kept their views to themselves. Stephen wondered if he could ask a polite question and show up the absurdity of the idea. Just get Lockhart to talk them through one part, any part, and describe in detail what would happen to it following its failure and return to the central store. What was meant to happen when it got there? Compared in every aspect to its genuine counterpart that an experienced, specialist manufacturer had designed? It wasn't worth asking.

The team spent the rest of the day working at their laptops before setting off for home. Stephen would again be crossing the country by train.

Inevitably, the following morning, Felix wanted to hear what had been said. He listened, nodded, and shook his head before suddenly interrupting, "And the central store? As far as I've heard, it couldn't be further away from the root mean square average travelling distance if it tried."

"Yes. I read that somewhere."

"And when it all goes tits up?" said Felix. "What will Lockhart do then?"

"Obviously, it will be someone else's fault."

"Yours, for example? Did none of your lot have the bottle to tell him what a load of crap he was talking?"

"In this blame culture? Our feet wouldn't have touched the ground. But I've got his phone number in case you want to do it."

Suppliers' representatives were now paying fewer visits to operating companies. "From what I've heard," said Felix "they're all rather amused. They'll be losing business, but they've still got loads of sensible customers. They know that, sooner or later, this nightmare will end and we'll have to go back to them. And they won't have to stick to the tight prices that we had negotiated over the years, so they'll more than make up for any lost income. But you should still be trying to stop this insanity."

"Put my head above the parapet?" asked Stephen. "There's no point. Eadie had slandered me to everybody and anybody. Lockhart let that slip a few weeks ago, so who'd believe anything I said? But to be honest, I'm actually enjoying watching all the work we've done over the years being torn apart. It's not as if we can do much about it, but at least we'll learn how bad things could have become if we'd been as inexperienced in our jobs. But that still doesn't stop me sympathising with the folk like Jason, who day in, day out, do their best."

There was now news that the divisional managing director was leaving. What had she done for the place, apart from causing embarrassment? But, of more importance, who would be appointed instead? That was soon answered. Eadie's replacement named him.

"What do you think?" Felix asked Stephen.

"I can understand why he was chosen, but I bet you anything you like that he wasn't responsible for the success of the business he came from. Our new people couldn't tell if he created success or was simply associated with it. But, if you want a prediction, I think he'll make some initial improvements, but ultimately he won't be successful. He would need to find out how the company grew and how it could continue that evolution. I'm certain he'll avoid some mistakes, but understanding how to replicate the successes, I'm not so sure."

"You're saying that we've had it?"

"I'm not saying that, but to be honest, it's of no interest to me."

Back at his desk, Stephen simply read his e-mails. Lockhart had arranged a meeting with a major supplier and his team had to attend.

It was only when people began moving to the coffee machine that he realised how much time had passed. Afternoon tea break. He stood up and stretched. Sitting still was bad for the health; reading what he had was even worse.

What was Felix up to? "Come in," Felix answered. Joe was there already and Stephen sat down beside him. Felix was typing something, an e-mail. Joe already had his coffee so Stephen got up and walked back to the machine. Only Alistair was now ahead of him in the queue. He looked round as Stephen approached.

"Busy day?" asked Alistair.

"Just the usual," Stephen replied. "E-mails that can't be ignored even though they're simply a waste of time. They do nothing to help the company move forward. They're all from new folk trying to make themselves look useful." Stephen bit his tongue, but rather too late. He shouldn't have said that to Alistair, but it was the truth. Wasn't it?

Back in Felix's office, the e-mail, or whatever it was, had been completed and he and Joe were obviously finding something very funny.

"So, what am I missing?" asked Stephen.

"I suspect the main board members are now all employed by a competitor in order to run us into the ground."

"So, they're cleverer than we thought."

"Definitely not," said Joe. "How can you even joke about that? Now that Eadie's away, there's nobody left who knows anything about how to run this business. Just look at the share price if you want to see how bad things are."

"I think there are more immediate indicators than the share price. Just phone any of our depots. Ask a friend in another opco to phone their depots. Morale is still getting worse everywhere, but at the coal face, they're really finding it hard to keep their heads above water," said Stephen.

Felix butted in. "That's what you've always said. The law of gravity acts downwards. The folk at the coal face always have to fight to stay afloat at the best of times, but when repair and replace starts to overtake preventative maintenance, the workload goes up and up and it's the beginning of the end."

"It is as simple as that. You could start the chain of improvements within minutes. But it would take a great deal of courage for someone to say that," said Stephen.

"That's true. But Joe's right, the main problem is that there's now nobody at the top who would understand what you're saying."

"On that cheery note, I'm going back to my desk to spend the rest of the afternoon being annoyed," said Stephen.

And that's exactly how things went. Doing, but not achieving. Joe had always said that if you buy cheap, you buy twice, and Stephen really couldn't have put it better.

Another announcement. It had been decided that the company had too many vehicles for the level of business it was currently doing. That was a statement from the top. Certainly, if depots had been allocated more vehicles than were required for each day's business and planned maintenance activities, major repairs were not a problem. However, if the number of spare vehicles didn't match that requirement, it made life rather stressful for the staff in question. Spare vehicle capacity was simply being imposed from the top in order to balance the books; it bore no relation to the actual requirements of the operation.

The true number required could be calculated, depending on a number of criteria including vehicle type and average age. Then, analysis of the depot maintenance workload could be made, and any problems investigated and solutions produced.

This was the role that Stephen and his equivalents in the other operating companies had carried out over the years, and if modesty allowed, they had proved to be quite good at it. It was the word puzzle; this is where we are, and here is where we want to go. And this is how we'll get there.

While there was, in theory, an agenda for the current projects, almost none of his time was being spent dealing with it. Instead, there was a list of questions from Lockhart, and there was little in common between the two.

No pause for lunch, just a coffee and a bar of chocolate. Non-stop reading and typing made the afternoon pass quickly. He would soon have to print out some papers and then log off.

All there was to think about now was the following day's meeting. One of Stephen's colleagues lived in the area and so he would probably drive. The others would no doubt be taking an early train but there had been no phone calls from any of them to discuss the agenda. Had they all been switched off?

One last check of his e-mails before logging off. What was this? The divisional MD had been replaced. No loss there, depending of course upon where the replacement had come from.

Stephen assumed that this was one of the first actions of Eadie's replacement. And since the replacement hadn't come from this industry, maybe this new MD did. If so, things might just be on the point of improving. Yes, it said so there. They had both served on a committee together and so they would no doubt know each other very well. And they must have been comfortable working together. Another good sign.

*

Stephen had booked a seat on the train and made a reservation in a hotel close to the supplier's premises. The journey itself was uneventful, and after dinner, he wondered if there would be something interesting on television. There wasn't.

He therefore went back to his e-mails and focussed on one from the new divisional MD. The language used had obviously been chosen to impress but unfortunately, the content let it down.

There were difficulties to be addressed, it said, and it would take some time to resolve them. 'No, it wouldn't', Stephen wanted to shout back. He had been in the organisation from the beginning; this guy had not, and so it was tempting to respond. But should he?

He sent an e-mail to Mike asking him what his impressions were. As usual, Mike gave little away, but after a few exchanges, he said that Stephen should. Was Mike keen to see the response, but not willing to risk his career by asking the question?

Stephen therefore drafted a reply, but tactfully omitted to say that the issues could be resolved within weeks, if not days, if the appropriate actions were taken. He forwarded the draft to Mike. Go ahead, was the reply.

There was no response that night. Nor had there been any contact regarding the agenda for the meeting the next day.

Breakfast was good. The room was busy with people helping themselves, but there was no queue-jumping. The majority of people were smiling and chatting, and giving the impression that they were business people looking forward to going off to a meeting. Lucky them.

The sun was bright, and the short taxi journey from the hotel was quite relaxing. Out here in the suburbs, it was visibly free of the morning rush-hour. The day had started well.

Stephen signed in at the desk and was given a visitor's pass. As usual, he took a seat and picked up a magazine to read. It was the supplier's propaganda, of course, but it was quite interesting, nevertheless. He started to read about current research and development. Nothing technical, of course, in case anything useful fell into a competitor's hands.

"Good morning. How are you? Not too tired?" It was the manufacturer's service manager.

"Not at all," said Stephen. "I came down last night by train. Am I the first?"

"You're the second. We're all meeting up in the cafeteria."

Stephen followed his guide down the stairs and picked up a coffee and a biscuit from the bar before sitting down beside the others. They were now four.

Three to come. He toasted his hosts and asked, "How are things on your side of the table?"

"Very well. Our new vehicles are proving very popular. No new problems to report." Yes, the service manager would be expected to say that.

Stephen had wanted to ask for the unofficial response to the compressor issue but he didn't want to be in the middle of that when Lockhart arrived. His colleague didn't seem to be particularly interested either, so he simply asked if anyone had made holiday plans.

He had almost got a response when he heard a cheerful 'Good morning' from the staircase from reception. Lockhart.

"A coffee here, or shall we just go up to the meeting room?" asked one of the hosts.

And that's where they went.

The meeting took up most of the day, the most interesting part being lunch. The first item to be dealt with had been the air system. The manufacturer reminded them of the importance of ensuring that preventative maintenance was carried out correctly, particularly the frequent replacement of air filters, and ensuring that they were genuine parts approved by the manufacturer. Not aftermarket equivalents. Ouch. That was unfair. But deserved.

There was good news. The manufacturer announced that there was now an improved compressor available, and if this was phased in, the problems would reduce significantly.

Lockhart said that he would recommend that to the board. And no doubt take the credit for the solution. Stephen had wanted to interrupt and say that this compressor should have been specified when the vehicles were being ordered, and if his air filter modification was adopted, the problem would be solved completely.

The other items on the agenda were covered and action points agreed for the next meeting. It was then time to set off home. Stephen was given a lift to the station and he made sure that he bought a newspaper before boarding the train. He would need some crosswords and sudokus to bring back his sanity.

*

Interestingly, the following morning's news was that the new divisional MD had appointed Lockhart to specify new vehicles in future. It was of, course, something that needed to be done, but couldn't he have found someone better suited to the task?

Whatever optimism Stephen had had about things improving, the news of Lockhart being given such an important responsibility simply said that things would in fact get worse. That was then confirmed by news that the idiot who had moved the vehicle wash at head office was going to assist him. This truly was the end.

Stephen had, rather bravely, just opened his second e-mail when Felix appeared at his desk. "Well. How did it go?" Felix asked.

"How did what go? My meeting yesterday? That's old news. Look at Lockhart's latest e-mail. It's official. All of us in the central team have to examine and approve a number of these lookalike parts. And when we've done that, we'll get more. Until everything we buy has been replaced with a kid-on equivalent."

"And if you don't approve them?"

"That hasn't been said in as many words, but it's a threat. Do it, or you're out the door."

"So why not just approve them?"

"Don't be ridiculous. But have you seen the other e-mail where we've been told that Lockhart will now also be specifying new vehicles?"

"I'm afraid I have. It's all over, isn't it?"

"If it's of any consolation, I'm in complete agreement with you."

Chapter 20
Farewell

Eventually, the only thing that helped Stephen get through each day was a spreadsheet that he had set up on his computer. For his last eighteen months with the organisation, the organisation that had been his life, he crossed off each day, one at a time.

He began to think about where he would spend his summer holiday. It would have to be very carefully planned if he was going to be sufficiently engrossed in it to forget about the job. He knew that because his colleagues were also finding it difficult to switch off.

Things changed when a routine visit to his general practitioner gave him a health scare. Probably a stress symptom, he was told. Would rage not be a better word, he mused? The word, of course, did not matter. His summer holiday was spent, along with some of his savings, undergoing an exploratory operation. He was mobile just in time to return to work, but at least he could cross off sixteen days from the table.

The next few months' activities were simply more of the same. Responding to e-mails and taking part in the weekly telephone conferences. He didn't even bother contacting Lockhart after any of them to advise him of alternative action to that which had been agreed. It wasn't worth the usual bristling response, even if his advice was eventually taken.

"I don't know how you remain so polite," Joe had said, after one of Lockhart's rants.

"It was the way I was brought up. Stand up when a lady enters the room. Put other peoples' needs before your own," was Stephen's reply.

But now not everything was the same. The weekly after-work drink that Stephen, Felix and Joe had always anticipated, and nearly always enjoyed, was a thing of the past. They still met up at work if some activity required two or all three of them, but otherwise, they sat at their computers and read through the endless e-mails. Most of them seemed to be from people in other group companies simply trying to be seen toeing the line, and probably because of that, they were now achieving less than they used to.

They no longer dared use their experience to support colleagues at the coal face to keep vehicles on the road and bring in customer revenue. The business was now all packaging and no content.

Stephen began to feel more remote, less aware of how the business was doing in the operating company where he was based, quite apart from across the group where his established contacts were no doubt in a similar situation. Stephen had no particular question to ask, but one morning, he received a phone call from a colleague in the central team. "What are you up to?" he asked.

"Up to my neck in rubbish," said Stephen.

"What kind of rubbish?"

"The same as you, no doubt. Home-made vehicle spares. I'm just wondering how to word my memo to Lockhart. He's asked me to approve them but they're rubbish. I can't give my approval for them." Stephen reflected for a moment and continued. "He gave me three items to take away and approve at the last meeting, and luckily, I didn't have to ask anyone to fit them to a vehicle and monitor them."

"What did you do?"

"I went down to a workshop and cut them open. Luckily the photos were self-explanatory. I didn't really need to say anything. They were just poor copies of a genuine spare part. From the outside, they looked genuine, but the internal structure was very poor and they certainly wouldn't have performed as well as a genuine part. I didn't have the material properties investigated by a specialist; I didn't need to go as far as that, but that was certainly an option."

"Have you sent your report to Lockhart?"

"I have, but there's been no reply so far."

"I'll see if I can stall him for a while. Let me know if you do get a response, Stephen."

"Will do."

Stephen hadn't been surprised by that exchange, but he was slightly apprehensive about the next contact that Lockhart would make with him. When it finally came, it was an e-mail to the others in the vetting team and it highlighted the advice that Stephen had given him. Stephen had simply been copied in.

A moment of relief, but across the division, there was no longer a desire to exchange notes with colleagues in other group companies, some of them friends going back many years. No enquiries about what had happened during the week, the good and the bad. There was also no interest in what might lie ahead, what they might achieve, individually or collectively.

Almost without exception, everyone now came to work because they had to, not because they wanted to. The exceptions were the new people appointed by Lockhart for the purchasing project. They were too new to know how to contribute to the business. Lockhart had once boasted about having spies, but these people didn't show enough interest in the business to spy. What could they tell him? We arrived late. We left early. We've asked about our annual leave entitlement.

Another e-mail. Stephen had to meet up with Lockhart next week for his annual appraisal. And, when the day came, it was Stephen who had to travel across the country.

"What have you achieved this year?" he was asked.

Stephen unenthusiastically ran through the list of the major issues in which Lockhart knew he had been involved.

"Yes. Good," said Lockhart. Notes were taken as each project was discussed. "You'll be able to retire in a few months, but you're aware that it isn't compulsory?"

'I can't wait,' thought Stephen before saying, "Yes, I am aware of that, but I will be retiring." Retiring without a pension from an organisation that probably wouldn't have survived without him. When Stephen had rejoined the group some fourteen years earlier, Derek had gone out of his way to ask HR to put him in the scheme before the closing date. They did bugger all. Did that count as gross misconduct?

"Have you thought about consultancy?" asked Lockhart.

'Of course, I have. How will I survive otherwise?' he thought. "No, I haven't," he said.

"Bear it in mind," said Lockhart. "There's still time."

The blame culture continued. An experienced and effective depot engineering manager was dismissed. Had he failed to salute? Had he failed to polish his protective footwear?

One morning, Felix opened a threatening e-mail from Lockhart. Why had he questioned a delivery from a new supplier? "What do I reply to that?" Felix asked.

"Tomorrow's Saturday," said Stephen. "We could meet in your office and I'll draft something for you."

On Monday, Stephen was called over to read Lockhart's response. 'Well done,' it said. 'You did exactly what I would have done.'

Stephen looked up and shook his head. "He's shameless, isn't he?" Lockhart would apparently give the supplier a wrap over the knuckles. "Is that what it's like having children?" Stephen asked.

Back at his computer, Stephen opened an e-mail from Jason and he noted that Mike had been copied in. Jason was obviously wanting to make a point. However, instead of responding, Stephen put on his high viz vest and walked over to see what the problem was.

"Read this e-mail," said Jason.

"I've seen it."

"I know you have. We're all copied in. Read it and tell me how I should reply."

"He's only asking how vehicle reliability can be improved. He's mentioned two of yours but remember that we persuaded the manufacturer to improve the fuel tank design. They say they'd modified them all, but it's worth checking that they didn't miss these two, or if their agent didn't carry out the modification correctly."

"Thanks."

Press cuttings were often circulated to staff, but only the good ones. Newspapers and even the trade press were often less flattering.

"Have you seen that?" asked Felix. "I wonder if our competitors feel sorry for us."

"I doubt it," said Stephen. "They probably think we're all tarred by the same brush. At least it's winter and we can go around under the cover of darkness."

He was about to add, 'at least I'll be retiring in four weeks' time, but he stopped himself at the last minute. He didn't want any kind of formal send-off. One was probably already being planned but he didn't want to raise the issue.

What was there to celebrate? A wasted life?

He found out from HR that the day before his birthday would be his last with the organisation. "Remember to return all the company's property: your laptop, your mobile phone, etcetera," they said.

"Can you give me a hand rewording an e-mail?" Felix had appeared out of nowhere.

"Sure."

"I'll be back at my desk."

That was the one pleasure left in this evil empire: telling someone senior what they didn't know and managing to build in a sting in the tail that they wouldn't notice. Even vehicle manufacturers were visiting less regularly, no longer doing small favours or asking how things were going. The threatening letters and phone calls from the centre had certainly distanced them.

Eventually, Stephen's last day had arrived and no doubt everyone assumed that he would still be there the following day.

From midday, his desk became progressively tidier as things were filed away. E-mails were still arriving and receiving responses. Just before the secretaries were due to go home, Stephen picked up his laptop and mobile phone and took them through to their office.

They both looked genuinely shocked when he told them that he was leaving. Task completed? No, Felix stopped him on the way back to his desk. "What are you up to? You can't be leaving."

"You've got it in one."

"But you can't. We'll have to arrange something for you."

"Of course," said Stephen. "We'll go for a drink some time. We can try and work out why we failed to influence the centre. Were we not up to it, or did we simply not try hard enough?"

"No, we didn't try at all. We acted out what we had learned during our time in the business, we did our jobs as well as we could, but we didn't lift our heads too far above the parapet. And that's probably true of many people in other organisations. Basically, they all have to do as they're told. If they don't, they'd be disciplined or dismissed."

"My job was initially to advise the chief executive, and if I found a problem, I would tell him. But finding out that something was a problem usually also directed you to the solution. If something had turned out the wrong way, you simply looked to see what would have made it a success. Problem solved.

"Anyway, I'm leaving the place now. And at least I'll enjoy my retirement."

"No, you won't," said Felix, and Stephen knew that he was right.

*

A few days later, Stephen happened to meet a friend in the street.

"You look different," he was told. "I've never seen you so relaxed."

He knew that he had been stressed out over the last few years, but he was disappointed that he obviously hadn't been able to disguise his feelings.

He knew that he had been blamed by Eadie for something, and for some reason, Eadie had told Lockhart that Stephen was potentially dangerous for the organisation and that he should be micro-managed. Lockhart had certainly done that, and that was the principal reason for Stephen retiring as soon as he could.

His subconscious mind had begun to ask itself why the final years at work had been so stressful and it was quite clear that Lockhart's micro-management, as well as the harm that he had done to the organisation to which Stephen had given so much, had been the cause.

Yes, Lockhart had given himself away at a meeting with a supplier when he had rudely interrupted Stephen's explanation of pricing structures. And now Alan's description of something questionable that Eadie had done during the creation of the group also had come to mind.

A supplier to the parts company that Stephen had been encouraged to fix had involved a member of a regulatory authority in his attempt to find out more about the previous ownership of the company. It might have owed him some money; why else do such a thing?

Did the regulatory authority then approach Eadie? And did they say that Stephen had involved them, or had Eadie simply jumped to that conclusion? In a brain containing only testosterone, that was very possible.

Why had Stephen not realised that something like that must have happened when Eadie had shown him the door seventeen years earlier? Quite simply, he had paid the price for being well brought up, for not always fighting his corner. Yes, he should have cornered Eadie, who would, of course, have backed down. Stephen had never forgotten Eadie's reaction to his response to his bullying not long after they had first met.

A lesson learned, albeit too late.

*

Work might have gone but e-mails remained a part of his life. 'Congratulations on your retirement' was the typical message. A more direct one was from Felix. 'Some of your friends want to take you out for a meal. Let me know when you're free.'

The local supermarket had a large choice of newspapers in its café and a morning visit to keep up with national and international events now became a new routine for Stephen. He felt no immediate need to revisit the organisation and risk bringing back bad memories. The supermarket visits lasted a few months but slowly his thoughts began to recall the good times, moments of satisfaction obtained simply from solving a problem or helping a colleague by making their working day less stressful.

He had always said that he only went to work because he needed the money; if he hadn't, he could have done whatever came into his mind: a holiday, researching something of interest in a library, learning a language. But because he had to devote a major part of his waking life to work, he had always been determined to get every last drop of satisfaction from it. Memories of the good moments started to convince him that perhaps things hadn't been so bad after all.

*

A phone call from Felix. And, after an exchange of polite chat, there was the invite to join some colleagues for dinner. Would he accept? Of course. It was a kind offer, and it would be good to see them all again.

There were six people at the table: one director, two colleagues from other departments, Felix, Joe and Stephen.

"I'll buy the wine," Stephen said. "As I recall, the main board used up the group's entire drinks budget."

"So, what's it like to be away?" Joe asked.

"What's it like still to be there?"

As if they had rehearsed it, the others all groaned.

"But since you ask," Stephen continued, "I'm as busy as ever but now I'm a student again."

"What are you studying?"

"Writing. My biggest regret was staying with this place – that place – instead of doing my PhD. So, I'm catching up on reading. The next stage will be to read up on the economy. I recently attended an interesting talk by a visiting lecturer on economics. So maybe there will be room for a fresh opinion. But how is 'that place'?"

As expected, Felix spoke up first. "You wouldn't have believed it possible, but it's still getting worse. Some more people have left, some have been sacked, and it's so amateurish."

"Yes," said Stephen. "I've been keeping an eye on it. These new experts tried to sell some depots that I helped to improve about sixteen years ago. In the end, the competitors just moved in and took over the customers."

"You're right," said Felix. "That's a new low, even for us. And it's not the first time it's happened in the last few months. Everyone's just waiting to see who gets sacked next."

"So, nothing amusing has happened?" said Stephen.

"There's been an injection of new vehicles, expensive-to-maintain fuel guzzlers," Felix replied.

"We're just waiting for it to dawn on them that they didn't specify them correctly and then a few years down the road the board will have cleared off before it becomes obvious that we aren't able to maintain them. As long as they get themselves another six-figure salary."

"It's seven we go for now," said Joe.

"Before I forget," said Felix, "the folk back at the ranch signed a card for you."

That would be a good souvenir.

Stephen read through the signatures, and a face and a voice briefly represented each one. And each face had a smile, a souvenir of happier times.

"You're looking emotional," said Felix.

"Am I letting it show? I didn't mean to."

"Well, maybe emotional is too strong a word, but I think that you're glad that you've got it."

Stephen nodded, then looked around the table. Everyone was engaged in conversation, listening, interrupting, laughing. No doubt the wine was helping, loosening tongues, allowing them to recall enjoyable events from the past. He had been stressed out by the pressure that he had been under over the last few years. Perhaps they hadn't, or were they simply better at concealing it?

"Your glass is empty." He looked up. Joe was standing at his side with two bottles.

"Red or white?" asked Joe.

"Red, please. You'd make a good wine waiter."

"I'm just trying out a number of possibilities in case I get shown the door."

"And what other careers would you consider?"

"Is this a serious question? You definitely need more wine. Come on. Tell me what this one's like."

Stephen took a mouthful. "It's very good."

"Better than the last one?"

"Yes, it is."

"It's just the same as the last one."

He'd been caught out. His defences were down. But he no longer needed them. He could now simply be someone sitting on a park bench, watching the world go by. Though sitting in a restaurant, as he was now, was much more interesting.

He was with one of his families, and it was amusing watching them chilling out in an environment so different from the one in which they had co-existed for so many years.

They hadn't all worked closely together; they were in different functions of the business, and they had all got to know each other well through the years. Stephen wondered what they would find to talk about and he was surprised to note how much they all knew about what the others had been doing on a day-to-day basis. This was no doubt the informal organisation at work again. The workplace equivalent of the brain's synapses.

He was just glad that he had been invited and they had all seemed genuinely pleased to see him.

*

Over the next few months, the e-mails became less frequent but a growing recommended reading list replaced them. More little epiphany moments, and the better ones noted down in a diary.

His phone rang. "Hi, it's Felix. Did you know that Lockhart's handed in his notice?"

"I hadn't heard."

"He must be missing you or missing being able to present your work as his."

"A nice thought," Stephen replied. "But it could be that he's finally realised how insane that purchasing project was."

"In that case, it's taken about a year for the penny to drop."

"Just because he had a big head doesn't mean it contained any bright ideas," Stephen replied.

"But the question remains. Why didn't you tell Eadie what a danger Lockhart was to us? It was your role to tell him."

"Yes, I should have told him. That was my role."

Chapter 21
On looking back

"The usual?" Felix asked, although he knew that was unnecessary.

"Please," said Joe.

"We're early. Stephen isn't due for another half hour."

"Gives us plenty of time to gossip."

"Let's sit over there," said Felix, "and we can keep an eye on the door. Cheers."

"Cheers, although I don't know why we said that," Joe continued. "When you look back to when we all first met, you couldn't have imagined then what would have happened to the place."

"But we didn't think about that at the time. We were too busy working out how to fit in. We would just assume that the place would stay the same or get better, but you wouldn't think for a minute that it would fall apart."

"Can't disagree," said Joe. "You assumed that the old folk had been there all their lives and you would eventually end up like them. If you asked your journeyman a question, he could answer it. If you made a mess of something, he would correct it for you, show you what you'd done wrong. Now you've got new folk at every level, and almost none of them from our business."

"Don't mention that to Stephen," said Felix. "He blames himself for that, for all of it. Apparently, he once told Eadie that he wished the place was more like the army. He only wanted the place to be better organised."

"His human machine?"

"Exactly. He always told me that he wanted the place to be better disciplined so he could push through improvements more quickly. No 'double handling' as he would say. Wait, there he is now. Over here!"

"You two look very comfortable," said Stephen. "In for the long haul?"

"Only as long as memory lane," said Joe, standing up. "What are you drinking?"

"I'll have what you're having," Stephen replied, taking off his coat.

"How's life?" asked Felix. "Have you recovered from the place yet?"

"I'm still fond of it," Stephen replied, "but, yes, I'm glad to be away."

"Do you remember when you and I first met?" Felix asked.

"As if it were yesterday. I'd joined the organisation a year earlier and I was with the work study team based in the central workshop. I was responsible for producing job times for repair and maintenance work, but when I told management how we could avoid the early failures of one particular unit, they suggested that I apply to join the technical team up in head office. I did, and that's when we met."

"I'd started as a management trainee, but I didn't have any clear idea of what my next step would be."

"Your drink," said Joe. "Felix and I were talking about the old days…"

"The good old days," Felix corrected him.

Joe raised his glass. "So, how did it all begin?"

Felix toasted the other two. "Begin, or begin to go wrong?"

"Well, both."

"The organisation as we know it today probably began where we did," said Stephen. "The three of us learned the business there, and we were probably lucky to have joined an organisation that felt like a large family: people who had been here for a number of years, were quite confident in their roles, and understood how they interfaced with each other. They didn't feel threatened by newcomers, and that in turn meant that I didn't feel threatened when I started. However, that doesn't mean that I didn't feel slightly insecure."

Felix put his glass down and said, "Since I'd started as a management trainee, I just did as I was told and eventually, I understood how to perform my tasks and how they related to what my colleagues were doing, how we were contributing to the functioning of the organisation."

"Me too," said Joe.

"I wasn't at the beginning of my career," Stephen continued, "but I was certainly regarded as somebody new. I had studied the theoretical approach to solving problems, but suddenly, I had to learn how to do it for real."

"When you visited your first depot and the foreman looked you up and down as if to say 'What does he know about this business'? That's right, isn't it," asked Felix.

"You remembered," said Stephen.

"How could I forget? You told me about it often enough." Felix laughed.

"Sorry about that, but it did make an impression on me: one of my epiphany moments. But the first one had been when an older member of the work study team said to me that…"

Felix butted in. "Work study does not ask what is done; work study asks what is achieved."

"You remembered that as well?" said Stephen.

"I did."

"And so did I," said Joe.

"Should I go home and leave you two in peace?" asked Stephen.

"Definitely not. You're getting the next round," said Joe. "But do you remember the first time that we met?"

"Of course. We were discussing the modification that we had devised to repair the structural problems that we were experiencing on one type of vehicle, the type that made up the majority of the fleet at that time. You told me that Eadie had called you up to his office and given you a bad time."

"I'd missed a day-release class, but I hadn't thought he'd have been aware of that. He got wired into me to the point I thought I should maybe leave."

"And why didn't you?"

"My parents would have continued where he left off."

"So, your parents effectively made you stay?"

"They did. But when Eadie left, I began to enjoy coming to work again. I was part of a team, a family away from home. People got on with their own jobs, but they were experienced enough to know what other folk did, and if any of them were struggling, they would help them out. Teamwork."

Stephen interrupted this time. "Synergy. The whole is greater than the sum of the parts."

"You mean, one plus one equals three?"

"Thank you, Felix. That's one way of putting it."

"And what about Eadie promising to take you and your team leader out for a meal after you helped prepare him for a conference."

"Yes. I certainly learned something that day," said Stephen.

"What did you learn?" Joe asked.

"I learned that not all people at work are motivated in the same way. Some really don't care about the company or the other people in it; they just care about themselves," Stephen replied.

"And is that a bad thing?" asked Joe.

"Not in itself. Not if they seek their rewards through making the company more successful." said Stephen.

"And did Eadie make it more successful?" asked Joe.

"What do you think?" answered Stephen. "He had nothing to offer except determination. For him, size mattered. It was as simple as that."

"And buying companies for more than they were worth and then making them worse than they were before," Felix interjected.

Joe smiled before turning back to Stephen.

"But Eadie, he took your advice for a while?"

"Until somebody slandered me," Stephen replied. "That's probably why Lockhart saw his job as keeping an eye on me. It took me a while to work out what happened but then I remembered something that Alan said to me just before he retired. I put two and two together. Eadie had blamed me for something that somebody else had done, and Lockhart seemed to have picked up that I was somebody dangerous."

"You, dangerous?" Felix nearly choked. "If anybody was, it was Lockhart."

"Well," said Stephen, "if you're being fussy, the problems began with the appointment of Harold as head of engineering. He knew almost nothing about our business."

"So, who chose him? Eadie?" Joe asked.

"The board no doubt approved of the appointment," said Stephen, "but yes, Eadie probably had the final say. And Harold's boss, the newly appointed director, again with no experience of our business, was no doubt delighted when Harold said we were overstaffed. Think of the praise he would get when he told the board about all the money he could save them."

"Wait a minute," Felix said, butting in. "Was he the one who told his colleagues, 'Get your nose in the trough, this won't last for ever'?"

"So, I was told."

"And does that mean that you're saying that all directors should have come from our business?"

"No, I'm not saying that," said Stephen. "The board should be able to manage the company, all aspects of the company, and be able to guide it through its environment. And that includes looking out for opportunities and threats and being able to understand and manage them. Board members should also work as a carefully designed team that ensures that the organisation is efficient and successful."

"And it also means no bullying? We used to say that good morale's like an extra pair of hands and low morale's like the handbrake going on," said Joe.

"You did, and you're even using Stephen's analogy of the human machine." Turning to Stephen, Felix went on, "Joe and I were talking about that just before you arrived, and I don't think it's as stupid an idea as I did before. And now obviously Joe's adopted it."

"I'm glad," said Stephen, "because I still think that it's a really useful model. If you ignore music, my main interest in life is motor cars. I love them. And if you look closely at a car, it's made up of thousands of components, each one designed to do a specific job without being overstressed. So, a team of people should be designed to do a specific job, the whole team carefully assembled in order to ensure that all requirements are covered and each member of the team is comfortable with the role they're playing. And I saw that again in just-in-time manufacturing.

"Stress can certainly come from bullying, but it can also come from being forced to play a role for which people haven't been fully trained – or a role they don't like. And that's a very common problem."

"I've certainly seen the effects of that," Joe replied. "Not so much in my team, but certainly in the operating depots."

"But another reason I like the comparison with a machine is because it catches peoples' attention," said Stephen. "Their first reaction is to think that it's a stupid analogy. I remember seeing the film Modern Times starring Charlie Chaplin. At one point, his character is working on a production line and he gets swept into the huge, uncaring machine. So, people are immediately shocked by the comparison, but when they think about it, they understand exactly what I'm saying. Design teams of people with care, let them play a role that they enjoy, thank them for their work, and they become unstoppable."

"You've said that before," said Felix.

Joe took another sip from his glass before putting it down. "I hear what you're saying."

Stephen continued. "To go back to cars, a roadwheel has been designed to play its role, and do so reliably. It's happy doing what it was designed to do. A steering wheel's different. It's happy as well, providing you leave it on the end of the steering column, but it wouldn't want to replace a roadwheel. Would it?"

"That's so true," said Joe. "I'm lucky that my team are one step back from the day-to-day activity of the business and we get left pretty much alone. We're relatively happy at work these days."

"While we're discussing bullying and motivation," said Stephen, "when Eadie invited me to rejoin the business twenty years ago, twenty-one years ago, I turned up in the group's first major acquisition and met the team there. The business had been run down quite deliberately by the previous owners to make it look more profitable, so things were a bit tough. The engineering director showed me around and it was quite apparent to both of us what actions had to be taken.

"It was the end of my first week there when Eadie turned up out of the blue. He started his bullying routine and I nearly walked out. I thought, why should I waste my time helping to fix a mess that he and his board hadn't been able to deal with. Stupidly, I stayed. It was a really enjoyable, satisfying year but I should have thought more about my career and gone elsewhere. That's probably one of the greatest regrets of my life. That, and not undertaking a PhD after my business course."

Felix looked concerned. "And you still regret that now?"

"Yes, very much so."

"So, what about the first major acquisition? Do you also regret that?" Felix then asked. "Because you carried on with the same approach when you started back here, when, five years later?"

"As I said, I found the job satisfying. Once you've found out how to fix something, and then find yourself in a similar situation, all your instincts are simply to do what you did before. Experience makes things so much easier, providing the new situation's sufficiently different to present a challenge."

"We'd certainly been run into the ground," Joe said, sighing.

"But that didn't stop Eadie being made to pay twice what we were worth, did it?" Felix added. "None of us will forget that."

"I won't either," Stephen said. "Something I've never forgotten was turning up at a depot just after I'd started back and seeing the drivers' car park full of brand-new, high-end cars."

Felix explained. "When our MD forced Eadie to pay twice what the company was worth, all employees got a share. You came back too late, didn't you? Anyway, Stephen, you haven't really answered the question. Why did you stay with the first major acquisition?"

"Simply because I enjoyed being able to make continuous improvements, to see people's morale improve on a daily basis. But the main question for me was, who should be allowed to be a manager? Or a director?"

"Another lesson learned?" asked Felix.

"Yes, Felix, it was. I believe that senior managers need to be chosen with more care than they are."

"Now tell us what you learned next."

"Is this an interview, Felix?"

"We're the jailers; you're the prisoner. Now get on with it."

"In that case, confession time. Like most people, I go to work because I'm poor: I need the money. So, while I'm spending the greater part of my waking day away from home, I want to ensure that I find each day as satisfying as I would if I could have been attending concerts, reading books, learning new things."

"So, what made you stay?" Joe still wanted to know.

"Loyalty. I was brought up to put other peoples' needs before my own. And I paid a price for that, a big one. But to be honest, if some people didn't act like that, the world would be a worse place than it is today."

"Another drink?" asked Felix. "After that, you deserve one. Mind you, it's your round."

"I assume it's the usual?" Stephen said before going over to the bar.

"Felix, would you be loyal, I mean, as loyal as that?" Joe asked when they were alone again.

"Maybe not as loyal as that, but yes, I'm loyal and so are you. Most of us are."

"But bullying can affect that."

"So, Jason was right all these years ago. The folk at the top think about themselves and the folk at the coal face think about the business."

"I think he was, but it's not just here. I meet folk from competitors, I meet friends in the street, and it really is a universal problem."

"Sorry to interrupt," said Stephen. "Can you each grab a glass?"

"Sure. Thanks, Stephen, but carry on. What did you do next?"

"I moved up to head office and I assumed that it would be for a few months. It ended up as three and a half years. The new acquisition was based there, but I had a few weeks to look around. I went to the main depot where I'd put in the new vehicle cleaning system a few years earlier. It was interesting to see the core business operating in a different setting, but that was when I first met Sandy."

Felix put his glass down. "I remember him saying that."

"In fact, a small project suddenly appeared from nowhere. He was having problems with the brakes on his vehicles, and they had only started after the new acquisition began relining his brake shoes in their workshop. The problem was that one vehicle type demanded that the shoes were removed and refitted in pairs. Now, doing them in bulk, that gave Sandy a problem. We just made a tool to measure them and match them in pairs again. But while I was doing that, I also got a chance to see the new acquisition in operation."

"And how was it?" Felix was determined to learn more.

"It was a good purchase in theory, but not in practice. It had simply been overvalued. When Thomas was explaining how it was managed, it was obvious he had a poor understanding of what was going on. And when Eadie, in turn, asked me to explain what I'd found, I assumed that I'd done my job. I had expected to be given another project."

"And you weren't?"

"No, I spent three more years trading through overvalued stock until the company was worth what they'd paid for it."

"What happened then?"

"They sold it, and Eadie told me I should leave."

"After all that, he just said you should go. No wonder you were desperate to retire. But were there any good moments?"

"Of course, there were. For example, I'd like to think that I taught them due diligence."

"Show me the evidence," Felix interjected.

"You've got me there. But, as I was saying, on looking back, being micro-managed was another reason that I should have walked out."

"And, again, you didn't. So, effectively, when you started back here, you were in disgrace," Felix laughed.

Stephen was reminded of something else. "Do you remember the day that Thomas turned up with his new sidekick and was asking about glass costs?"

"I do," said Felix. "And I asked you to explain to him how the costs arose."

"He gave me some slimy look and asked if I was behaving myself."

"Yes. I couldn't believe that."

"My instinct was to reply that I was the better brought-up of the two of us and I always behaved well. As usual, I said nothing, but it did make me wonder why he'd said what he had. And now we know."

"Oh, what a tangled web we weave," said Felix.

"Walter Scott's Marmion. I didn't know you liked poetry, Felix," said Stephen.

"I don't. I read that in a Christmas cracker."

Joe just shook his head. "But if you were a bad employee," he said, "what about that head of purchasing and his board-approved plan to buy pretend spare parts in order to save a fortune?"

"Now that you mention him," Felix said, "I read somewhere that he later said that you always learn from your mistakes."

Joe countered with, "That's not acceptable at that level. If you're an apprentice, you can learn. But those in a senior position are there because they've got beyond that. What about an airline pilot, what about a brain surgeon?" Joe nodded. "That's teamwork again, isn't it? And on that note, should I get another round?"

"Please."

Joe went back to the bar and Stephen and Felix emptied their glasses.

They were both lost in thought for a few moments until Felix said, "It is all about teamwork. When people are encountering something they've never seen before, they have to understand it. Feeling that they're part of a team helps them put new things into context. But, as you've always said, evolution is normal. Sometimes step-changes require to be addressed, new technologies arrive, new legislation has to be met. And the teams have to be able to adapt."

Joe arrived back with the drinks. "What are you two talking about?"

"Change. New vehicle types. New legislation. You name it."

"That's easy," Joe said, putting the glasses down on the table. "Stephen keeps going on about it. All problems are solved backwards. You've told us that often enough."

"We weren't talking about that," said Felix, reaching for his glass. "We were talking about people working together."

"I know you were," said Joe. "I was just winding you up. But, if change is required, you have to be clear where you're going before you set off, otherwise you could end up anywhere. It's the game where you have to change one word into another, one letter at a time, but still making a complete word at each move. The business has to continue operating at all stages of the process. Am I right?"

"You are indeed," said Felix. "If you need to train people, you do. And, if you need new skills, you employ the appropriate people. If you can take an objective view of what's happening, it's not difficult."

"You make it sound easy," Joe sighed, "but that's not my experience of how things usually happen."

"You're right," said Stephen, "because there are so many variables. Personal ambitions, qualifications, experience to date, but as he's just said, if you are clear where you want to go, you can design a team to achieve exactly that."

Felix smiled. "After three pints, I should want to disagree with that. But I can't. I just hope our place is fixed. Do you agree, Joe?"

"Totally."

"Well, I hope for both your sakes it is fixed," said Stephen.

"And what are you doing now?"

"I've gone back to university," said Stephen.

"To design your human machine?"

"Why didn't I think of that? Your good health."

Chapter 22
The limits of mankind

Receiving the phone call wasn't a complete surprise. Stephen assumed that his name must have come up when Charles had last met Felix.

"What are you doing tomorrow evening?" Charles asked. "I'll be in your part of the country visiting some clients, and it would be good to catch up."

Stephen was pleased to receive the call.

"Just say where and when, and I'll choose the venue. And you'll be my guest," he replied.

"I could be as early as five if everything goes to plan. And let's make it that great restaurant with the roof terrace; you know the one? But we'll go fifty-fifty. I remember that you would never let suppliers invite you."

"Five o'clock tomorrow evening. I'll be waiting."

*

"You seem really engrossed in that."

Stephen looked up. "I'm always engrossed. But it's great to see you. Take a seat. You'll see I'm on white wine. What can I get you?"

"I'll have the same."

Stephen signalled the waiter and pointed to the glass. "You're looking well, Charles."

"But not as well as you. How do you feel to have escaped?"

"Mixed feelings. I miss the job; it was a really important part of my life. And I miss my colleagues. But the atmosphere in the place had become so awful that I retired as soon as I was sixty-five."

"But that's normal, isn't it?"

"It's normal, but not compulsory. I think the government would have been happy that another old person was still in work. But now I might be able to start achieving things again."

"Such as?"

"Undertaking a PhD. I had actually enquired about doing that when I was about to complete my MBA. And one of the professors was quite interested. Unfortunately, I gave all my attention to my job and I now regret that. My dissertation was going to be on the economy. What is money and where does it come from? The goal would be to learn how to control it."

The waiter discreetly put the glass down on the table.

"Your health," said Charles. "And good luck with that, Stephen. But, for interest, why did you choose the career that you did?"

"The main profession in my family was medicine; there were a couple of lawyers and my father was a civil servant. I was well aware of that from a very young age, but motor cars were the things that had always fascinated me. And, later, when most of my school friends were spending their weekly pocket money on comics, I saved up and spent mine on a monthly car magazine."

"That explains a lot."

"It does. I studied engineering, and in the final year of the course, I was introduced to work study and I was fascinated by it. As soon as I graduated, I found a job in the work study department of a healthcare organisation. I enjoyed it, but I missed road vehicles. So, when I saw a transport company advertise for a work study practitioner, I applied and I was lucky. And that's where I learned to distinguish between doing and achieving. That leads you straight on to job design."

"Making people work faster?"

"Charles, what a cruel idea. No, the answer is quite the opposite. Work study has two main approaches: work measurement and method study. Measurement teaches you to apply a rating to the speed of work and method study teaches you to be able to design jobs.

"You can certainly incentivise people to work faster but I first looked for greater gains from analysing working processes. The fact that learning curves can show that improvements of ten times or more possibly made me focus on job design."

"But people learning a new job will always speed up as they master the techniques."

"Very true, but that's not what I'm talking about. I'm looking at the whole manufacturing process, including both their job and those of their colleagues. You can also get the benefits of synergy."

"The last time I saw Felix, we discussed your human machine."

"Exactly."

"But don't you also have to ensure that everybody pulls their weight?"

"I wondered about that at first, but I later learned that it needn't be a problem."

"And where did you learn that?"

"After completing my business course, I got a job in the electronics industry where they manufactured wiring harnesses and circuit boards for major clients. I arrived at the same time as they had employed external consultants to convert them from batch production to just-in-time."

"Yes, I've seen that in action. Some of my suppliers use it. It's impressive."

"Converting raw materials to finished products was reduced from weeks to hours. And nobody worked faster than before. And, with operators in the JIT cell waiting for the first product of each customer order to reach their stage of the operation, you might even say that sometimes they worked more slowly than before."

"That seems too easy. Things don't always run so smoothly, do they?"

"They do not. So just imagine how much potential improvement is out there, just waiting for us to identify it and benefit from it."

"So, why haven't we identified it?"

"As a former colleague said, some people think about the job and others think about themselves."

"True. I've found that problem throughout my time in business, not in my own organisation, but with customers. But because I need to make sales, I just tailor my approach to the type of person I'm talking to."

"I don't envy you having to meet new people all the time and be nice to them, no matter how they speak to you. My job was just problem solving and so I didn't usually upset anyone. Suppliers were pleasant to me, and the majority of my colleagues were as well. I'd known many of them for years, and we became friends, almost family, and the newer colleagues at least realised that my role was to help them, and touch wood, I was always able to do that."

"So, why were you so anxious to retire if you loved the job so much?"

"Because it had changed so much. And the problems came from new people at the top. They didn't know the industry. We all assumed that they were simply in search of a high salary, and since they couldn't teach any of their juniors, they survived by ducking and weaving. And bullying."

"So, who appointed them?"

"That's the million-dollar question. If that could be solved, you would have the answer to just about every problem in business. And politics. Part of the problem is the CV that some people present. Some of the ones I've seen are genuinely impressive, but when we saw those of some of our new senior colleagues, they suddenly became unbelievable. They were lying, often presenting other people's work as their own."

"I never had to think about things like that, but I'm in total agreement. Anyway, Stephen, I suspect that the conversation is going to become even more intense. Shall we go through to dinner? And bring your glass. If you hadn't been talking so much, you would have noticed that mine was empty."

"Sorry. I was getting a bit carried away."

They both read the menu and placed their orders. Charles spoke first. "I suspect that this conversation is heading towards a well-designed organisational structure."

"That's exactly where it's going."

"Yes, Felix has told me that much."

"You mentioned that you've seen just-in-time manufacturing with some of your suppliers? Well, this is simply one step beyond that. The JIT team is formed to make one particular product. When the next product is being manufactured, it might require different processes and a reconfigured team. The organisation structures of most companies have evolved over a period of time to match their activities, and that's fine. However, when you look more closely, it's often apparent that some people aren't enjoying their jobs and it's always worth finding out why in case you can do something to help."

"What do you mean, 'help'?"

"Some people who are new to the job haven't been fully trained, and they can't keep up with the rest of their team. That can make them feel guilty or, in some cases, they'll be made to feel that they're not pulling their weight. And some people simply don't like the job and they leave. If you can train them, or move them to a role that they prefer, then you've helped."

Their orders arrived at the table.

"Interesting," said Charles, "but before you go on, you haven't touched your wine. You're making me feel guilty."

"Sorry. I suddenly felt that I was back at work, chatting about all the stupidity we saw around us."

"By 'around us', you really mean stupidity at the top?"

"Yes. It was as unambiguous as that. We all wanted to see more capable people at the top: people on the main board who could react to the marketplace and most importantly, know how to implement any changes that were necessary."

"It's easy when you know how. I assume that's what you're saying, even in such a roundabout way."

"That's exactly what I'm saying."

The waiter broke the flow of the conversation. "Is everything to your satisfaction?"

They had barely started the main course and therefore both nodded their heads. Stephen smiled.

"I didn't think you liked surprises, Stephen," said Charles. "Anyway, eat up or you'll be getting another one."

"Life would be boring without surprises, but I like good ones. Here, or at work. Life would be boring without change. Tasks at work become satisfying once you've mastered them, but once you have, you start looking for something new. Slow but progressive change is good. Evolution is normal, but revolution can be traumatic, and I saw that in the workplace. Work practices can change when, for example, new computer systems are introduced. People have to be trained in the new system, and then it takes them a while to master it. Vehicles were, of course, at the heart of our business…"

"They still are," said Charles helpfully.

"Quite so. And as I was saying, if a new vehicle type is introduced, operations staff and maintenance staff have to get used to it. But once they have, day to day operation settles down again. People know what has to be done and they are all comfortable in their roles. They enjoy the satisfaction they take from their work and they enjoy being part of an extended family. And that spills over from their own team to others. They know that people in other teams are also contributing to the overall operation."

"I agree totally with you, Stephen. Even in my company that's relatively small, people get satisfaction from their actions, helping the company move forward and they know what part each of them plays. And if anyone is off on holiday, the others are perfectly happy to adapt to covering their role."

"And you must have played a role in designing your team by understanding each role inside out. I assume that you've played every role in your company?"

"Yes, I have, but I've never really thought about that before."

"Well, there you are. That was another thing I learned from my business course. With so many disciplines today so advanced and complex, no one individual could fully understand them all. Therefore, a chief executive, for example, must create around him a team that can manage each activity necessary for the business."

"Again, I agree."

"And the components connect all the way to the coal face, where the product is delivered to the customer. That's all there is. It's universal."

"But do most organisations not already have that?"

"In principle, they do. Organisation structures usually match the needs of the business, but when changes are required, the response by management isn't always the right one. I've seen cases of workload going up because of a poor decision made at board level, and people simply having to try and live with the consequences."

"I see your glass is empty this time. I'll get you another one."

"Thanks, Charles. But to go back to the issue of the accuracy of CVs, there is of course an answer to that. Imagine you're a custom official. 'Is this your case, sir? May I look inside it'?"

"Unless you're a customs official who went to the same school as the traveller?"

"You've got it in one. And I believe that's more of a problem at senior levels in organisations."

"But at more junior levels, you would hope that the interviewer is simply trying to assess if the applicant could not only do the job, but also fit in."

"And if it's an internal applicant?"

"Well, if there's a vacancy, why not? That would be natural. And if there's a vacancy, it's usually better to promote from within. You know that you're getting experience, but it also improves the morale in the rest of the team."

"My own organisation's too small to allow me to predict what larger ones would do, but I understand what you're saying."

"Yes, most of the organisations I've worked for have been quite sizeable, and watching people at work has shown me that the more experienced people are usually more efficient than their newer colleagues," said Stephen.

"And is there a conclusion that you've drawn from that?"

"Yes, several. People perform best if they are good at the job. Sounds like a tautology, I know. But, like some wines, not this one, they get better with time, and so experience is important, very important. And most jobs interface with other ones. So, team players are important. And if people work together for long enough, they develop close bonds; they tend to look after each other. They know what they're meant to achieve as a team, and they set about their work collectively to make sure it's achieved."

"You're right, Stephen. But one of the reasons I work is to look after my children."

"Yes, I remember you mentioning that. The financial reward is important, but so too is job satisfaction. Solving problems and learning along the way. But helping people is also satisfying and being part of a team doing well is especially satisfying. Remember, humans are gregarious."

"My own team seem to get on well. I'm not always there, of course, but I get the impression that they regard the office as a home from home."

"We both seem to be quite clear that people have to be competent in their jobs, and happy, but the tasks they are given should also be designed to ensure that the business meets the needs of the customer. In our case, that includes managing the costs of the service we provide. As a supplier, I'm sure you're very aware of the problems that our purchasing people have caused."

"That's an understatement. When we first met, I think you were all relieved to get your hands on spare parts as soon as they were needed in order to get vehicles back on the road. And I think the prices we were charging were never an issue."

"Probably our hierarchy of needs. Get the vehicle back on the road, then make sure that our costs are managed."

"You studied Maslow's Hierarchy of Needs?"

"Yes. I found it remarkable. It allowed me to put things including business into some form of context: what human activities depend upon another? But to get back to purchasing, the major players in this business had brought component prices down to very competitive levels and that was never really an issue that required to be addressed. Our purchasing people at that time were sufficiently experienced to know that original-equipment quality had to be maintained otherwise vehicle reliability might be compromised. But the most important issue was the ownership cost of each part, not its purchase price. We looked at that in pence per mile operated."

"I was concerned when, out of the blue, your new purchasing people began to demand price cuts, and if I hadn't been able to comply, I'd have lost the business."

"To whom?"

"There were several competitors who were quite happy to buy on price, with no regard to quality. The customer is always right."

"The customer certainly should be right in our case. Our problem was that the board allowed the purchasing director to speak on our behalf. The person claiming to speak on our behalf should have been better managed. The chairman, or the chief executive, should have ensured that the director controlling each function of the business fully understood how that function operated – that it was designed to carry out its role in the day-to-day operation. If an individual director is incapable of doing that, he should either not have been appointed, or the other board members should have used their skills and experience to guide him in the right direction. That's what they're paid to do."

"I was concerned when I began getting these incessant demands to reduce prices. By keeping in touch with the operating companies, I knew where my products fitted into their operations. I also knew that this industry had a reputation for negotiating tight prices and so I'd given high discounts from the beginning. Then in order to meet these further demands, I had no choice but drop the quality of what I supplied."

"You certainly weren't the only supplier in that situation. We were having to deal with more and more poor-quality parts on a daily basis. We were being driven back into the swamp from which we'd worked so hard to escape."

"Felix was explaining how bad things are when I met up with him last week. And you're right. The mess you were in should have been quite apparent at board level, surely."

"It should have been, but either it wasn't, or they didn't know what to do."

"That's an interesting point. I think that I know everything about my business; I've been in it since I graduated. I know my staff; I know my customers and I know my suppliers. But I remember you talking about new-to-the-world products. And I would agree that not every change in the marketplace can be predicted."

"Yes, Charles, that term was one I learned from my business course, and why it stuck with me was that it reminded me of studying engineering. In the first two years we used slide rules, but in years three and four, they had been replaced by the electronic calculator. I wondered if slide rule manufacturers had seen that one coming."

"I'm not anticipating anything dramatic taking place in my industry, but I certainly couldn't rule it out. It would depend upon how quickly I became aware of the threat, but because of prices being driven down, I've already started to diversify: spread the risk."

"Good idea. I don't know if it's particularly relevant here, when you're speaking to colleagues, or in your case, customers; it's always interesting to try and read between the lines of what they're saying, what they really mean. I learned a lot from that, but I learned so much more by watching television programmes about wild animals. Mothers looking after their offspring, teaching them. The young then having to mix with their peers.

"And there's so much innate behaviour, and we see a lot of that in the things that people do. Road rage, for example. Civilisation truly is the very thin veneer over human behaviour, the acceptance that we all have to compromise some of our desires in order to benefit from collective living. We can't always get our own way, but that's a very small price to pay for the benefits that it brings us: street lighting, healthcare."

Charles put down his glass. "It's obvious when you think about it."

"But in nature, you see dominant males, determined to lead the group. It's normal for people to accept a leader, or a manager, but you are a manager. I assume that you treat your people well. You wouldn't consider bullying, for example."

"Never. I know my business inside out and I ensure that everyone in it is trained for the tasks they perform. Why should I want to do anything like that? I certainly wasn't brought up to behave like that and I don't think that anyone should behave like that. What do they say? What you do not want done to yourself, do not do to others?"

"We used to say, pull people, don't push them."

"I suppose that's one way of putting it. I always thank people for their efforts, and some of the more innovative ideas in my company have come from staff. They deal with customers on a daily basis and they can identify problems in our relationship with them."

"And what do they do?"

"They develop solutions, and then bring the issue to my attention and ask if we should make any changes to our procedures."

"And do you agree to these changes?"

"I do. And if there's any financial benefit obtained from them, I pass on that reward to them."

"Good for you. I'm sure not all people in your position would do the same thing. A lot of research these days relates to psychopathic behaviour in organisations. People who are determined to get to the top and are often successful because they're good at reading other people."

"Can that be avoided?"

"That's the million-dollar question again. Apparently looking at their CV can give a clue. If they've habitually moved from one job to the next, that's one thing to look for, but if the interviewer is experienced, he or she should be capable of asking the right questions."

"So, you would say that senior people in a company are part of your human machine? They don't run it?"

"They are part of the machine. It's the customer who runs it. It's the customer who puts the foot on the accelerator, turns the steering wheel or applies the brakes. Management simply has to recognise what the customer wants and speed up, change direction or slow down, depending upon the customer's wishes."

"What if the customer has got bored and simply wants to go home?"

"Then management could simply obey that command. But if the machine is well designed, it may be able to entice the customer to go for a longer journey, be intrigued by on-board devices."

"So, who designs this human machine to enable it to do all of that?"

"A designer, a consultant. But remember, cars have warning lights on the dashboard. The machine itself knows when something is wrong. And we're now in the age of artificial intelligence. Cars might soon be able to fix themselves."

"So, there's nothing to rule out management being able to fix the company?"

"If management are truly part of the machine, they would be able to fix it. If they weren't part of the machine, if they were just some baggage being carried around, increasing the fuel consumption, that would be a problem. And, from what I've seen, it often is."

"Well, Stephen, that all seems a bit pessimistic. Wouldn't you agree?"

"No, I wouldn't. It can be done. And if the management team were also well designed, there would be no problems. Anywhere."

"Anywhere?"

"Initially, I enjoyed my role analysing vehicle reliability and working out how to improve it. After studying business, I enjoyed fixing companies and I now believe that if you can fix an organisation, you can fix a country."

"Aren't you exaggerating?"

"Not at all. I know that I keep going back to efficiency, but politics today reminds me of a game of tug-o-war. One team pulling to the left and the other pulling to the right. All that energy being put to waste. Very sad. There are cleverer ways of designing control systems."

"If you put it that way."

"What other way is there to put it? Apparently, steam locomotives had an efficiency of around nine per cent while voltage transformers for the national grid were nearer ninety-nine point five. A diesel car engine seems to be around thirty-five percent, and I've read articles suggesting that the efficiency of the average office is similar. That's disappointing, but it's still probably way ahead of today's political processes."

"But could you say that to a politician?"

"Of course, you couldn't. Imagine someone from outside your discipline saying that you've got it all wrong. What would your innate reaction be to that?"

"I'd have had a squirt of adrenalin."

"I get such thoughts, but I don't respond. I give them careful consideration."

"In that case, how do you give feedback to politicians?"

"Plant thoughts, and hope that they can adapt to being more logical in their thinking. Offer win-win situations. But the longer solution for everyone is education. As I said earlier, I really learned a lot from watching television programmes about the behaviour of wild animals. What I would have once termed bad behaviour, I would now term natural behaviour. Humans are simply another type of animal. Their advantage over other species is that they can think in a much more complex way. However, they still display natural responses to certain situations. Civilisation is simply learning, or being taught, how to avoid making these natural responses. It's an artificial way of behaviour but it's vital if mankind is to reach its potential."